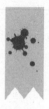

KILLER'S ART

KILLER'S ART

MARI JUNGSTEDT

First Published in the United States in 2013 by
Stockholm Text
Stockholm, Sweden

stockholm@stockholmtext.com
www.stockholmtext.com

Copyright © 2012, 2013 by Mari Jungstedt, by agreement with
Stilton Literary Agency

This edition is published by arrangement with Transworld Publishers, a division
of The Random House Group Ltd. All rights reserved.

English language translation © Tiina Nunnally 2010
Cover design by Ermir Peci
Photograph of Mari Jungstedt by Anna-Lena Ahlström
Printed and bound by RR Donnelley, Chicago, Illinois

1 3 5 7 9 8 6 4 2

ISBN 978-91-87173-45-5

Prologue

Two seconds. That was all it had taken to destroy him. To tear his life apart. Two pitiful seconds. He never imagined that the truth could be so merciless. He had fallen headfirst into the blackest abyss.

The malevolent thoughts that raced around his head at night refused to let go. For weeks they'd been keeping him awake. Not until dawn did he finally slip into a liberating slumber. He could escape his thoughts for a few hours. Then he woke again to the hell that had been forced upon him. A lonely, private inferno that raged beneath his controlled exterior. Sharing it with anyone else was impossible.

It took a while before he understood what he had to do. Slowly and irrevocably the realization had crept in. He would have to set to work on his own. There was no going back, no back door that he could slip through and pretend to the world and himself that nothing had happened.

It had started one day when he'd discovered a secret. He didn't know what to do about it and carried the knowledge inside him for a while. But it itched, chafed, and irritated him like a sore that had split open and refused to heal.

Eventually he could have put it out of his mind. Convinced himself that it was best to leave it be. If only he had done that.

If only curiosity hadn't prompted him to investigate further, so he couldn't forget, so he had to find out more. Even if it hurt.

The fateful day arrived, although he didn't know it at the time, not at first. Not in his mind, at least. Maybe his body had sensed the danger instinctively. Maybe not.

He was home alone. For a large part of the night he had lain awake, thinking about the thing that had preoccupied him for the past few weeks. When he heard the day coming awake outside the window he got out of bed with effort.

He had no appetite, and he barely managed to get down a cup of tea. He merely sat at the kitchen table staring at the overcast sky and the high-rise building opposite; he had no idea how long he sat there. Frustration finally drove him out of his apartment.

The morning was well under way, but as always in November, it never got truly light. The snow on the pavement was a dirty brown, and people were hurrying through the slush without looking anyone else in the eye. The cold was raw and damp, not conducive to strolling.

He decided to go back to that place. He had no real reason to do so, he was just obeying an impulse. If he had known what was going to happen, he wouldn't have gone. But it was as if the whole thing were predestined.

When he turned down the street, the man was just locking the door. He followed the man at a distance as he walked to the bus stop. The bus arrived almost at once. It was packed with people, and he practically rubbed shoulders with the man as they stood crowded together in the center aisle.

The man got off at the NK department store and with determined steps pushed his way through the hordes of Saturday shoppers. He walked briskly toward the city center in his elegant woolen coat with a scarf nonchalantly flung over his shoulder, smoking a cigarette. Abruptly he turned off on to a side street.

The man had never taken this route before. His pursuer's pulse quickened but he kept back at a safe distance. Just to be sure, he walked along the opposite side of the street, but he still had a good view.

Suddenly he lost his quarry. He crossed the street and found a metal door that was so unobtrusive it merged with the shabby facade of the building. He cast a surreptitious glance in both directions. The man must have disappeared through the door, and he decided to follow. He didn't know how devastating the consequences would be as he pressed down the door handle.

Inside, a faint red light on the ceiling provided scant illumination. The walls were painted black. A steep staircase, its steps marked by tiny lights, led straight down to a basement apartment. Not a sound was audible. Hesitantly he descended the stairs and ended up in a long, empty corridor. It was dimly lit, and he could only sense that people were moving about in the dark up ahead.

It was the middle of the day, but that wasn't evident in the basement. The world outside didn't exist. In here other codes prevailed. He understood that after only a few moments.

Seemingly endless corridors wound their way in a complicated labyrinth. Shadowy figures came and went, and he couldn't distinguish the face of the man he'd been following. He strained not to take in what he was seeing, wanting to protect himself. Impressions tugged at his attention, tried to get under his skin.

He got lost and ended up next to a door. That cursed door. If only he hadn't opened it.

Two seconds it took him to register what was happening inside, to comprehend what he was seeing.

That sight would ruin his life.

At dawn there was already a tension in the air. Egon Wallin had slept badly, tossing and turning all night. The terraced house where he lived stood at the shoreline, just outside Visby's ring wall. For hours he had lain awake, staring into the dark as he listened to the sea outside. The cause of his insomnia was not the stormy weather. After this weekend his well-ordered life would be turned totally upside-down, but he was the only one who knew what lay ahead. He had formulated the plans over the past six months, and now there was no going back. His twenty-year marriage would be over when Monday arrived.

It was no surprise that he'd had trouble sleeping. His wife, Monika, lay wrapped up in the covers with her back to him. Neither his restlessness nor the awful weather seemed to trouble her in the least. She slept soundly, taking long, deep breaths.

When the digital clock showed 4:45, he gave up and got out of bed. He slipped out of the bedroom and pulled the door shut behind him. The face he saw in the bathroom mirror was unshaven and bags were clearly visible under his eyes even in the dimmed light. For a long time he let the shower water run over his body.

11

In the kitchen he made coffee. The hiss of the espresso machine blended with the howling of the wind whipping around the corner of the house. The storm seemed to match his emotional state, which was just as agitated and chaotic. After twenty-five years as an art dealer and owner of Visby's foremost gallery, with a stable marriage, two grown children, and a relatively humdrum existence, his life had taken a drastic turn. He had no idea what the future would bring.

This irrevocable decision had been a long time coming. The change he had undergone during the past year was both amazing and dramatic. He no longer recognized himself; at the same time he was closer to his real self than ever before. Emotions surged inside his body as if he were a teenager, as if he had awakened from a torpor that had gone on for decades. The new parts of himself that he'd discovered both enticed and frightened him.

Outwardly he behaved as usual, trying to appear impassive. Monika knew nothing of his plans; it would come as a shock to her. Not that he cared. Their marriage had died long ago. He knew what he wanted, and nothing else mattered.

His resolve calmed him enough that he was able to sit down on one of the bar stools at the modern kitchen island and enjoy his double macchiato. He opened the newspaper, looked for page seven, and studied the advertisement with satisfaction. It was positioned at the top right of the page, and it looked good. A lot of people would show up.

Before he started off on his walk into town, he went to the shore and stood there for a moment. The mornings were getting lighter earlier each day. Even now, in mid-February, it was possible to sense that spring was coming. The stones scattered on the beach were typical of Gotland, as were the boulders sticking out of the water here and there. Seagulls flew low over the surface, opening their beaks wide to shriek. Random waves rose up with no discernible rhythm or pattern. The air was so cold it brought tears to his eyes. The gray horizon seemed full of promise. Especially when he thought of what he would be doing later that evening.

The thought cheered him up, and he set off for town, covering the half-mile distance at a brisk pace.

Once inside the ring wall, the wind was not as blustery. The narrow lanes were silent and deserted. At such an early hour on a Saturday, not a soul was around. Up near the heart of town, at Stora Torget, which was the central marketplace, he encountered the first sign of life. A bakery van stood outside the ICA supermarket. The doors at the back of the store were open to accept deliveries, and he could hear a clattering sound from inside.

As he approached the gallery his stomach twisted into a knot. On Monday he was going to leave the art business to which he had devoted his entire professional life. He had put his heart and soul into this gallery; he couldn't begin to count the number of hours he'd spent here.

He stopped and stood outside on the street for a moment, gazing at the facade. The big modern glass windows faced the open square and the thirteenth-century ruins of St. Karin's church. Inside the medieval church were arches and underground passages from the same period. Against this historic backdrop he had created a modern and discriminating gallery using light, airy colors, adding a few unique details that gave the place a personal touch. Visitors to the gallery often praised him for his exquisite combination of the old and the new.

He unlocked the front door, went up to his office, and hung up his coat. Not only was this weekend going to be a turning point for him personally, it marked the opening night of the first art show of the year. It would also be his last. At least here in Visby. The sale of the gallery had gone through all the legal red tape, and the new owner had signed the contract. Everything was now in place. And he was the only person on Gotland who knew it.

He went back downstairs to survey the gallery space. The paintings had all been hung as they should. He straightened one that was slightly crooked. The invitations had been sent out several weeks earlier, and the advance interest indicated that they could expect a large turnout.

The catering company would arrive soon. He made one last check of the paintings and the lighting. He was always very particular about such things. The paintings had been carefully arranged to showcase each at its best. They were very striking, exploding with strong colors. Expressionistic and abstract, filled with youthful energy and power. Some were brutal, violent, and horrifyingly dark. The artist, Mattis Kalvalis, was a young Lithuanian, until now unknown in Sweden. So far his work had been shown only in the Baltic countries. Egon Wallin enjoyed taking a risk on unknown quantities, new artists who had their whole future ahead of them. He went to the front of the gallery and put the black-and-white photo of Mattis Kalvalis on display in the window.

As he raised his eyes and looked out at the street, he noticed a man standing a short distance away, staring right at him. He had on a baggy, black down jacket, with a knitted cap pulled low over his forehead, and surprisingly he was wearing big, dark sunglasses in the middle of winter. There wasn't even a hint of sunshine.

It was odd how he just stood there. Maybe he was waiting for someone.

Unconcerned, the art dealer continued pottering about the gallery. The local radio station was playing listener requests, and at the moment Lill-Babs was singing, or Barbro Svensson as he preferred to call her.

He smiled a bit as he straightened one of the more violent paintings, which had an almost pornographic theme. What a contrast to the tune coming from the radio: "Do you still love me, Klas-Göran?"

When Egon turned around to face the street again, he gave a start. The man he had seen in the distance had moved. He was now standing very close to the big display window, so close that the tip of his nose was practically touching the glass. For some reason the stranger was looking Egon right in the eye, although he made no sign of offering any sort of greeting.

Instinctively Egon took a step back and nervously began looking for something to do. He pretended to be arranging the wine glasses that had been set out the night before. Then he moved on to the platters for the hors d'oeuvres that the catering company would be bringing.

"Klas-Göran" had faded away, to be replaced by Magnus Uggla singing a lively pop tune from the eighties.

Out of the corner of his eye Egon saw the mysterious man still standing in the same place. An uneasy feeling crept over him. Was he a nutcase released from the mental institution? He wasn't about to let this idiot provoke him. *He'll leave soon,* Egon thought. *He'll get tired of standing there if he can't see me.* The front door was locked, he was sure of that. Because of the opening reception, the gallery wouldn't open until one o'clock.

He climbed the stairs to his office, went in, and shut the door. He sat down and started fiddling with some papers, but the feeling of uneasiness refused to let up. He needed to do something. Confront that man on the street. Find out what he wanted.

Annoyed at being interrupted in this way, he got up and went briskly back downstairs, only to find that the man was gone.

With a sigh of relief, Egon went back to work.

A fierce wind woke him. The windowpanes were rattling and a branch was slamming against the wall of the house. The sea was roaring, and a whistling sound came from the treetops. The covers had slipped off onto the floor, and he was cold. The few electric heaters weren't enough to warm the cottage properly. It wasn't usually rented out in the wintertime, but he had managed to persuade the woman who owned the place to make an exception. He had claimed that he was doing research for the Agricultural Ministry about the threat to the Gotland sugar industry, but it was on a freelance basis, which meant that he couldn't afford a hotel room. The owner hadn't really understood his explanation, but she didn't bother to ask any further questions. Renting the place didn't involve any more work for her; it was just a matter of handing over the key.

He climbed out of bed and pulled on a shirt and trousers. He had to go out, despite the bad weather. The cottage had both a kitchen and a toilet, but the water had been turned off.

He was met by a blast of wind when he pushed open the door, which slammed shut behind him as he stepped outside. He went around the corner and took up a position as close to the wall as possible at the back of the cottage, which faced the woods. There it was somewhat calmer. He unzipped his fly and aimed the stream at the wall.

Back inside the kitchen, he ate a couple of bananas and opened a protein drink, which he downed as he stood at the counter. Ever since he'd come up with the plan two months earlier, he'd felt a certainty, a conviction that there was no other option. Hatred had invaded his body, making his tongue sour and his thoughts sharp. Methodically he had worked out all the preparations, ticking them off point by point with meticulous precision. Everything had been done in secret. The fact that nobody knew what was going on gave him confidence. He was in control, and that was an advantage that would make all his plans succeed. Time after time he had gone over the details until not a single flaw or potential pitfall remained. The time had now arrived. It was a cunning and ingenious idea, but it would not be easy to execute.

He leaned forward and peered out of the window. His only concern was the damn wind. That would make it more difficult for him, and could even upset the whole plan. At the same time, it presented certain advantages. The worse the weather, the fewer people would be out, and that minimized the risk of discovery.

His throat felt scratchy. Was he coming down with a cold? He pressed his hand to his forehead. Damned if he didn't have a fever. Shit. He found a bottle of acetaminophen and swallowed two tablets with water from a container on the counter. This was no time to be getting a cold; he was going to need every ounce of muscular strength.

The backpack with all the equipment was ready. One last time he checked to see that he had everything he needed. Then he quickly zipped it shut and sat down in front of the mirror. With practiced movements he applied the makeup, inserted the contact lenses, and glued the wig in place. He had tried out this disguise many times before to ensure it would be perfect. When he was done he paused to study the transformation for a moment.

The next time he looked in the mirror, he would be seeing the face of a murderer. He wondered if it would be obvious.

M attis Kalvalis was nervous and had to go out for a smoke practically every ten minutes.

"What if nobody comes?" he kept saying in his strident Eastern European accent. His face was even paler than usual, and his lanky body was in constant motion among his paintings. Several times Egon Wallin had shown him the advertisement in the paper and patted him on the shoulder.

"Everything will be just fine—trust me."

Kalvalis's manager, who had come with him from Lithuania, wasn't much help. He mostly sat outside the gallery smoking and talking on his cell phone, apparently not bothered by the icy wind.

Egon had anticipated a good turnout for the opening of the show and when he unlocked the door of the gallery, there was a long queue of people waiting outside, stamping their feet in the cold.

Many familiar faces smiled at him, their eyes bright with anticipation. He looked in vain for a certain person in the crowd now streaming into the gallery. There was still plenty of time. It was going to be hard to feign indifference.

He noted with satisfaction that the cultural reporter from the local radio station had just come in. After a while he caught sight of yet another journalist from one of the local papers, interviewing the artist. His PR campaign, with press releases and follow-up phone calls, had apparently worked.

A good-sized crowd soon filled the gallery. With three thousand square feet spread over two levels, the space was disproportionately large for Gotland. But the premises had been passed down through several generations, and Egon Wallin had tried to keep it in its original state as much as possible. And he liked giving works of art plenty of space so as to make the best impression. The gallery really did do these paintings justice: the rough walls presented an intense contrast to the brilliant colors and the expressive and ultra-modern style. The gallery visitors strolled among the works, sipping sparkling wine. Music could be faintly heard between the rooms—the artist had insisted on the songs of a Lithuanian rock band that sounded like a mixture of Frank Zappa and Kraftwerk.

Egon had at least persuaded him to turn down the volume.

Mattis was now looking much more relaxed. He walked through the crowd, talking loudly, laughing and gesticulating with his large hands, the wine splashing out of his glass. His movements were abrupt and uncontrolled, and every once in a while he would burst into hysterical laughter, almost doubling over.

For one terrible moment Egon suspected that the artist must be on drugs, but he quickly brushed that thought aside. He was probably just releasing nervous tension.

"Hell of an opening, Egon. Really well done," he heard someone say behind him.

He would recognize that hoarse, ingratiating voice from miles away.

He turned around and found himself face to face with Sixten Dahl, one of Stockholm's most successful gallery owners. He was wearing a black leather coat with trousers and boots to match and tinted glasses with orange frames; he was fashionably unshaven. He looked like a bad imitation of George Michael. Sixten Dahl owned a gorgeous gallery on the corner of Karlavägen and Sturegatan in Östermalm, Stockholm's most exclusive part of town.

"You think so? How nice. And it's great you could make it," Egon said with feigned enthusiasm.

More or less as a joke, he'd seen to it that his competitor in Stockholm had received an invitation. Dahl had tried to get his mitts on Mattis Kalvalis, but Egon had emerged from the battle victorious.

Both art dealers had been in Vilnius at a conference for gallery owners from the Baltic region. There the singular style of the young painter had caught their eyes. During one of the dinners, Egon Wallin happened to be seated next to Mattis Kalvalis. They hit it off, and amazingly enough, Kalvalis had chosen the gallery on Gotland instead of Dahl's gallery in the capital. Many people in the art world were surprised. Even though Wallin had a respected reputation, it was considered extraordinary that the artist had chosen him. Dahl was equally well known, and Stockholm was a much bigger city.

But the fact that Egon's biggest competitor would turn up in Visby for the opening was not so strange. Dahl was known for his persistence. *Maybe he still believes that he can convince Kalvalis to change his mind,* thought Egon. He wasn't going to have any luck. What Dahl didn't know was that Kalvalis had already asked Egon to be his agent and represent him in all of Sweden. The contract had been drawn up and was just waiting for a signature.

The opening was a success. The desire to buy a painting seemed to spread like an epidemic. Egon never ceased to be astounded by the herd mentality of people. If the right person paid the right price quickly enough, there would suddenly be many others who were willing to open their wallets. Sometimes it seemed as if luck was more important than quality when it came to evaluating art.

A Gotland collector had raved about the work and put a hold on three of the paintings almost at once. That was enough to inspire others, and there was even a bidding war for a couple of the pieces. The prices were jacked up considerably. Egon Wallin was practically rubbing his hands. Now the rest of Sweden would be sitting at the artist's feet.

The only fly in the ointment was that the person he'd been expecting hadn't yet turned up.

The art connoisseur and valuer Erik Mattson had been assigned to make an extensive evaluation of a large estate in Burgsvik in southern Gotland. The head of Bukowski's Auction House had asked him and a colleague to make the trip. A landowner on Gotland had a large collection of Swedish artwork from the early twentieth century that he now wanted to sell. The collection included about thirty pieces, from Zorn etchings to oil paintings by Georg Pauli and Isaac Grünewald.

Mattson and his colleague had spent all of Friday in Burgsvik, which had certainly been an experience. The estate turned out to be a unique example of a genuine old Gotland limestone manor, and they were impressed by both the surroundings and the collection. They were well received by the owners, who invited them to stay for dinner. They then spent the night at the Strand Hotel in Visby.

Erik wanted to get plenty of rest before Saturday. He had a lot on his agenda. He was going to start the day by visiting the place he loved above all others, although he hadn't seen it in years.

Right after breakfast he jumped in the car and set off. The day was overcast, and the weather forecast predicted snow. But he wasn't going far. His destination was just a few miles north of Visby.

Just as he was about to turn down the driveway marked by a sign that said "Muramaris," he noticed a car coming out. That surprised him. It seemed unlikely that anyone would be coming here in the wintertime.

The parking area close to the road was designated for visitors, but since it was February it was deserted. When he got out of the car, he paused on the gravel path to face the sea, which was only just visible from this distance. The waves rolled in, as steady and inevitable as the passing of the years.

On either side of the path stood dense rows of trees, growing low to the ground and crooked, clearly stunted by the harsh autumn storms. He knew that there were no neighboring houses.

As he walked down the long slope, his eyes filled with tears. It was so long ago that he was last here. The treetops whispered around him, and the gravel crunched beneath his feet. He was alone, and that was precisely what he wanted. This was a sacred moment.

As he rounded the bend and saw the house, snow began to fall. The flakes gently drifted down from the sky, settling softly on top of his head. He stopped to study the area spread out below: the dilapidated main building, the gardener's residence, and farther away the red-painted cottage that had its own special history.

What a contrast it all was to the last time he was here. Back then it was summertime, and they had stayed for two weeks, just as the visiting artist and his lover had done, although that was almost one hundred years earlier.

Erik had enjoyed every second they were here, sleeping in the same room where the artist had slept, simply being under the same roof, eating breakfast in the kitchen where he had once sat; not even the old cast-iron stove had changed since then. Eric could only imagine the stories the walls could have told.

Right now he had a panoramic view of the home called Muramaris. The name meant "hearth by the sea." The rectangular, sand-colored main house was two stories and had been built of limestone. Its architectural style was a unique blend of Italian Renaissance, with a loggia facing the sea, and a traditional Gotland estate. Large windows with white mullions graced each side, opening onto the woods, the water, and the austere Baroque garden at the back with its sculptures, fountains, flagstone paths, and decorative flower beds.

The man who'd had such an influence on Erik's life had often visited this place, spending sunny summer weeks here, swimming, taking walks along the beach, painting, and spending time with the controversial artist couple who had built their dream house on this plateau at the beginning of the twentieth century. Even though so many years had passed since then, the artist's presence was still strong.

With some difficulty Erik opened the green wooden gate; it moved reluctantly, creaking loudly. He wandered around to the back. The house had stood empty for years, ever since the new owner had taken over, and the neglect was evident. The stucco was peeling off, the wall surrounding the property had crumbled in several places, and some of the sculptures in the garden were now missing. The once-proud building was sorely in need of renovation.

He walked slowly along the flagstone path. Unlike the house, the garden had retained some of its former grandeur, with carefully pruned hedgerows. Near the pond in the middle of the garden he sat down on a bench. It was damp and cold, but that didn't bother him any more than the snow, which was coming down heavier now. His eyes were fixed on a particular window belonging to the guest room on the ground floor, next to the kitchen. It was there that one of the most myth-shrouded paintings in Swedish art history had been created—at least that was the rumor, and there was no reason to doubt the claim. The artist had worked on the large oil painting during the same year that he had designed the garden here at Muramaris, in the midst of a raging world war. The year was 1918.

That was when Nils Dardel painted "The Dying Dandy." Erik whispered the words as he sat there on the bench.

The dying dandy. Just like himself.

After a successful opening reception, the whole gang from the gallery celebrated with a fancy dinner at the Donners Brunn restaurant in central Visby. Mattis Kalvalis sat in the middle and seemed to enjoy all the attention. Everyone at the table was in high spirits, and Egon Wallin thought the evening was a happy ending to his old life. They sat at the best table in the magnificent cellar dining room, basking in the glow of the candles, the superbly prepared food beautifully arranged on their plates.

He raised his glass for yet another toast, and they all cheered for the new star in the firmament of art. Just as the shouts died out, two new guests appeared: Sixten Dahl, in the company of a younger man whom Egon had never seen before.

They greeted everyone politely as they went past, and Sixten once again praised the exhibition, giving the artist a long look. *What the hell is he up to now?* thought Egon. As luck would have it, they sat down at a table on the other side of the room so that Egon was sitting with his back to them.

Later, when he got up to go to the restroom, he discovered Mattis Kalvalis and Sixten Dahl together in the restaurant's smoking room. They were alone, deeply immersed in what looked like a serious conversation. Anger surged up inside Egon at once. He opened the glass door.

"What are you doing?" he snapped in Swedish to Sixten.

"What's wrong with you, Egon?" said his competitor, feigning surprise. "We're having a smoke, and this is the smoking room."

"Don't try any tricks. Mattis and I have a contract."

"Is that so? I heard that it wasn't signed yet," said Sixten, stubbing out his cigarette and nonchalantly heading out of the door.

Naturally Mattis didn't understand a word of what was said. Yet he seemed visibly ill at ease.

Egon decided to let the matter drop. He merely turned to the artist and said, "We have a deal, don't we?"

"Of course we do."

It was past eleven by the time Egon and his wife finally returned home. Monika wanted to go to bed at once. He explained that he was going to sit up for a while, to unwind and reflect on his day. He poured himself a glass of cognac and sat down in the living room.

Now it was just a matter of waiting. He thought about the incident at Donners Brunn, but decided it had been nothing. Of course Sixten would keep trying. But the contract with Mattis was going to be signed the next day. They had agreed to meet at the gallery. Besides, the opening had been a success. He was confident that Mattis would remain loyal.

He took a big gulp of the cognac. The minutes crept by. He tried to stay calm and restrain his eagerness. If Monika followed her usual routine, she would spend ten minutes in the bathroom, then crawl into bed and read a few pages of a book before turning off the light and falling asleep.

That meant that he had to wait about twenty minutes before he could leave the house and walk over to the hotel. There wouldn't be anyone on duty at the front desk this late at night, so there was no risk of being recognized.

His whole body was looking forward to the rendezvous.

H is wife's nighttime regimen took longer than he had estimated, and Egon Wallin was feeling extremely annoyed by the time he finally set off. It was almost as if she had known that he had plans and so had read her book for longer than usual. Maybe even several chapters.

He had tiptoed past the bedroom several times, as quietly as he could, noting that her light was still on as his body itched with eagerness, almost like eczema. Finally she turned off the light. Just to make sure that she was actually asleep, he waited another fifteen minutes. Then he cautiously opened the door and listened to her regular breathing before he dared leave.

When he came out onto the street, he breathed a sigh of relief. Anticipation burned on his lips and tongue. Briskly he set off. The lights were out in most of the windows that he passed, even though it was Saturday and not yet midnight. He had no desire to run into a neighbor—around here everybody knew everyone else. They had bought the terraced house when it was new and their children were young. Their marriage had been relatively happy, and their lives had taken the expected path. Egon had never been unfaithful, even though he did a great deal of traveling for his job and met all sorts of people.

A year ago he had gone to Stockholm on one of his customary business trips. Passion had struck him like lightning, and in the course of one night, everything changed. He had been completely unprepared. Suddenly his life had assumed a new purpose, a new meaning.

Having sex with Monika had become almost unbearable. Her response to his half-hearted initiatives had been cool over the last few years. Their activities in bed finally ceased altogether, which was a great relief; they never spoke about the matter.

But now he felt desire burning inside him. He chose the quickest route past the hospital and the hills near Strandgärdet. He would be there soon. He took out his cell to say that he was on his way.

Just as he was tapping in the number he tripped and fell. In the dark he hadn't noticed the big tree root sticking up in the path ahead of him. He hit his head hard on a rock, and for a few seconds he lost consciousness. When he came to, he felt blood running from his forehead and down his cheek. For a moment he just sat there on the cold ground. Fortunately he had a tissue in his pocket so he could wipe off the blood. The cuts on his forehead and right cheek were quite painful.

Damn it, he thought. *Not now.* Cautiously he touched his face with his fingertips.

Luckily the cuts didn't seem serious, but a big bump had started swelling above his right eyebrow.

Feeling dizzy, he had to walk slowly at first, but he soon reached the wall. From there it wasn't very far to the hotel.

He had just passed the small opening in the wall facing the sea, the so-called Kärleksport, or Gate of Love, when he sensed the presence of someone very close to him. All of a sudden he felt something sweep past his ear before he was pressed backward.

Egon Wallin would never make it to his intended rendezvous.

Siv Eriksson woke as usual several minutes before the alarm clock rang. It was as if her body knew when it was time to get up, and she always managed to turn off the clock before her husband, Lennart, was woken by the noise. Cautiously she got out of bed, trying to be as quiet as possible. It was Sunday, after all.

She padded out to the kitchen in the pink woolly slippers that Lennart had given her for Christmas and put on the coffee. Then she took a hot shower and washed her hair. Afterward she ate her breakfast in peace and quiet while she listened to the radio and let her hair dry.

Siv Eriksson was looking forward to this day. Her work hours were shorter on Sunday, only from seven to noon. After work Lennart was going to pick her up so they could celebrate the fifth birthday of their only grandchild. Their daughter and her family lived in Slite, in northern Gotland, so it would be a bit of a drive. Siv had taken care of the presents, which were neatly wrapped and sitting on the table in the hall. Lennart would bring them along when he left the house; she had written a note to remind him.

After finishing her coffee and brushing her teeth, Siv got dressed. She gave the cat some food and fresh water.

He didn't show any interest in going outside, just looked at her lazily before curling up in his basket. She glanced at the thermometer in the window, noting that it had become even colder; it was now minus 14°F. She'd better wear both a hat and a scarf. Her woollen coat was old and a little too snug.

The apartment where they lived was on the top floor of a building on Polhemsgatan, with a view of the northeast side of the ring wall. When Siv came out onto the street, it was still quite dark. The walk to the Wisby Hotel where she worked was a couple of miles, but that didn't bother her. She liked to walk, and besides, it was the only exercise she ever got. She enjoyed her job setting out the cold buffet; she and a colleague were also in charge of the breakfast service. At this time of year the hotel had few guests, which suited her just fine as she was not the type who thrived on stress.

She cut across the street and set off along the path near the soccer field, where the grass was covered with a thin layer of snow. In the parking lot outside the municipal offices for culture and recreation, she slipped on the icy asphalt and almost landed on her back.

At the crossing on Kung Magnus Road, which ran parallel to the east side of the ring wall, she paused for a moment to look in both directions, even though it really wasn't necessary. On Sunday mornings there was little traffic, but Siv Eriksson was a cautious person who never took any unnecessary risks. She walked through Östergravar, a small grassy area next to the wall. This particular section of her route was so isolated that it always made her rather nervous early in the morning when it was still dark. But she would soon reach the medieval ring wall that enclosed the central part of the city. There she would pass through Dalman Gate to enter the city proper. The gate was part of the Dalman Tower, sixty feet high and one of the grandest of the medieval defense towers.

About thirty yards away from the gate, Siv Eriksson stopped abruptly. At first she couldn't believe her eyes. Something was dangling from high up in the opening. For several bewildering seconds she thought it must be a sack. But when she got closer, she realized to her astonishment that a man was hanging by a rope that had been fastened to the grating above the gate opening. It was the type of portcullis that could be lowered in ancient times if an enemy was about to attack.

The man's head was bent forward, and his arms dangled limply at his sides.

Siv skidded on the icy bridge and almost fell again, but she grabbed hold of the railing just in time. She looked up at the man. He was dressed in a black, ankle-length leather coat and black trousers. On his feet he wore a pair of low boots. He had dark hair and looked to be in his fifties.

She had a hard time distinguishing his facial features in the dim morning light. She took a few uncertain steps forward as she fearfully glanced around. When she got close enough, everything seemed to come to a standstill inside Siv Eriksson's head. She recognized the man; she knew him well. She pulled her cell phone out of her pocket and punched in the number for the police.

Detective Superintendent Anders Knutas arrived at Dalman Gate half an hour after the call came in. Normally he would have stayed at police headquarters to divide up the job assignments, but this was something he had to see. A man most likely been murdered in cold blood and hoisted up for everyone to see in the middle of the biggest and grandest of the gates in the ring wall. This was something so out of the ordinary that he made an exception. The patrol that had arrived on the scene first had immediately sounded the alarm, saying that it didn't look like a suicide; rather, there was every reason to believe foul play was involved. The reason for this was that the body had been hung several yards up in the air. It was also at least a yard away from either side of the wall. Nobody could have stood up there or climbed up to where the noose was attached in order to take his own life.

When Knutas arrived, both Detective Inspector Karin Jacobsson and technician Erik Sohlman were already on-site. Karin looked even shorter than her five foot three inches, and her face was so pale it was almost translucent. She had walked over from her centrally located apartment inside the wall. Knutas could tell at once that she had already seen

35

the body. Karin never seemed to get used to the sight of corpses; but then neither did he.

A crowd of neighbors had gathered, and they were all looking up in horror at the body with its back to them in the gateway. None of them would have believed that something as gruesome as a murder would ever take place on their peaceful street.

Dalman Gate was part of the ring wall in the middle of Norra Murgatan, a long and narrow cobblestoned street that ran parallel to the wall's eastern side. Low, picturesque houses lined both sides. It was downright idyllic, with lace curtains in the windows, ceramic pots made in the typical Gotland style, and little gardens behind fences. The houses closest to the wall had been built directly attached to it.

Jacobsson and Knutas walked past the cement sculpture in the shape of a sheep that prevented cars from driving through the gate and stepped over the blue-and-white police tape.

Knutas stopped short at the sight of the victim.

At first glance, it looked like a tragic suicide. The rope was attached to a strong hook that had been fastened to the portcullis above the gate. The dead man's head was bent forward, his body was limp.

The scene reminded Knutas of the year before, when several people had been ritually murdered and then hanged.

"I feel like I've seen this before," he said to Jacobsson.

"I know. The first thing I thought about was finding Martina Flochten last summer." Jacobsson shook her head and stuffed her hands farther into the pockets of her down jacket.

When Knutas got close enough to see the face, he froze.

"Dear Jesus, it's Egon Wallin, the art dealer."

Crime-scene technician Erik Sohlman, who was in the process of photographing the body from various angles, lowered the camera and took a closer look at the man's face.

"You're right, it's him," he exclaimed. "My God. I was in his gallery only a week ago and bought a painting for my mother's sixtieth birthday."

"We've got to get him down from there as soon as possible," said Knutas grimly. The body could be seen from the road, and by now people were starting to wake up.

He nodded toward Kung Magnus Road, where several cars had already pulled over. People were getting out and pointing toward the gate. In the morning light, the macabre scene was exposed to everyone who passed.

"Hurry up now," Knutas urged his colleagues. "He's hanging there as if he's in a display window."

He scanned the area. It was always hard to strike the right balance as to how much should be cordoned off, but all his years of experience as a detective had taught him that the larger the area, the better.

The police couldn't yet rule out suicide, but if Egon Wallin had been murdered, which is what Knutas believed, then they would need to secure all conceivable evidence. He made a quick decision that they would need to isolate the entire green area, from Osterport to Norderport. There were footprints everywhere, clearly visible in the snow, and some of them might belong to the killer.

Knutas studied the portcullis where the rope of the noose had been fastened. It seemed impossible for Egon Wallin to have managed the whole thing on his own. There was absolutely nothing to climb on. The noose was so high up that Knutas realized he would be forced to call in the fire department to get the body down.

He pulled out his cell and rang Forensic Medicine in Solna. A medical examiner would fly over from the mainland in a police helicopter as soon as possible.

From experience Knutas knew that the ME would prefer them to leave the body untouched until he did his first examination, but in this case that wouldn't be possible. The dead man was hanging there as if he were the victim of a public execution. If it turned out to be a homicide, the media frenzy would descend upon them before they knew it.

Knutas had no sooner thought this than he felt the first camera flash behind him. Alarmed, he turned around, only to witness more camera flashes.

He recognized the photographer from the newspaper *Gotlands Allehanda*, accompanied by one of the paper's most persistent reporters. His face flushed with anger, Knutas brusquely grabbed her by the arm.

"What in hell do you think you're doing? This might be a suicide case. Right now we don't know anything for sure. Absolutely nothing! The family hasn't even been informed yet. He's only just been found!"

"Do you know who it is?" she asked quickly as she pulled her arm away, ignoring Knutas's agitation. "I think it looks like Egon Wallin, the art dealer."

"Didn't you hear what I just said? It's not certain that any crime has been committed here. Get out of here now and let us do our job in peace!"

Suicide at least was something that journalists in Sweden respected and didn't usually report. Not yet, at any rate. But with the sort of developments that were occurring in the media, it wouldn't be long before they began reveling in such cases.

Knutas was even angrier because he knew and respected Egon Wallin. Not that they'd actually spent much time together, but they'd met on various occasions over the years, and Knutas had always liked the man. There was something very straightforward and candid about him. An honest individual who had both feet on the ground and who was content with his life, unlike so many others who complained nonstop. He seemed to be a thoroughly decent guy who treated everyone well. A real mensch. They were about the same age, and Knutas had always looked up to Egon Wallin. He had an appealing aura about him that made people want to be his friend. And now here he was, hanging from the gate—dead as a doornail.

Every minute that passed without taking the body down was a torment. He was already dreading having to tell Wallin's wife about the tragedy.

More journalists had appeared on the other side of the police tape. He did understand that they had a job to do. If this turned out to be a homicide case, the police would be forced to schedule a press conference.

Knutas was grateful at least that so far no TV crew had turned up. But the next moment he caught sight of Pia Lilja, the most zealous TV cameraperson he'd ever encountered. She worked with Johan Berg at Swedish Television. At the moment she was alone, but that didn't prevent her from filming. They were in a public place, after all, and as long as she stayed outside the cordoned-off area, there was nothing he could do to stop her.

Knutas sighed. He cast one last look at the body before he left the scene, accompanied by Jacobsson.

It was going to be a busy day.

Usually Sundays were calm in the editorial offices of the Regional News division at the headquarters of Swedish TV in the Gärdet district, and today was no exception. Johan Berg was feeling hungover and worn out as he sat at his desk, listlessly scanning the daily papers. Absolutely nothing was going on. Not in Stockholm, on Gotland, or in Uppsala, which were the areas covered by Regional News.

The previous evening had turned out to involve far more drinks and had lasted much longer than he had planned. He'd gone out for a few beers with his best friend Andreas, who was also a journalist. They'd ended up at Kvarnen, and had then stupidly accompanied several colleagues from Swedish Radio's Eko news program to a party out in Hammarbyhöjden. It was four a.m. when had he stumbled through the door of his one-bedroom apartment on Heleneborgsgatan.

Adding to his distaste for spending Sunday on the job was the fact that the editor in charge was a substitute in whom he had very little faith. He had hardly taken off his jacket before she was enthusiastically proposing one mediocre assignment after another. She seemed to be nervously grasping at every straw. Good Lord, there were still ten hours left before the five-minute fluff piece they usually broadcast on Sundays. And besides, they had a report in the can. Calm down, for God's sake, he thought morosely. The mere sight of her made him tired. She was also the newscaster, so she was the only person around to talk to. On Sundays the resources were so meager that one person had to be both editor and newscaster.

He glanced through the various press releases that had been sent to the editorial offices over the weekend. Ninety-five percent had to do with various PR gimmicks for different functions going on in town, including announcements about hip-hopper Markoolio being the master of ceremonies when the new Tumba Center was opened, something about a lace workshop at Skansen, and publicity for a guinea pig race at the Sollentuna exhibition hall.

He hated all these different "days" that had been invented over the past few years. First there were Children's Day and Book Day and Women's Day, which were okay—but lately there had been a plethora of days that had to be celebrated. Days officially designated to honor cinnamon rolls, the suburbs, go-karts, and so on. This Sunday was apparently Mitten Day. What could that possibly mean? Was everybody supposed to go around wearing homemade mittens, waving their hands around and looking happy? What purpose could that possibly serve? Were they going to sell pastries shaped like mittens and exchange knitting patterns? He almost felt like doing a report on the topic just because it sounded so dumb.

The rest of the press releases were either from groups dissatisfied with the public-transportation system, or from obscure groups of activists protesting about everything imaginable: a dangerous road outside a school in Gimo, a daycare centre in Vaxholm that was about to be closed, or the long line at the welfare office in Salem. Johan shook his head as he tossed one press release after another into the wastebasket.

The cameraman for the day showed up and joined him with a cup of coffee. They sat and commiserated about the fact that there were no worthwhile stories to report. Now and then Johan could feel the editor glancing at them, but he chose to ignore her. For just a little while longer.

He tried to ring Emma several times, but the line was always busy. *Should she really be spending so much time on the phone when she's taking care of Elin?* he thought with annoyance. He felt a familiar stab of yearning. His daughter was now eight months old, but he saw her only sporadically.

He put down the phone and looked over at the editor's desk; she was putting in calls to all the small police stations in their area to find out if anything was going on that might be newsworthy.

He suddenly felt guilty and realized that he needed to pull himself together. It wasn't her fault that he was tired and out of sorts. Or that Sundays were always hopeless news days. Maybe he could use his police contacts to fish out some tiny morsel that with a little effort could be turned into a story. Good enough for a Sunday, at least.

He was just about to pick up the phone on his cluttered desk when his cell phone rang.

He recognized Pia Lilja's voice at once. She was the cameraperson he most often worked with whenever he went over to Gotland.

"Did you hear the news?" she gasped.

"No, what is it?"

"They found a dead man hanging from one of the gates in the ring wall this morning."

"Are you joking?"

"No, damn it. It's true."

"Was it suicide?"

"No idea, but I'm going to find out. I can't talk any more. I've got to go and see what's happening."

"Okay. Ring me again as soon as you know anything."

"Sure. Ciao."

Johan punched in the number for Detective Superintendent Anders Knutas. When he answered, he sounded out of breath.

"Hello, Johan Berg here."

"It's been a long time. Are you back on the job again?"

"Hey, don't you ever watch Regional News? I've been at it for weeks."

"Good to hear that you're back on your feet again. That's what I meant."

Johan chuckled. He'd been off sick for several months after having been stabbed in connection with a homicide case that he'd been involved with the previous summer. His wounds had been quite serious. Knutas had come to see him in the hospital several times, but that was a while ago, and they hadn't spoken since.

"So what's going on over there?"

"We found a dead man hanging from Dalman Gate this morning."

"Was it murder?"

"Don't know yet. That's something the ME's examination will determine."

"So there's nothing to indicate that it might be murder?"

"I didn't say that."

"Come on, Knutas. You know my situation. I'm sitting over here in Stockholm. I need to know whether it's worth me coming to Gotland or not. What does it look like? Murder or suicide?"

"Unfortunately, I'm not at liberty to answer that question." Knutas's tone was a bit less stern.

"Do you know who the victim is?" A brief pause.

"Yes, but he hasn't been formally identified. And as you very well know, we can't give out the name just yet. Not until the family's been notified."

Knutas was breathing hard. Johan could hear that he was walking as he talked.

"How old is the victim?"

"He's middle-aged. That's as much as I can tell you. I've got to go now. We'll be sending out a press release later on. There are lots of journalists here, asking questions."

"When will you know more?"

"We'll probably have a preliminary report by lunchtime, at the earliest."

"I'll get back to you then."

"Do that."

Johan frowned as he put down the phone. It was incredibly frustrating not being able to determine whether he should go over to Gotland. He was also acutely aware of how late he'd be in reporting the story if it did turn out to be murder. His Gotland colleagues would obviously have a big head start.

For several years he'd been fighting to establish a permanent reporting team on Gotland, but so far he'd had no success. He thought it was unbelievable that his bosses couldn't see that a permanent team was needed over there. The island encompassed a relatively large area. And there were almost sixty thousand residents. At the same time, life on the island was changing; the college there was flourishing, as were its cultural life and art community. Gotland was no longer just a place that came alive in the summertime when it was invaded by hundreds of thousands of tourists.

A few minutes later a news bulletin from the TT news service appeared on his screen.

TT (Stockholm) A man was found dead just before seven o'clock Sunday morning on Gotland. The man was found hanging from Dalman Gate in the Visby ring wall. His

*identity has not yet been established. The police are not
ruling out foul play.*

Just to be on the safe side, Johan booked a seat on the next
flight to Visby. Time was of the essence. If it was confirmed
that this was a homicide, he needed to get there quickly.
The fatigue he had felt was gone and the adrenaline was
flowing, as it always did when there was something major
happening. If this was murder, he was convinced it would
be a big story on all the Swedish TV news programs. A
corpse found hanging from the historic ring wall in idyllic
Visby. Jesus Christ.

He couldn't help thinking that if he did end up flying to
Gotland, he'd be able to see Emma and Elin sooner than
expected. And he found himself in the absurd situation of
hoping that the man at the gate had been murdered.

It didn't take long before the national news editor came
rushing into the office to ask them what Regional News was
planning to do about the story.

Johan didn't get a chance to answer before his phone
rang again. It was Pia Lilja.

"I'm almost certain it's a homicide, Johan. I think you'd
better come over here."

"What makes you think it's murder?"

"My God, I've been at the scene! He's hanging from a
noose attached to the portcullis above the gate—and Dalman Gate is really high. The opening itself is over fifteen
feet. It would have been impossible to get up there on his
own. Plus the police have cordoned off a big area. Why
would they do that if there was no crime involved?'

"Okay," he said excitedly. "Did you get any material?
Have you interviewed anyone?"

"No. The police aren't saying a word. Not to anybody,
if that's any consolation. But I did get some good footage.

I managed to make my way round to the other side of the wall before they put up the police tape, so I got some fucking great angles of the body itself before they took it down. Talk about a macabre sight! I think we're the only ones on the story at the moment."

"Yes, I haven't seen any other talk about it. See you soon."

The minutes seemed to crawl by. It was unusual for the ferry to be late, and of course it would have to happen on this particular morning. He began fidgeting as he sat in a lounge chair in the quiet lounge on the foredeck. There were few passengers on board. Ahead sat an elderly couple who had already taken out a thermos and sandwiches, which they ate as they did the crossword. A man about his own age, his jacket spread over him, was dozing in the row of chairs behind.

When the ferry finally pulled away from the dock, he heaved a sigh of relief.

For a while he'd been convinced that the police were going to come rushing onto the boat and arrest him. Gradually he'd allowed himself to relax. In three hours and fifteen minutes they would reach the mainland. He was longing for that moment.

In the cafeteria he ordered pasta with chicken and a salad. He also had a glass of milk. After the meal he began to feel better. The mission had been a success. With surprise he recalled that it hadn't been difficult, even from an emotional viewpoint. Like a soldier in the field, he had carried out the operation with great concentration, keeping strictly to the plan. He had stayed focused on the task at hand. Afterward he had felt a sense of calm and satisfaction that he hadn't experienced in a long time.

When they reached the open sea he got up from his chair, took both plastic bags, and went up to the top deck. There were no other passengers outside in the cold, but he needed to act quickly before anyone turned up. He made sure that no one was around. Then he heaved the bags over the side.

When they disappeared into the foaming waves far below, the last remnants of pressure lifted from his chest.

The results of the first examination that crime tech Erik Sohlman had made of the body were unambiguous. All indications were that Egon Wallin had been murdered. Knutas immediately summoned his colleagues to a lunchtime meeting. The investigative team consisted of four individuals besides Knutas: the police spokesman and assistant head of the criminal unit, Lars Norrby, Detective Inspector Karin Jacobsson, and Thomas Wittberg, whose title was the same as Jacobsson's. Only Sohlman was missing; he was still at the crime scene waiting for the ME. Also in attendance was the hardened chief prosecutor, Birger Smittenberg, who had interrupted his day off so he'd be able to follow the investigation from the very beginning.

Knutas stressed that they had to get started on all fronts as soon as possible—the first twenty-four hours after a murder were crucial.

Someone had shown enough foresight to order meatball sandwiches and coffee. After everyone at the table had helped themselves to the food, Knutas began the meeting.

"Unfortunately, we're dealing with a homicide. The victim is the art dealer Egon Wallin. His body was discovered by a woman on her way to work at 6:45 this morning. As you probably all know by now, he was found hanging from the very top of Dalman Gate. The injuries to his neck show that Wallin was murdered. Erik is on his way here and will be able to tell us more. The ME has just arrived from Stockholm and is at the crime scene."

"This is insane," exclaimed Thomas Wittberg. "Another hanging victim like last summer? What the hell is going on?"

"Yes, it's strange," Knutas agreed. "But at least Wallin doesn't seem to have been subjected to a ritual killing. The witness who found the body is being interviewed," he went on. "She was first taken to the hospital, where she was examined and given something to calm her nerves. She was clearly in a state of shock."

Knutas got up and used a pen to point to a map on the wall at the front of the room. It showed the eastern side of the ring wall, with Dalman Gate and the green area called Östergravar.

"We've cordoned off all of Östergravar along Kung Magnus Road from Östergravar to Norderport. We're going to have to maintain the restricted zone for an unspecified amount of time, until any and all evidence has been secured. On the inside of the wall, we've cordoned off part of Norra Murgatan and Udden Lane, closest to the gate, but we're going to have to open it up very soon. Not because there's a lot of traffic up there at Klinten, but still. That's the area where the techs have been focusing their attention first. It seems reasonable to assume that the perpetrator came from that direction."

"Why's that?" asked Karin Jacobsson.

"Because according to Sohlman, the victim was probably not killed at Dalman Gate. The body was transported there from some other location."

"How could he figure that out so quickly?" Wittberg fixed his blue eyes on Knutas in surprise.

"Don't ask me. He just said that the site of the murder was not the same as where the body was found. He'll have to explain when he gets here. But if the perpetrator—or perpetrators—killed Wallin somewhere else, they must have had a vehicle. Lugging around a corpse wouldn't be easy. And I don't think they would have driven across Östergravar."

"Are there any witnesses?" asked Birger Smittenberg. "Didn't anyone who lives nearby see or hear anything? The gate is right in the middle of a street with houses on both sides."

"We've started knocking on doors, and we can only hope that it'll produce something. There's actually only one house that has windows directly facing Dalman Gate. The location was well chosen if the killer wanted to be undisturbed, considering it's right in the center of town. With a little luck, it would be possible to do something like this at night without being seen by anyone."

"It still seems incredibly risky," Wittberg objected. "I mean, it would take time to drag the body out of a car and hang it up there like that."

"And physical strength," added Norrby. "Not everyone could hoist a body up that high. Provided there wasn't more than one person involved, that is."

"No matter what, whether it was one or more killers, they've probably been to the gate several times before, to check it out and make preparations. That's what I mean. We need to find out if anyone in particular had been noticed at the gate over the past few days."

Knutas sneezed loudly. As he blew his nose, the prosecutor seized the opportunity to ask a question.

"Is there any concrete evidence so far?"

As if on command, the door opened and Erik Sohlman came in. He greeted everyone briefly before hungrily reaching for a sandwich and pouring himself a cup of coffee. Knutas decided to let him finish eating before plying him with questions.

"So what do we know about the victim?" Knutas looked down at the papers in front of him. "His name is Egon Wallin, and he was born in Visby in 1951. He has lived here all his life. Married to Monika Wallin, with two grown children. He lives in a terraced house over on Snäckgärds-vägen. His wife has been informed of his death. She's been taken to the hospital, and we'll interview her later. The two children have also been contacted; both live on the main-land. Wallin is well known in town, of course. He and his wife have run the art gallery for twenty-five years. He took it over from his father, and it's been in the family for as long as I can remember. Wallin has no criminal record. I've met him many times over the years, although I can't say we really knew each other. A hell of a nice guy, and he seemed to be well liked. Is there anyone here who knew him?"

They all shook their heads.

By this time Sohlman had washed down two sandwiches, so Knutas assumed that he was ready to talk.

"Erik, what can you report?"

Sohlman went over to the computer in the middle of the room. He signaled for Smittenberg, who sat closest to the door, to switch off the lights.

"This was the sight that Siv Eriksson encountered this morning on her way to work. She was walking along the path from Kung Magnus Road when she discovered the body hanging in full view from the top of the gate. Egon Wallin was fully clothed, but he had neither his wallet nor his cell phone on him. We'll be sending his clothes to the National Crime Lab later today for analysis. A scarf was found on the ground beneath the body. We don't know whether it belonged to the victim or not, but it's going to the NCL too."

Sohlman clicked through images of the body taken from various angles.

"I've only given him a preliminary examination, but I'm

almost positive that we're dealing with a homicide. And that's because of the wound on the neck. When we took the body down, I was able to get a closer look, and it seems likely that he did not die by hanging."

He paused for effect and gulped down some coffee. Everyone around the table was listening closely.

Sohlman used a pen to point at the image.

"Wallin has visible injuries that have nothing to do with the noose around his neck. Both of the thin parallel marks that we can see here go all the way round his neck, just above the larynx and continuing around the back. The marks indicate that he was strangled from behind with a thin, sharp cord—a piano wire or something similar. Either the killer wasn't sure that his victim was really dead after the first attempt, or else Wallin struggled and his attacker had to try again—hence the two parallel lines. There are reddish ruptures inside the marks, indicating that it was some sort of cord that caused his death. In addition, we can see this thicker mark, which probably resulted from the rope that was put around Wallin's neck when he was hanged. There is no sign of bleeding or discoloration. That indicates that he was already dead before he was hanged. Otherwise his injuries would look very different."

More photographs showed the victim's face. Knutas flinched. It was always worse if he happened to know and like the victim. He could never disconnect his own feelings completely.

Sohlman, on the other hand, seemed to have no trouble doing so. There he stood with his unruly mop of red hair, wearing his usual brown corduroy jacket, speaking in a calm and pleasant voice as he informed them of the details of the horrifying crime that had been committed. Now and then he took a sip of coffee, as if he were showing them his holiday snaps. Knutas would never be able to understand how Sohlman did it.

He cast a quick glance at Karin. Her face was as white as chalk. Knutas was full of sympathy; he knew how hard she struggled. The pictures of the victim showed everything in close-up. Wallin's face was reddish, his eyes were open. On his forehead a cut and a bruise were visible, and there was a scratch on his cheek. Knutas wondered if he got those injuries as he fought for his life.

As if Sohlman had read his mind, he now went on, "These injuries on his face are inconsistent. I have no idea where they came from. I suppose we can't rule out the possibility that they were sustained in connection with the hanging, but that seems strange, and the wound on his neck indicates that he was attacked from behind. But I'm happy to leave the interpretation of the facial wounds to the ME. He's got to have something to do too."

Sohlman grinned.

"How long has he been dead?" asked Jacobsson, whose face had now returned to its normal color.

"Difficult to say. Judging by the body temperature, I'd guess at least six hours. But that's just a guess, of course. You'll have to wait for the preliminary post-mortem results from the ME."

"Any other evidence?" asked Knutas.

"We haven't found much of interest in the gate area. A few cigarette butts and some chewing gum, but they could have been there before. There are some fresh tire tracks near the gate and also some footprints. The Östergravar area is crawling with footprints, of course. We've had the dogs go over that section, too, but so far there's been nothing of interest."

"Could this be about something as simple as a robbery?" said Wittberg, giving his colleagues an inquisitive look.

"Even if the robber lost his head and ended up killing

his victim, why would he go to the trouble of hanging him from the gate?" said Jacobsson doubtfully.

Sohlman cleared his throat. "If there's nothing else right now, I'd like to get back to the crime scene."

He shut down the computer and turned the lights back on before he left the room.

Knutas gave the remaining members of his team a sharp look. "Let's leave the question of motive for the time being. It's much too early to speculate about that right now. What we need to get started on is mapping out Egon Wallin's life: his art business, his employees, neighbors, friends, relatives, his past—everything. Karin and Thomas will be responsible for that. Lars, you'll handle the press—the reporters are going to be on us like hawks. The fact that the victim was hanged in this fashion isn't going to make things easier. You know how much the tabloid hacks love a scandal—they're going to be drooling over this."

"Shouldn't we hold a press conference today?" suggested Lars Norrby. "Otherwise we're going to spend all our time on the phone. And everyone is just going to ask the same questions."

"It seems a little early for that," Knutas objected. "Wouldn't a press release be sufficient for the time being?"

"Hmm, I don't know. It sounds like this could be a major case. Wouldn't it be better to take care of everybody at once?"

"Okay. Let's send out a press release right after the meeting, confirming that this is a homicide case, and then we'll schedule a press conference for this afternoon. How's that?"

Norrby nodded.

"And then we'll put all our efforts into finding out as much as we can about Wallin and what he did on the days leading up to his death. Who did he meet? What did he do on the day of the murder? Who was the last person to see him alive? This murder didn't just happen by chance."

On the plane Johan had time to think about Emma. Everything had happened so fast that he hadn't been able to try calling her again. Now they'd be seeing each other sooner than planned. In his mind he pictured her as he last saw her, with her dark eyes, pale complexion, and sensitive mouth. He thought that she had looked at him in a new way when they parted. As if he meant more to her than previously. For three years they had struggled with their relationship, and yet he was happier than he had ever been before Emma came into his life.

He leaned back in his seat and looked out of the window. The fleecy clouds reminded him of the misty shore where Helena Hillerström had got lost and then met her killer three years earlier. She had been Emma's best friend, and it was in connection with the murder investigation that they had first met. Johan had interviewed Emma, and then they began an affair. She was married at the time, and the mother of two young children. How long ago that seems, he thought. Now Emma had been divorced from Olle for over a year and had given birth to another child— and this time Johan was the father. Elin was eight months old and a true miracle. But it hadn't been easy to cultivate their new relationship. There were so many factors in the way, so many different people involved.

As far as his job was concerned, Johan was stationed in Stockholm, and there wasn't much he could do about it. And Emma had to take her other children, Sara and Filip, into consideration. Her ex-husband had started getting difficult again and was blocking all attempts to negotiate when it came to the children.

It was an understatement to say that they were fighting an uphill battle. On many occasions Johan had been convinced that their relationship was over, but each time they had found their way back to each other. Now their love felt stronger than ever. Johan had accepted that Emma needed time with her own children, that she wasn't yet ready to move in with him, even though they had Elin.

They tried to see each other as often as possible. Johan went to Gotland at least once a week for his job, but it wasn't enough. At the end of the summer he was going to take paternity leave, and then he would move into Emma's house in Roma. That was going to be their trial by fire. If things went well, they would get married the following year and finally move in together permanently. That was what Johan hoped, at least. Another child was also on his wish list, but on that topic he knew he had to proceed with caution. Emma had strongly rejected the idea every time he'd tried to bring it up.

He barely had time to drink his coffee before the captain announced that they were starting their descent into Visby airport. Johan was surprised every time at how quick and easy it was to fly over to the island. When he was back home in Stockholm and missing Emma and Elin, Gotland always felt painfully far away.

Pia was waiting for him with the car belonging to Swedish TV when he arrived. Her black hair stuck out in all directions, as usual, and her eyes were just as heavily made-up as always. A purple gemstone glittered in one nostril. She smiled and gave him a hug.

"Great to see you again. Things are really starting to cook." Her brown eyes shone. "The police put out a press release a little while ago. They suspect foul play." With a triumphant expression she handed over a piece of paper.

This was what Pia loved best. Action. Drama.

Johan read the brief statement. A press conference was scheduled for four o'clock. He took out a notebook and pen and asked Pia to turn on the radio so they could follow the news reports on the local station.

"Have they said anything about how he was killed?"

"God, no."

Pia rolled her eyes as she drove through Norderport, where she made a sharp turn and headed up the steep slope of Rackarbacken.

"On the other hand, I happen to know who the victim is," she said with satisfaction.

"Really? Who is it?"

"His name is Egon Wallin, and he's well known in the city. He runs—or rather ran," she quickly corrected herself, "the biggest art gallery in Visby. You know the one, right on Stora Torget."

"How old was he?"

"In his fifties, I'd guess; married with two children. A native of Gotland, originally from Sundre, and married to a Gotlander. Seemed totally trustworthy and honest. So it's unlikely this has anything to do with some kind of dispute among criminals."

"Could it have been a robbery?"

"Maybe, but if the perp was just after his money, why would he kill him and then hang his body from the gate? Doesn't that seem a little over the top?"

She brought the car to a halt with a lurch in the parking lot opposite the cathedral. Undoubtedly it had the best view of any parking lot in Sweden, thought Johan as he looked out over the city with its magnificent cathedral, clusters of buildings, and medieval ruins. And forming a backdrop beyond was the sea, although at the moment it was barely visible through the gray haze.

They hurried over to Dalman Gate.

The street was swarming with activity. Police officers had been posted to make sure no one went inside the area that had been cordoned off. The small parking lot next to the gate was filled with police vehicles, and police dogs were searching the area. Johan pushed his way forward. Over by the gate he saw Knutas talking to an older man whom he recognized as the ME. He managed to catch Knutas's eye, and the superintendent signaled for the ME to wait a moment. Johan was on good terms with the police after the serial murders of the previous summer, when he had actually helped the authorities solve the case.

Knutas gave Johan a firm and heartfelt handshake. They

hadn't seen each other since Johan had started working again.

"How's it going?"

"I'm fine now. I've got a whale of a scar across my stomach, but hopefully that'll just make me more interesting at the beach in the summertime. So what can you tell me about all this?" Johan nodded toward the gate.

"I can't tell you much except that we're certain it's a homicide."

"How was he killed?"

"You know I can't discuss that right now."

"How can you be sure he didn't take his own life?"

Johan was still fishing, hoping to get the superintendent to let something slip unintentionally.

But he was out of luck. Knutas just gave him a stern look.

"Okay, okay," said Johan, backing off. "Can you confirm that Egon Wallin, the art dealer, is the victim?"

Knutas sighed in resignation. "Officially, no. Not all the family members have been notified yet."

"How about unofficially?"

"All right. It's true. The victim is Egon Wallin. But you didn't hear that from me."

"Could I do a short interview with you right here and now? An official one, that is?" Johan grinned.

"Be quick about it." Knutas didn't say much more than what Johan already knew. But there was still a lot to be said for interviewing the officer in charge at the crime scene. Besides, it also showed all the work going on in the background. That was television's strength: taking the viewer to the actual scene.

Johan and Pia interviewed a number of people who were in the vicinity. When they were finished, Johan looked at his watch.

"We've got time to swing by the gallery too. The place

is probably closed, since it's Sunday, but we can still get an exterior shot. Maybe I can do a piece-to-camera there."

"Sure, of course." Pia folded up her equipment.

When they parked the TV car on Stora Torget, they saw flowers and burning torches on the pavement outside the gallery. A "Closed" sign was posted on the door. All the lights were off, and through the dark Johan could just make out some of the big paintings hanging on the walls. Suddenly he gave a start. Out of the corner of his eye he saw someone going up the stairs inside. He peered through the window to try to get a better view, and knocked on the door several times.

Even though he waited there for a long time, no one came to open it.

Knutas spent all of Sunday dashing madly between police headquarters and Dalman Gate. Late in the afternoon he suddenly realized that he had forgotten to call home.

As soon as he heard Lina's voice he remembered they were planning to have dinner with his parents at their farm up in Kappelshamn in northern Gotland. Damn. He knew how particular they were about everything going according to schedule. In his mind he could already hear the disappointment in his father's voice as Lina reported that his son wouldn't be joining them. His father had never fully accepted the fact that Knutas had become a police officer. Not really. And his opinion still had an effect on Knutas, even though he was fifty-two years old. When it came to his parents, he would never be truly grown-up.

Lina, on the other hand, usually accepted a change in plan with equanimity, whether it was a postponed holiday in the mountains or a parent-teacher meeting that he had to miss.

"It'll work out," she would simply say, and it always did. He was rarely made to feel guilty because of his job, and that made his life so much easier. His Danish wife had an easygoing temperament that often made him think how terribly lucky he'd been. They'd met just by chance when he went to a restaurant in Copenhagen while attending a conference for police officers. Back then she was working as a waitress while completing her studies. Now she was a midwife at Visby Hospital.

There was standing room only at the press conference. Because the victim was so well known on Gotland, the story was big news for the local media. And the fact that he'd been found hanging from a gate in Visby's ring wall was enough to spark the interest of the media all over Sweden. Besides, it was a Sunday.

When Knutas and Norrby entered the room where the press conference was being held, the high level of anticipation was palpable. The reporters were seated in rows with their notepads ready on their laps. The camera people were setting up their equipment, and microphones had been affixed to the podium at the front of the room.

Knutas went over the most important information and revealed the identity of the victim. There was no reason to keep that secret. All of the family members had now been contacted, rumors had begun spreading in Visby, and flowers were piling up outside the gallery on Stora Torget.

"Do you suspect a robbery?"

The question came from a representative of the local radio station.

"We can't rule out the possibility of a robbery at the moment," said Knutas.

"Did the victim have anything of value in his possession? A wallet, for instance?"

Knutas gave a start. Johan Berg, of course. He and Norrby exchanged glances.

"That kind of detail is under investigation, so I can't go into it right now."

"How can you be so certain that it's a homicide?"

"A preliminary examination of the victim has been done, and he has sustained injuries that could not have been self-inflicted."

"Can you describe the injuries?"

"No."

"Was a weapon used?"

"I'm not going to answer that question either."

"How was he hoisted up so high in the gateway?" asked the same aggressive reporter from the local newspaper who had been at the crime scene. "You had to get help from the fire department to get the body down."

"We assume that we're either dealing with more than one perpetrator or with a man who is unusually strong."

"Are you looking for a body builder?"

"Not necessarily. Those types of guys often look much stronger than they actually are."

Someone laughed.

"Do you have any theories about whether the perpetrator is from Gotland or the mainland?"

"We're keeping that question open."

"If the murder didn't result from a robbery, what do you think was the motive?"

"It's much too early to speculate about that. We're working on a broad front and keeping all avenues open. Nothing can be ruled out at this early stage."

"What are the police doing at the moment?"

"We're interviewing people, knocking on doors, and going over tips that have come in. And we're asking the public to come forward if anyone thinks they saw or heard anything, either on the night of the murder or the day before. We think that the perpetrator may have gone to Dalman Gate to survey the area before the murder took place."

"Egon Wallin's gallery had a big and well-attended opening the same day that he was killed," said Johan. "What do you think is the significance of that?"

"We don't know, but we're asking everyone who attended the opening on Saturday to contact the police."

Not much else was said. Knutas and Norrby ended the press conference and stood up to leave the room.

All the reporters immediately crowded around Knutas to get individual interviews. He tried to refer as many as possible to Norrby, who gladly dealt with one reporter after another.

Most people asked the same questions, and they didn't vary greatly from what had been asked during the press conference.

After an hour, it was finally over and Knutas felt completely drained. He regretted offering to participate at all. Especially at such an early stage in a homicide investigation, when it was important for him to be available to his colleagues and not to journalists. Lars Norrby could just as well have handled the press conference on his own. He was the police spokesman, after all.

K nutas shut himself up in his office for a while after the press conference. Exhaustion overcame him as he sat there in silence. He took out his pipe and began filling it, pondering how to get Norrby to take responsibility for the press and devote less of his time to the actual investigation. Knutas didn't feel he had the patience to deal with the media to the same extent as he had in the past. It seemed senseless for the person in charge of the investigation to waste his time on keeping the press informed, especially when the police had so little to report.

Generally he and Norrby got on well together. His colleague could be a bit slow and long-winded, but there was nothing wrong with the way he did his job.

Knutas and Norrby were about the same age, and they had worked together for twenty years. It was not at all clear in the beginning that Knutas and not Norrby would be the one to be promoted to head of the criminal division. That was how it had turned out, but Knutas couldn't really explain why.

Lars Norrby was a likeable person, divorced, with two teenage sons who lived with him. The most striking thing about his appearance was his height. He was almost six foot seven. The fact that he was thin, bordering on gaunt, made his height all the more impressive.

If Norrby felt slighted because it was Knutas who had become detective superintendent, he concealed his feelings well. He had never shown even a hint of jealousy. Knutas respected him for that.

He stuck the unlit pipe in his mouth and rang Wittberg on his cell, but the line was busy.

A list of those who had attended the opening at the gallery was being put together. The employees who had been at the dinner afterward had been contacted, and interviews were going on.

Knutas had asked Wittberg to find the artist and his manager at once. According to the victim's wife, Monika Wallin, who had undergone an initial interview at the hospital, both the artist and his manager were supposed to stay on Gotland until Tuesday.

Knutas hoped to clear up various matters by speaking with them. The fact that Wallin had been killed on the very day that he held the first exhibition opening of the season, which had also attracted a great deal of interest, might not be a coincidence.

He had asked Jacobsson to help out with the interview as his own English wasn't adequate.

The phone rang. It was Wittberg, and he sounded out of breath.

"Hi, I'm at the Wisby Hotel."

"Yes?"

"Mattis Kalvalis isn't here. His manager either. The clerk at the front desk ordered a taxi to take them to the airport this morning."

"What? You mean they've run off?" Knutas tapped his chin.

"Apparently. I called Gotland Air to find out if they really did take the flight to Stockholm. And they did. The plane left at nine this morning."

Emma had just come through the door when the phone rang. She set Elin down on the floor. Dressed in a heavy snowsuit, her daughter sat there motionless, looking like a tiny Michelin man.

"Emma Winarve."

"Hi, it's me, Johan." Why did she always feel a burning in her stomach whenever she suddenly heard his voice?

"Hi!"

Elin started to cry. Emma kept her eyes fixed on her daughter as she spoke.

"I'm in Visby. Tried to call earlier, but no one answered."

"No, I've been out for a long walk. But listen, could I call you back in ten minutes? I've just stepped in the door with Elin."

"Sure. Do that."

Emma quickly got Elin undressed, turning her head away when she noticed the stink of her daughter's diaper. She took Elin into the bathroom to get her changed. She thought about Johan as she tended to Elin. She'd missed him more than usual lately. Not for any practical reason. She was doing fine, and Elin was an easy child to take care of. Sara and Filip had also adapted to their new routine and were beginning to get used to the idea of life after the divorce. Sara was in third grade and Filip in second. There was only a year between them, and sometimes she thought they were almost like twins. Nowadays they enjoyed playing together, and they got along even better than before the divorce. The children had drawn closer together because of their parents' separation. At the same time it was also rather sad, as if their faith and trust in their parents had diminished. At such a young age they had been forced to realize that nothing lasted for ever and nothing can be taken for granted.

For the sake of the children, Emma was cautious about her new relationship. Of course the relationship was the reason why her marriage had failed, but she wasn't yet ready to throw herself into a new family arrangement. She had consciously kept Johan at a distance, even though she was more in love with him than ever.

Her life had been turned completely upside down since they met, and sometimes she wondered if it was all worth it. Yet in her heart she had no doubt. That was why she had decided to carry their child to term, even though the pregnancy was unplanned and Elin had come into the world at a time when her relationship with Johan was on very shaky ground.

The fact that Johan had almost died—when Elin was only a month old—had shocked Emma more than she'd at first been willing to admit. Since then she had no doubt whatsoever that she wanted to live with him. It was just a matter of doing everything at the right time and in the proper order, for the sake of the children.

She picked up Elin and nuzzled her soft neck. Dinner would have to wait. She sat down on the sofa and punched in the number of Johan's cell. He answered at once.

"Hi, sweetheart. How are things?"

"Fine. How come you're here? Has something happened?"

"A man was found dead in Dalman Gate. He was murdered."

"Oh my God. When did it happen?"

"This morning. Didn't you hear about it on the news? They've been talking about nothing else all day long."

"No, I missed it. Sounds awful. Do you know who it was?"

"Yes, the art dealer on Stora Torget."

"What? Egon Wallin? Is that true?"

"Do you know him?"

"No, but everybody knows who he is. Was he robbed? Is that what happened?"

"I don't think so. It seems a little much to go about hanging a person in that way, so I suspect there's something else behind it."

"You mean he was hanged from the gate? God, how macabre. It sounds like those horrible murders from last summer. Do you think somebody was incited by them?"

"You mean a copycat killer? Let's hope not. Although I don't know exactly how Wallin was murdered, only that he was found hanging from the gate. The police aren't saying much. But Pia and I are up to our eyeballs in work. We're doing stories for Regional News, Rapport, and Aktuellt."

"So you're busy tonight?"

Johan's voice took on a softer tone. "I was thinking of asking you whether I could come over later. After I'm done."

"Sure, do that. That would be great."

"I might not get there until around nine or even later, depending on whether anything happens about the murder."

"That's okay. It doesn't matter. Come over whenever you can."

K nutas could hear excited voices coming from the conference room as he arrived for the meeting with the investigative team on Sunday evening. Everyone else was already
there, crowded around one of the computers on the table.

"Those damned reporters," growled Wittberg. "Don't they
have any brains at all?" He tapped his finger on his temple.

"What are you talking about?" Knutas came over to find out
what was going on. The front page of the online version of the
evening paper showed a photo of Egon Wallin hanging from
Dalman Gate. The headline was simple and terse.

"MURDERED" it said in big black letters. The only miti-
gating detail was the fact that the face was partially hidden by
a police officer, making it impossible to identify the victim.

Knutas shook his head.

Wittberg went on. "Don't they have any consideration for
his family? Good Lord, the man has children!"

"That picture isn't going to turn up on the front page
of the printed edition, is it?" asked Jacobsson. "Surely that
would be going too far."

"I'm beginning to wonder whether it's even worth holding
press conferences anymore," said Wittberg. "They just seem
to get the reporters all worked up."

"Maybe we got a little ahead of ourselves this time," Knutas admitted.

He'd been foolish enough to let Norrby convince him that a press conference would calm down the media and give the police more chance to do their work in peace. But the result seemed to be the complete opposite.

He felt his irritation growing. A persistent headache throbbed at the back of his head.

"The clock's ticking, and we need to start talking about more important matters," he said, taking his usual seat at one end of the table.

Everybody sat down so the meeting could begin.

"We're now positive that we're dealing with a homicide. I've received an initial statement from the ME, who agrees with Sohlman that the victim's injuries speak quite clearly. The body will be transported by boat to the mainland this evening, to be taken to forensics. I'm hoping that by tomorrow we'll have a preliminary post-mortem report. Wallin also has a number of peculiar facial injuries, and we'd like to find an explanation for them. Out of consideration for his family, we'll wait to search both his home and the gallery. I just had an interesting conversation with one of his employees, a woman named Eva Blom. She told me that a sculpture is missing from the gallery. It's a small piece made of Gotland limestone. It's called "Yearning" and it was done by the sculptor Anna Petrus. Apparently it's a smaller version of a sculpture in the garden at Muramaris. That artist residence, you know, located right before the Krusmynta estate."

"When did it disappear?"

"On Saturday. According to Ms. Blom, it was there when the gallery opened at one o'clock. She remembers it specifically because she went around the whole place to make sure everything was in order."

"When did they close the gallery?"

"There were guests until around seven or eight. Then Egon Wallin, his wife, the artist, and the gallery employees all went to Donners Brunn for dinner. They locked up the gallery and set the alarm, as usual."

"Is she sure about that?"

"A hundred percent sure."

"So that means the sculpture disappeared sometime during the opening?"

"It seems so."

"Is it valuable?"

"No, apparently it's quite small, and the material isn't anything special. The artist is relatively unknown, so according to Ms. Blom there wouldn't be much point in stealing it to make money."

"Then why would anyone take it?"

The question was left hovering in the air, unanswered.

H is eyes were stinging with fatigue, and Knutas realized that it was about time for him to go home. He
hadn't had a minute to himself all day and wanted to sit
down in the privacy of his office to gather his thoughts
for a moment.

He sank into his old, worn oak chair with the soft leather
cushion. He had decided to keep it, in spite of the extensive refurbishment that police headquarters had undergone
six months earlier. All of the furniture had been replaced
but he'd had this chair for his entire career in the criminal
division, and he refused to let it go. He'd solved so many
cases sitting in it. It could spin around and rock back and
forth, and that gentle movement always seemed to allow his
thoughts to float freely.

The work had been so intense ever since Wallin's body
had been found in the morning that Knutas was having a
hard time grasping everything that was whirling through
his mind.

He shuddered when he recalled the sight that he'd encountered at Dalman Gate. Such a pleasant man. What was
happening here on Gotland? The number of violent crimes
had increased significantly during the past few years, espe-

cially murders. On the other hand, violence was increasing all over Sweden. He thought back to the days when someone breaking into a kiosk was considered front-page news. Nowadays that sort of incident hardly got any attention at all. The social climate had become more brutal on all fronts, and he didn't care for this development.

He took out his pipe from the top drawer of his desk and began meticulously to fill it. When he was done, he leaned back in his chair and began sucking on the pipe without lighting it.

The fact that the artist and his manager had vanished so mysteriously was disturbing. And it had turned out that they were accompanied by one of the art dealers who had been at the opening. Sixten Dahl. It had been impossible to reach any of them during the course of the day. Oh well, he thought. We'll just have to keep at it tomorrow.

His thoughts drifted to Egon Wallin. He'd run into the art dealer many times in different situations. He and Lina had also visited the gallery now and then over the years, even though they usually just went to look. But one time he did buy a painting by Lennart Jirlow, a restaurant scene that reminded him of the place where Lina had worked in Copenhagen when they met. He smiled at the memory. It was for Lina's fortieth birthday, and she had never been so happy about anything else he'd ever bought for her. Gifts were not Knutas's strong point.

In his mind he conjured up an image of Wallin. The most striking thing about him was his attire. He usually wore a long leather coat and trendy-looking cowboy boots, which made him seem more like a big-city resident than a Gotlander. It was obvious that he dyed his hair a reddish blond, and the light suntan that he sported all year round was equally artificial.

Wallin's appearance formed a stark contrast to that of

his wife, who seemed colorless and ordinary; her face was so nondescript that it was hard even to remember what she looked like. Sometimes Knutas had rather cruelly wondered why Wallin took such trouble with his appearance while his wife clearly didn't give a thought to her own.

Knutas actually knew very little about Wallin's personal life. Whenever they met, they exchanged only a few words, and Knutas usually felt that the conversation ended too quickly. He would have liked to talk more with Egon Wallin, but had the impression that the wish was not reciprocated. Even though they were about the same age, they had no mutual friends.

Wallin's children were much older than Knutas's twins, Petra and Nils, who were nearly fourteen, so they hadn't had opportunity to meet through their children either. Wallin hadn't seemed interested in sports, even though athletic events provided a strong sense of community on Gotland. Knutas himself swam regularly; he also played floor hockey and golf. He assumed that Wallin spent most of his time with art aficionados, and Knutas definitely didn't belong to that social circle. He didn't have a clue about art.

It was a rash choice for a crime scene, considering that the gate could actually be seen from Kung Magnus Road. A police vehicle could easily have passed by while the perpetrator hoisted up the body. Maybe he was so doped up that he didn't care.

Knutas immediately dismissed the idea. Nobody drunk or on drugs would have been able to carry out such a complicated plan. Another possibility was that the killer didn't know that police headquarters was so close. Maybe he was from the mainland. The question was, what was his connection to Egon Wallin? Did the murder have something to do with his art dealings, or was it about something else entirely?

Knutas sighed wearily. It was past eleven. Sooner or later they would undoubtedly know the answer.

Johan woke up in the big double bed in the house in Roma. He stretched out his hand to stroke the smooth skin on Emma's shoulder and touch a lock of her hair. From the crib he could hear a gurgling sound, which quickly got him out of bed. The room was dark, but he felt Elin's soft body, warm with sleep, against his own as he lifted her up and placed her on the changing table.

With a light twist of the key he switched on the music box and hummed along with "Baa, Baa, Black Sheep." Elin grabbed hold of her feet and prattled with delight. He burrowed his head against her chubby belly, making a smacking sound so that she whooped with laughter. In the midst of the game he suddenly stopped and held perfectly still, with his face pressed against her little body. For several seconds he stood there like that while Elin relaxed and fell silent.

Finally he had a child, but it had been two weeks since he last saw her. What kind of life was this? She was growing up with her mother, sharing the daily routines with her. For Elin, Emma was the one who represented security. He was just a minor figure—someone who occasionally popped up like a jack-in-the-box and was around for a few hours, a day or two at most, only to disappear again. What sort of relationship was that? How had things got to this point?

When Johan was back in Stockholm and his days were filled with work, everything seemed more or less okay. It was in the evenings when he was at home that the sense of longing would set in. Of course, he'd only been discharged from the hospital a couple of months ago, so they hadn't really been living apart as parents for very long.

They'd spend most of the Christmas holidays together, which had been great. After that, daily life had rolled along as usual, and the days had slipped by, one after the other, turning into weeks. He came over to Gotland as often as he could. But now he realized that he couldn't keep going like this.

He picked up Elin, warmed up some formula in the microwave, and sat down on the sofa in the living room to give her the bottle. He was suddenly overcome by a great sense of calm. His old life had now come to an end. It was definitely over.

Emma appeared in the doorway, her light brown hair tousled and longer than before. It now hung to the middle of her back. It was thick and glossy. She stood there, wearing only underwear and his light blue T-shirt, peering at him sleepily. Even though she was pale and bleary-eyed, he thought she was beautiful. His feelings for her were clear, in spite of the fact that nothing else in their relationship seemed simple. Things had been complicated right from the start. Yet here he now sat, holding his daughter in his arms, with the woman he loved standing nearby. All the struggling had to come to an end. He didn't care whether he could find a job as a journalist on Gotland or not. That shouldn't be the deciding factor. He'd take any kind of work he could find, even at the check-out stand at Hemköp, or washing cars. It made no difference at all.

"Are you already up?" Emma yawned and headed for the kitchen.

"Come here," he said as quietly as he could. Elin was sleeping in his arms with her mouth open.

"What is it?"

"Sit down." Emma looked surprised, but sat down next to him on the sofa, tucking her legs beneath her. He turned to look at her. There wasn't a sound in the room; it was as if she sensed that he had something important to say.

"Enough is enough." Johan spoke calmly, his tone matter-of-fact.

A worried look appeared on Emma's face. "What do you mean?"

Johan didn't break the silence. Instead, he got up, went into the dimly lit bedroom and carefully placed Elin in her crib. She didn't wake up. He closed the door and returned to the living room.

Emma watched him uneasily. Johan sat down on the sofa again and gently took her face between his hands.

"I want to move over here," he said calmly. "Live here with you and Elin. You're my family. I can't wait any longer. All the stuff about my job and everything else will just have to be worked out. You have to let me take care of you, be a real father to Elin and a stepfather to Sara and Filip. I want to be your husband. Will you marry me?"

Emma gave him a stunned look. Several seconds passed. Tears began rolling down her cheeks. It wasn't exactly the reaction that he'd expected.

"There, there, sweetheart." He leaned forward and put his arms around her. She started sobbing against his chest.

"It can't be that bad," he said with an uncertain smile.

"I'm just so tired," she wept. "I'm so damned tired."

Johan didn't really know what to say; clumsily he stroked Emma's back. Suddenly she began kissing his neck, and her kisses became more and more passionate. She pushed back her hair and searched hungrily for his mouth, keeping her eyes closed the whole time.

Desire flared up inside him, and he roughly pushed her back onto the sofa. He kissed her wildly, almost biting her lips. Emma responded with a low groan in her throat, and all of a sudden she wrapped her legs tightly around him. They made love on the sofa, then leaning against the table, against the windowsill, and finally on the floor. Afterward, as he lay with her head resting on his arm, he found himself looking up at the underside of the coffee table, which was only a few inches from his sweat-covered forehead. He smiled as he kissed her cheek.

"I'll take that as a yes."

As on most mornings, Knutas walked to work along Östra Hansegatan, past the Swedish TV and Radio building. He saw lights on in the windows upstairs where Regional News now had its offices. He wondered whether Johan was already on the job. It wouldn't surprise him.

It was still dark outside, and the air was cold and brisk. The walk took less than twenty minutes and helped him to think more clearly.

When he opened the door to police headquarters, he felt the familiar tingling sensation that always came over him when starting on a new murder investigation. The fact that someone had been killed was of course terrible; at the same time, there was a certain excitement mixed with determination to catch the murderer. The hunt had begun, and that was something he enjoyed without feeling any shame. Knutas liked his job; he had felt that way about it ever since he was promoted to the criminal division twenty years earlier. He had thrived in his position as head of department for the past ten years—though he could do without the paperwork.

As usual, he greeted the young women at the reception desk and exchanged a few words with the duty officer before he went up the stairs to the criminal division on the first floor.

Every chair in the conference room was already occupied when he entered, two minutes before the scheduled start time. This first meeting after a major event had occurred was always special. The energy in the room was palpable.

Erik Sohlman started off by reporting on the latest news from the technical investigation.

"The killer arrived by car on Norra Murgatan and drove all the way up to the gate. There are signs that the body was dragged; the marks on Wallin's body also indicate that he was murdered somewhere else and then transported to Dalman Gate. All the items that were picked up in the Östergravar area will be studied, but they're not really of great interest given the perpetrator probably never entered that area at all."

"A first interview was conducted last night with the victim's wife, Monika Wallin," said Knutas. "We know that she was the last one to see Wallin alive. After the dinner at Donners Brunn on Saturday night, the couple returned to their terraced house on Snäckgärdsvägen. Mrs. Wallin went to bed, but her husband said he wanted to stay up for a while. In the morning when she woke, he wasn't there. He had apparently put on his coat and gone out. The rest we know."

"Could there have been a third person in the house?" asked Jacobsson. "I mean, maybe he received an unexpected visitor, or else someone broke in?"

"Unlikely. He seems to have left alone."

"Did his wife have any idea where he was going?" asked Wittberg.

"No," said Knutas. "But I'm going to see her today, so maybe I'll learn more. She was in shock yesterday."

"What about the tire tracks?" asked Norrby.

"Hard to say. They're from a larger type of vehicle. I'd guess a van or a small truck. We need to check on any stolen vehicles and talk to the car rental agencies," said Knutas.

"I really wonder what the motive was behind this whole thing," said Wittberg pensively, running his hand through his curly blond hair. "I mean, it takes a lot to kill somebody. Why would the killer then hang his victim from the gate? It must mean something specific."

Knutas thought Wittberg seemed unusually alert for a Monday morning. Normally he was good and tired after his weekend escapades. The attractive twenty-eight-year-old was the Casanova of police headquarters. His cornflower-blue eyes, his dimples, and his toned body charmed all the female employees on the force. With the possible exception of Karin Jacobsson, who seemed to regard him as a nice but slightly cocky little brother. Thomas Wittberg had had a constant stream of new girlfriends, but lately he seemed to have settled down. He'd just come back from a holiday to Thailand with his current girlfriend, and his deep suntan formed a sharp contrast to his pale and hollow-eyed colleagues.

"It can't be just a random killing," Jacobsson went on. "I mean, some kind of impulsive attack on the street or anything like that. Or some lunatic he just happened to run into. This seems very well planned. The murderer must have been someone he knew."

"We have a complete list of everyone who was invited to the gallery opening, plus we're checking whether anyone decided to crash the party," Knutas continued. "We're interviewing them all. And we need to pull out all the stops to get hold of the artist and his manager."

"They haven't checked out of the hotel over here, at any rate," said Wittberg. "Their belongings are still in their rooms, and they haven't paid the bill, so maybe they're just out for the day. I'll keep trying to track them down; so far they're not answering their cell phones. But I'm hoping to get hold of Sixten Dahl, at least. His gallery will be opening soon, and somebody there should be able to help us. It's very possible that he knows the whereabouts of the other two men."

The meeting was interrupted by the ringing of Knutas's cell. He pulled it out of his inside jacket pocket and took the call. Everyone waited in silence. They listened to the murmuring and grunting of their boss and watched his expression change from great surprise to worried circumspection. When he ended the conversation, everyone's eyes were fixed on him.

"That was Monika Wallin. A little while ago a moving truck parked outside their house. The movers had been hired by Egon Wallin with clear instructions as to what they were supposed to pick up. He'd paid for the entire job in advance."

The premises of the venerable Bukowski's Auction House were somber and elegant. The reception area faced Arsenalgatan, between Berzelii Park and Kungsträdgården Park in central Stockholm.

The art valuer Erik Mattson, clad in a gray suit and with his hair combed back, received the customer, whose attire was significantly simpler than his own and who seemed rather bewildered and ill at ease in the discreet and distinguished setting. The man had brought an oil painting, tucked under his arm and securely wrapped in newspaper and silver tape.

On the phone that morning the man had described the painting as an archipelago scene painted in various shades of gray, with an expanse of sky and sea and a little white house with a black roof. Even though the work of art was unsigned, Erik thought it sounded interesting, and he'd asked the customer to bring it in to be evaluated.

Now he was here, wearing a coat that had seen better days, and with a thin, old-fashioned scarf around his neck. His shoes could have used a good polishing; that was something that Erik Mattson always noticed.

Well-maintained shoes always indicated that a customer

took good care of himself. This was not the case with the man who now stood in front of him, nervously fingering the large package. He had beads of sweat on his forehead. The collar of his shirt was wrinkled, his coat was threadbare, and the gloves that he'd placed on the table had worn through the lining. He spoke with the distinct accent of Söder, the old working-class district of the city. Not many people talked that way anymore. It was almost charming.

Erik hoped that the painting wasn't stolen. He studied the customer carefully—no, he didn't look like a criminal. Besides, the painting probably wasn't worth anything; that was the usual situation with unsigned works. But he always liked to have a look. Every once in a while they'd find a real gem, and nobody wanted to miss out on such a possibility. The worst-case scenario was that the valuable item would then end up with their fiercest competitor, Auction Works, instead. That couldn't be allowed to happen.

Mattson showed the customer into the cramped but elegant valuation room. It was furnished with a Gustavian table with a chair on either side; a painting by Einar Jolin hung on the wall. There was also a bookcase filled with reference works. A laptop lay on the table, so that he could quickly check the history of a work or find information about its possible creator. If it was difficult to assess the value of a work, he might have to ask a colleague for help. Sometimes a painting would be kept for a few days if a more extensive examination was required. It was exciting work and Erik Mattson loved it.

Together they placed the painting on the table, and Erik felt a familiar sense of anticipation fill his chest. This was one of the golden moments of his job: when he stood next to a customer he had never met before, with a painting that had been described to him but that he hadn't actually seen yet. He felt the excitement of wondering whether it might be an unknown, perhaps forgotten, work by a great artist worth millions of kronor, or a worthless copy by some art student.

Erik had worked as an assistant to the curator of modern painting and sculpture at Bukowski's for fifteen years, and in that time he'd become an expert appraiser of the art they handled. Yet he hadn't advanced to the position of curator, as most assistants did after a few years. But there was a reason for this.

The newspaper rustled; it was hard to get the tape off.

"Where did you get the painting?" he asked, to ease the customer's obvious nervousness.

"It hung in Pappa's summerhouse in the archipelago for years, but when he sold the house, all of us children were allowed to take whatever we wanted. I'd always liked the painting, but I didn't think it was valuable." He glanced at Erik with an expression of both hope and concern. "A neighbor happened to see it on the wall, and he said that it was so expertly done that I ought to have it valued. I really don't think that it's worth anything, you know," he said apologetically. "But I thought it wouldn't hurt to find out."

"Of course. That's what we're here for."

Erik gave the man an encouraging smile, and he seemed to relax a bit.

"Where did your father get it?"

"My father and mother bought it at an auction sometime in the forties. Since then it always hung in the summerhouse. It's on the island of Svartso. You know, one of those old merchant's villas. They liked having a scene from the archipelago on the wall. So, that's about the whole story."

Now only the innermost paper was left.

Erik turned the painting over and was astounded by what he saw. He couldn't hide his surprise, and the customer stared at him with delight as he eagerly took out a loupe to study the authenticity of the work. Neither of them said a word, but their excitement resonated through the room.

Erik immediately recognized the style of the artist. This particular motif had been used by the painter several times, even though his total oeuvre wasn't extensive; there were less than a hundred known works. After an acrimonious divorce in 1892 and subsequent court proceedings in which he lost custody of his three children, the artist had devoted himself to painting. Stockholm's archipelago became his refuge. The lighthouses and navigational buoys, the sparse vegetation and the defiant rocks exposed to the elements all became symbols for the artist himself, struggling against the tides of the time and defending his right to think freely.

He was meticulous in his observations of nature; in grayish-blue nuances he had depicted the capricious weather of the archipelago. Erik Mattson had seen him use this motif at Dalaro. In the solitary beacon on a desolate shore under a dramatic sky, he had found a motif that suited him during that period. The fact that the artist hadn't signed the painting was not unusual. He had regarded painting as a sideline, something he turned to whenever he developed writer's block.

Yet he was considered one of the greatest artists of his day. Erik Mattson did a quick mental calculation and placed the value of the painting at between four and six million kronor.

The artist was none other than August Strindberg, Sweden's most debated author in the early twentieth century.

To say that Monika Wallin was plain was no exagger- ation. Her mousy brown hair was cut short and care- lessly styled, her thin lips bore no trace of lipstick, and her posture, though erect, was awkward. At first glance she seemed to be someone who would easily disappear in a crowd. She opened the door to the terraced house on Snäckgärdsvägen after Knutas rang the bell four times. She looked pale and tired, and there were dark circles under her eyes.

Knutas was surprised that he didn't recognize her. He knew that they had met several times before, although they had never actually spoken to each other. Yet Monika Wallin was not someone who made a lasting impression; that much was clear.

Knutas introduced himself and reached out his hand. "My condolences."

She shook his hand without changing her expression. Her handshake was surprisingly firm.

"Come in," she said, and led the way into the house.

Knutas could see as soon as he stepped into the hall that the house was occupied by art lovers. Covering nearly every square inch of the light-colored walls were paintings, both large and small, by all sorts of modern artists. Everything was of the highest quality; even Knutas could see that.

They each sat down in an armchair in the living room, where the windows faced the grayish-blue sea. Only the narrow road that ran toward Snack divided the property from the shore.

Knutas took out his notebook and pen. "So, why don't you tell me what happened this morning?"

Monika Wallin was holding a handkerchief in her hand, twisting and turning it as she talked.

"Well, I was sitting in the kitchen when a big removal van suddenly came roaring up our driveway. At first I thought it had taken the wrong turn. But when the men rang the bell, they showed me the contract that Egon had signed. He had hired them."

"Do you have a copy of the contract?"

"Yes, they left several documents." Monika Wallin got up and continued to talk as he heard her opening a drawer in the kitchen. "They left empty-handed, of course. It didn't really make any difference to them, since Egon had paid for everything in advance."

She came back and handed Knutas a sheet of thin, light blue paper. He saw that it was a copy of a contract, and that the moving truck was supposed to transport the goods to Artillerigatan in Stockholm.

"Artillerigatan," he mused. "Isn't that in the Östermalm district?"

Monika Wallin shook her head. "I don't know where it is."

"There's no number for a land line on the contract," murmured Knutas. "Just a cell number. Is it Egon's?"

"Yes."

"And you don't know anything about this?"

"No, it was a complete surprise. Unfortunately, it wasn't the only one. Egon has a desk here in the house with several locked drawers. Of course I knew where he kept the key, but I've never had any reason to snoop through his things. I opened the drawers just before you arrived."

She reached for a folder lying on the table. Her lips were thin and dry, and right now they narrowed even more.

"There's a divorce application in here, and he'd even taken the trouble to fill it out. There are also documents stating that he'd bought an apartment on Artillerigatan in Stockholm, and that he'd sold our gallery to a certain Per Eriksson," she said bitterly. "It's hard to believe."

"May I have a look?"

Knutas studied the documents intently, making his way quickly through the pile. It was clear that Egon Wallin had been making plans to decamp.

"I don't know how I'm going to make it through this," she said plaintively. "First the murder. And now this."

"I can understand how tough this must be for you," said Knutas sympathetically. "And I'm sorry that I have to trouble you right now. But I need to ask you a few questions. For the sake of the investigation."

Monika Wallin nodded. She continued to crumple the handkerchief in her hand.

"Tell me about Saturday, when you had the gallery opening," Knutas began. "What did you both do that day?"

"Egon left for the gallery early in the morning, before I was even awake. That wasn't unusual if we were having an opening. He liked to be there in plenty of time, to make any last-minute changes, see that the paintings were hung correctly, and so on. I always take care of the catering, and I arrived just after eleven, at the same time that the food arrived."

"How did Egon seem? Was his behavior different in any way?"

"He seemed jumpier than usual, impatient and irritable. I thought it was odd because everything was going so smoothly."

"Then what happened?"

"The artist, Mattis Kalvalis, showed up, and after that we didn't have a moment's peace. He was constantly asking for something—a glass of water, an ashtray, cigarettes, pastries, a Band-Aid, all sorts of things. He seemed totally wound up; I've never met anyone so nervous before. And incredibly self-absorbed. He showed no concern for the fact that we had other things to do. It was as if he filled up the whole room." She sighed and shook her head. "But then all the guests began to arrive, and after that it was nonstop activity until seven o'clock."

"Did anything unusual happen during the course of the day that you noticed?"

"Yes, actually there was something. Egon was gone for a long time. I went looking for him, but no one knew where he was."

"How long was he gone?"

"It must have been over an hour."

"Did you ask him where he'd been?"

"Yes, but he just said that he'd gone out to get more wine. There was so much to do that I didn't give it another thought."

She turned to stare out of the window, and for a while neither of them spoke. Knutas was waiting for her to go on without his prompting. During sensitive interviews, it was important to know when to keep quiet.

"How did he seem when he came back?"

"Exactly like earlier in the day—strangely agitated."

"Do you think one of the guests had upset him?"

"I don't know," she said with a sigh. "If so, it was most likely Sixten Dahl. He was the only one there that Egon didn't like. He's an art dealer in Stockholm."

Knutas gave a start. Sixten Dahl was the one who had accompanied the artist and his manager back to Stockholm on Sunday morning. For the time being, however, Knutas didn't let on what he knew.

"Why didn't Egon like him?"

"They would run into each other occasionally, and Egon always complained that he found Sixten overbearing. Maybe it was more the fact that they were very alike," she mused. "They often competed for the same artists and had the same taste in art. Mattis Kalvalis was one example. I know that Sixten Dahl was interested in him too, but Mattis had chosen Egon."

"What happened after the opening?"

"We went to Donners Brunn for dinner."

"Who was there?" asked Knutas, even though he already knew the answer.

"Egon and I, Mattis Kalvalis, and the others who work at the gallery."

"How many of you work there?"

"Four altogether. The others are Eva Blom and Gunilla Rydberg. They've both been with us for twenty years."

Knutas was busily taking notes. The mention of Sixten Dahl was extremely interesting. He hoped that by now Wittberg had managed to get hold of the art dealer and the two others. Eva Blom was an old acquaintance. She and Knutas had been in the same class as children, and he knew that she lived with her family in Vate parish. On the other hand, he didn't know Gunilla Rydberg.

"Are you aware that both the artist and his manager have left the hotel?"

"What? No, I didn't know that."

"They went to Stockholm yesterday morning. Do you know why they might have gone there?"

"No idea." Monika Wallin looked genuinely surprised.

"Mattis was supposed to come in today to sign the agent contract with Egon. Of course, that's no longer relevant."

"When are they due to return to Lithuania?"

"Tuesday afternoon. I know that for certain because we had planned to have lunch together before they left for the airport."

"Hmm." Knutas cleared his throat. "Let's go back to the night of the murder. Did anything significant happen during dinner at Donners Brunn?"

"No. We ate a good meal, had plenty to drink, and enjoyed ourselves. By then Mattis had calmed down; it was probably just nervousness, and he was finally able to relax. He told us lots of funny stories from Lithuania, and we all laughed so much that we cried."

"When did the party break up?"

"We left the restaurant around eleven. We said good-night outside, and then everyone went their separate ways. Egon and I took a cab home. I went to bed almost at once, but he said that he wanted to stay up for a while. That wasn't unusual. I fade away when it gets late, but he's always been a night owl. I almost always go to bed before he does."

"Where did you see him last?"

"He was sitting in his chair in the living room," she said pensively.

"His wallet and cell phone were both missing when he was found. Did he leave them at home?"

"I'm sure he didn't. Egon never went anywhere without his cell phone. He always had it with him, even when he went to the bathroom. And I find it hard to believe that he'd leave the house without his wallet. Besides, I would have found them in the house and I haven't."

"Could you try to call his cell phone? It might be hidden somewhere," suggested Knutas.

"Absolutely."

Monika Wallin got up to get her own phone. She punched in a number. Nothing happened. She tried again as she walked through the house.

"Nothing," she said with a sigh. "I just get his voicemail."

"Okay" said Knutas. "Thanks for trying. Could you write down his number for me?"

"Of course."

"Just one more thing about Saturday. We heard that a sculpture disappeared from the gallery."

"Yes, it's very annoying. One of the guests must have taken it."

She seems very composed for a woman whose husband has just been murdered, and in such a macabre fashion, he thought. And then to find out that her husband was planning to leave her and move out without even telling her.

Knutas wondered if he would have behaved the same way if Lina had been murdered and hanged like that. He thought he would probably have been sedated in the psychiatric ward of Visby Hospital. He shuddered inwardly and quickly brushed aside the thought.

"You have two children, is that right?" he went on.

"Yes. A son who's twenty-three. He lives in Stockholm. And a daughter who's twenty. She's studying to be a doctor in Umeå."

"What does your son do?"

"He works at a daycare center."

"I see."

"The children will be here later today."

"I understand," said Knutas. "Pardon me for asking such a personal question, but how was your relationship with your husband?"

Monika Wallin answered instantly, as if she'd been expecting the question. "Safe and boring. We had a good marriage in the sense that we were good friends, but over the years it had become more like a brother–sister relationship. We ran the gallery together, but otherwise there wasn't much."

"Why did you stay together? It couldn't have been for the children's sake."

Knutas could have bitten his tongue. He ought to tread more carefully with a new widow. The words had come out before he had thought about what he was saying. But Monika Wallin didn't seem upset.

"We both felt that things were fine as they were. The gallery took up almost all of our time; he devoted himself to art and his business trips, while I took care of the administrative work. We lived side by side but rarely crossed paths. But the fact is, I think he'd found someone else."

She stretched, and Knutas realized that he was actually beginning to think she was rather elegant. Upon closer inspection, her hair wasn't mousy at all; it had a soft, ash-colored sheen in the light coming through the window. Her complexion was smooth and clear. Her colorlessness was in fact quite beautiful.

"Why do you think so?"

"We no longer had any sex life. In the past Egon always had great needs in that area."

She cleared her throat.

"There were other signs, too. He seemed unusually happy and pleased after his trips to Stockholm. He began taking more interest in his appearance, and he stayed up late at night, sitting in front of his computer. He said that he was working, but I could tell he was chatting online with someone."

"But you never confronted him about this?"

"No. Why should I do that? It wouldn't have made any difference anymore. Our relationship was no longer what it had once been."

"So you have no idea who it might have been?"
"No clue at all."

The murder of the art dealer Egon Wallin in Visby had grabbed the attention of the whole country. Pia Lilja was the only one who had captured photos of the victim as he hung from the gate in the ring wall, and every Swedish newspaper had wanted copies. Max Grenfors, who was the head of Regional News, had been overjoyed when he rang Johan's cell phone on Monday morning, and he offered high praise for the previous day's reporting.

"Terrific! Great job. And amazing photos. Pia is unbeatable!"

"But shouldn't you—"

"Yes, yes, I've already called to congratulate her," Grenfors interrupted, as if he knew what Johan was going to say. "Have you seen the morning papers? All of Sweden is talking about the murder. And everybody is going to wish they had your job today," he continued effusively. "I need you to send in a report by lunchtime and another one for the afternoon broadcast."

Sometimes Johan got tired of his boss's cynicism. Pia's photo of the body hanging from the gate had been splashed across the front page of the evening papers. Since every

Swede at some time in his life visited Gotland on summer holiday, the picture had stirred strong emotions. That morning, Johan had already seen the story top the morning news on TV. Max Grenfors had wanted to show footage filmed at the scene, but he was stopped by the powers-that-be at the national news bureau, who thought that would be going too far.

Johan drove into the parking lot outside the TV and radio building on Östra Hansegatan and pulled into the spot reserved for Regional News. The editorial office used to be housed in a small building inside the ring wall, but it had been moved here, to the former premises of the decommissioned A7 military regiment. The building had been used as a stable for the military's horses, and the architect had wanted to preserve vestiges of its history in the renovation. This was especially evident in the doors, columns, and wide panels of the walls. The color scheme was mostly brown and white. Everything had been nicely done, and most of the occupants seemed happy with the move, even though the location was not as central as before. Regional News had been assigned two new rooms on the second floor with a view of the park. Pia was sitting in front of a computer, and she glanced up at once when Johan came in.

"Hi," he said.

"Anything new going on?"

"No, but check this out." She waved him over to the chair next to her. "Every damned newspaper has my photo. Have you seen this?"

She clicked on the websites of various papers. Poor Egon Wallin was on the front page of every one of them.

"Shit," said Johan in disgust. "Whatever happened to ethics? Even Grenfors was hesitant about using it, for once."

"Yes, but at the same time it's a good fucking picture," muttered Pia without taking her eyes off the screen.

"But think about his family. How do you think his children will feel when they see every paper in the country using that picture of their father on their placards? And why do you carry a still camera around when you're supposed to be filming for TV?"

Pia heaved a deep sigh and looked up at Johan.

"Remember I'm a freelancer. I always take a still camera with me. And I happened to get an opportunity to take a picture from an angle that no one else could get. Good Lord, it's fine to be nice and considerate if you've got a monthly salary. I've got bills to pay. I'm going to be living off this photo for months. And by the way, of course I realize this must be rough for his family. But we're in the news business, and we can't be super-considerate about everybody involved in what goes on in the world at the cost of filing our reports. I think the photo is okay. It only shows the body from a distance and not his face. Besides, his children are adults. And no one would be able to recognize him anyways."

"No one outside the family, maybe," said Johan drily. "So have you heard from Grenfors?"

He wanted to change the subject to avoid further discussion. Johan was very fond of Pia, but when it came to ethics, they had widely different views. Trying to persuade her to adopt his own, more cautious take was like pounding his head against a brick wall. The worst part was that the editors, with Grenfors in the lead, usually agreed with Pia. People who ended up caught in the middle were generally given little consideration, in Johan's opinion. He thought it was possible to report the news without trampling on others. Besides, in his position as reporter, he was responsible for the content—it was his name that appeared on the TV screen.

Whenever the discussions were at their most heated, Grenfors would shout at Johan that he was a damned bleeding-heart reporter, meaning that he always thought too much about the consequences of his reporting.

There was a school of journalism that advocated remaining neutral when it came to consequences; Grenfors belonged to that school, but Johan did not. He thought that journalists had a responsibility that extended beyond the publication of an interview. And this was especially true of crime reporting, when both the victim and family members became part of the story. This responsibility particularly came into play with TV because of its enormous and widespread impact.

He was tired of this discussion, which was constant. Every day there were new positions to be taken, which always prompted new disputes. He and Pia had spent half of Sunday evening bickering about the photo of Egon Wallin. Johan had been against publication, but both Pia and the editorial management disagreed with him. By a few minutes before broadcast, they risked dropping the entire spot if no decision was made. In the end he was forced to go along with a brief and distant shot showing the body hanging from the gate.

B ut today was a new day, and Johan and Pia had agreed to start off with the gallery, provided it was open after the events that had occurred. They at least hoped to find someone working there.

As they drove, Pia peeked at him from under the straggly black fringe that hung into her eyes. "You're not angry, are you?"

"Of course not. We just happen to disagree."

"Good," she said, patting his knee. "I wonder who that was inside the gallery yesterday," said Johan, just to change the subject.

"Maybe it was an employee who saw us arrive and didn't feel like talking," said Pia. "They must have to clean up the place after an opening."

"You're probably right."

"And maybe they needed to talk about what happened," said Pia, swerving to miss a big orange cat that ran across the road.

She expertly steered the car through the narrow cobble-stoned streets and parked in the middle of Stora Torget. That was no problem in the wintertime when the open mar-ketplace was empty of all the booths and vendors' stalls that filled the square in the summer. Pia set up her equipment on the street and began filming. Just as she turned on the camera, a plump older woman wearing a sheepskin coat and cap came walking over with a bouquet of flowers in her hand.

Johan quickly approached with a microphone. "What do you think about the murder?"

The woman looked a bit hesitant at first, but quickly collected herself. "It's dreadful that something like that could happen here, in little Visby. And he was such a nice man, Egon. Always friendly and amiable. It's hard to believe that this has actually happened."

"Why are you bringing flowers here?"

"It's the least I can do to honor Egon. Everybody is terribly shocked."

"Does it make you scared?"

"You do start thinking about the fact that a crazy man might be on the loose. And whether it's even safe to go out anymore."

The woman had tears in her eyes. She fell silent and waved her hand to indicate that Pia should stop filming. Johan asked whether he could use her in his report. She agreed and clearly spelled her name for him.

A modern sign made of steel was posted between the medieval masonry anchors in the rough stone facade, stating that the name of the gallery was Wallin Art. In the display window was a photograph of Egon Wallin with a lit candle in front of it. When they tried the door, they found that it was locked, but they could see people moving about inside.

Johan knocked on the door and managed to catch a woman's attention. She came over and opened the door for them. A bell rang as they entered. The woman introduced herself as Eva Blom. At a counter stood another woman, printing the words "Closed due to death of the proprietor" on a piece of paper.

"We're planning to stay closed today," Eva Blom explained, giving them a forced smile. "I assume that Monika wouldn't want us to try to conduct business as usual. Especially considering all the reporters who've been calling both yesterday and now this morning." She cast a glance at Pia, who was already in the process of filming the picture of Egon Wallin in the window.

Eva Blom was evidently fond of red. She wore a black jumper and skirt, with bright red lipstick that looked good against her milky-white complexion. She was a short woman, barely reaching up to his shoulders. She looked up at Johan, her blue eyes staring at him from behind red-framed glasses. "What do you want?"

He introduced himself and Pia. "We're doing a report on what happened, and we'd like to get your reaction, of course. You worked so closely with Egon Wallin," he said, giving Eva Blom a solemn look.

"As long as you don't take any pictures,' she said tersely. "I don't want to be on TV."

"Unfortunately that's the only way for us to report on anything; we work for Swedish television," explained Johan. "Could we at least take some footage inside the gallery?"

Grenfors wasn't going to be pleased that they hadn't got more interviews. And Johan had stubbornly refused to comply with his boss's request to get an interview with the new widow. There was a limit to what he would stoop to doing just for the sake of a good story.

Detective Inspector Karin Jacobsson was the person whom Knutas was closest to at his job. They had worked together for fifteen years. She was an astute and skilled officer, but it was Karin's personality that had drawn him to her from the very start. She was charming, lively, and spirited; she always had an opinion about everything, and he'd never met anybody who was able to get to the point so fast. At least when it came to work. She was a sweet, petite woman with dark hair and doe-like eyes. As was evident from her muscular physique, she spent much of her free time playing soccer. Her most remarkable feature was the gap between her front teeth, which was most apparent whenever she smiled or laughed. Karin almost always wore jeans and a shirt. In the summertime she would occasionally appear at work wearing a dress, causing a few raised eyebrows.

She was thirty-nine but looked younger, and she was still single, at least as far as Knutas knew. If she was involved in a relationship, she was keeping it to herself, which was practically impossible to do in a small town like Visby. Her parents lived in Tingstäde, and she saw them now and then. There was something enigmatic about Karin that Knutas couldn't work out.

Right now they were having coffee in his office, considering various motives for the murder of Egon Wallin.

"It does seem strange that the artist and his manager would leave for Stockholm on the very morning of the murder, but there could be a perfectly reasonable explanation," said Jacobsson. "Maybe it was something they'd planned long before."

"Well, I hope we can get hold of them soon so we can hear what they have to say. We can't dismiss the fact that it's a damned odd coincidence for them to end up on the same plane as Egon Wallin's biggest competitor. And a guy who had previously tried to get his mitts on Kalvalis."

"I agree. But then again, how many flights to Stockholm are there on a Sunday?" Jacobsson went on. "It may have nothing at all to do with the case. I think that first and foremost we need to ask ourselves why Egon Wallin went out in the middle of the night. What normal person goes home with his wife around eleven after a festive evening and then suddenly decides to take a walk? Besides, it was freezing cold on Saturday night. The only reason I can think of is that he went out to meet someone. A love tryst, to put it bluntly."

"I've also been thinking along those lines. But who is this lover of his and where can we find her? And why hasn't she come forward? Egon Wallin didn't take his car, nor did he call for a cab; we've already checked on that. So he must have left home on foot, and then he either ran into the murderer somewhere outdoors or he was killed at the home of his mistress."

"Others could also be involved," Jacobsson interjected. "Maybe his mistress had a husband who discovered what was going on, and he killed Egon Wallin during the night."

"Unless it was his mistress who did it," countered Knutas. "Though I have a hard time imagining that a woman would be able to hoist up his body like that. Provided she didn't have help, of course."

Knutas stopped to sneeze loudly. He took a few moments to blow his nose before going on.

"Good Lord, we can keep on speculating forever, but it won't really get us anywhere."

Jacobsson drained the last of her coffee and got up.

"How are things going, by the way?" asked Knutas. "How are you?"

He regarded her intently. There was something weighing on her; he'd noticed it for several days now. She's really cute, he thought as he observed her hesitation. Knutas was not the only one who had a hard time deciphering what Karin thought or felt about personal matters. She had a reserve as thick as armor, which meant that few dared ask any questions about her private life, at least initially. Unless, of course, it had to do with soccer.

The strange thing was that Knutas found it so easy to confide in her, even though she was reticent about confiding in him. He often turned to Karin when he had problems with Lina or the children. She was always sympathetic and willing to listen. But if he asked her about concerns in her own life, she was always evasive.

When she first arrived at Visby police headquarters, he thought for a while that he was falling in love with her, but then he met Lina and forgot all about his budding interest in Karin. Yet he was still very fond of her, and he sometimes worried that she might look for a more challenging job. Although Karin had worked on the Visby police force for sixteen years, he wouldn't feel secure until her personal life prompted her to settle down permanently. As things now stood, if she met someone over on the mainland, she'd be gone. Or if she was offered a job that she couldn't refuse.

Sometimes he felt like her father, even though there were only thirteen years between them. Knutas had become dependent on having Karin Jacobsson as part of the team, and he certainly didn't want to lose her.

She paused for a moment before answering his question. "I'm fine, thanks."

"Sure?' Her expression was inscrutable as she met his gaze. "Of course. I'm fine."

Even though he could see that something was bothering her, he knew better than to ask any more questions.

Emma had been caught completely off guard by Johan's sudden proposal of marriage. In a sense it was inevitable, as if they would have to come to that decision sooner or later. They had a child together, after all. By the time she had chosen to keep the baby and break up her marriage, she'd already made up her mind. And yet she had kept wavering back and forth. When she thought about how she'd behaved since meeting Johan, it seemed a miracle that he still wanted to be with her. That he hadn't grown tired of her long ago.

He had left the house for the city and his job a short time ago. He had kissed her before leaving, but had not said any more about the matter or pressed her for an answer. She had watched him walk down the snow-covered path toward his car, studying his dark curly hair, his brown leather jacket that was nicely worn, and his washed-out jeans.

It was really quite simple: she loved him and it was obvious that they should get married. At the same time she was terrified that her relationship with Johan would end the same way her marriage with Olle had. The dreariness of daily life would come creeping in once the elation of living together had waned. The excitement would fade, gradually but relentlessly leading to the point when they were no longer excited by each other. Their sex life would wither and become mechanical and obligatory because neither of them had the energy to sustain the passion that once existed.

She shivered under the blanket, where she could still smell Johan's presence. They just couldn't let that happen. She got up, stuck her feet in her slippers, and put on the T-shirt that was still lying on the sofa. She went into the bedroom and leaned over the crib where Elin was sleeping.

In the kitchen, sunlight was streaming in through the window. It was almost unreal after so many weeks of gray skies. She'd nearly forgotten what sunshine looked like.

She made coffee and toast, then sat down in her usual place near the window and peered out at the snowy land-scape. There was enough snow for the kids to go sledding, and that made her happy. There was a hill nearby, and the kids loved to take their sleds over there. Soon Elin would be old enough to go along with Sara and Filip.

Right now they were staying with their father. She was actually getting used to this every-other-week existence and was now able to enjoy being alone with Elin half the time. She looked at the kitchen chair across from her. That was where Olle had sat all those years, drinking his green tea; the smell had always made her slightly sick. Johan didn't drink green tea, thank God.

She wondered what bad habits would come to light if they moved in together. Things Johan hadn't mentioned yet, but which would become apparent as soon as he moved in with all his belongings.

That's where he'll sit from now on, she thought, trying to picture Johan occupying the chair opposite. How long would love last this time around?

She sighed and put another slice of bread in the toaster. She realized that she was still suffering the effects of a failed marriage, and that her thoughts were much too negative. There was nothing to indicate that this time things would go as badly.

After she finished eating and cleared away the breakfast things, she looked in on Elin again. She was still asleep.

As she left the bedroom, Emma caught a glimpse of herself in the small round mirror in the hall. She stopped, took the mirror from its hook and carried it back to the bedroom. Then she lay down on the bed and held the mirror overhead.

For a long time she lay there, staring up at her face, so pale in the wintertime. Her eyes looked sleepy and sad, her lips colorless. Her hair was still lovely, flowing over the pillow. Who was she really? And what did she want? She had given birth to three children, yet she still felt like a lost little girl. In her heart she didn't know what to make of the person she saw in the mirror. She was loved by many, but she felt rootless. She'd never been a particularly self-confident person.

Suddenly she realized that she'd never made any of her own choices. Not really. She had allowed circumstances to steer her. When she met Olle, he had courted her and usually taken the initiative. He was cute, pleasant, considerate, and very much in love with her. Had she simply slipped into the relationship like a passive dolt?

She moved the mirror a bit farther away, and stared into her own eyes. What was she thinking? It was time to make up her own mind about what direction her life was going to take.

And when it came right down to it, the decision wasn't hard to make. Not at all.

L ate in the afternoon Knutas finally received answers to several important questions. Wittberg came into his office and dropped onto the chair in front of his desk. His hair was tousled, his cheeks red with excitement.

"You're not going to believe this. There's so damned much to tell you that I hardly know where to begin."

"Just go ahead and start."

"I got hold of Sixten Dahl, Mattis Kalvalis, and his manager, Vigor Haukas. It's true that they all traveled together to Stockholm. At the gallery opening Dahl made the artist an offer he couldn't refuse. Since he still hadn't signed the contract with Egon Wallin, he agreed to go and see Dahl's gallery on Sunday, to meet his co-workers and discuss the details of the offer. So far, nothing strange about that. But when it comes to the sale of the gallery here in Visby, it turns out that Egon Wallin sold it to a certain Per Eriksson from Stockholm."

"Yes, we already know that."

"What we didn't know was that Per Eriksson is just a front. The real owner is Sixten Dahl."

Wittberg leaned back with a triumphant smile.

"You've got to be joking." Knutas had to take out his pipe.

"We're going to have to do some more digging into that. Are those two guys from Lithuania coming back here?"

"They're already at the hotel. But they're leaving for home tomorrow, late in the afternoon. I took the liberty of telling them to be here tomorrow at noon."

"Good. What about Sixten Dahl?"

"The Stockholm police are going to interview him early in the morning."

"Great job, Thomas."

The phone rang. It was the ME, who wanted to give Knutas a preliminary post-mortem report. The superintendent placed his hand over the receiver.

"Is there anything else?"

"You can bet there is."

"Okay, we'll take it up at the meeting later. I have the ME on the phone." Wittberg left.

"Starting with the cause of death," said the ME. "Wallin was strangled several hours before he was hanged from the noose. Judging by his injuries, he was probably attacked from behind and strangled with a sharp wire, such as piano wire. He has defensive marks on his arms, skin scrapings under his fingernails, and scratches on his neck, all indications that he fought back. At the same time the wire cut so deep into the flesh so that—"

"Thanks, that will be sufficient. I don't need to know any more at the moment."

Knutas's sensitivity was not just limited to seeing victim's injuries, but hearing about them as well.

"Of course." The ME cleared his throat and then let a slight hint of disappointment enter his voice as he went on. "As far as the rest of the injuries go, he has several cuts on his face, a bruise over one eyebrow, and a scratch on his cheek. He probably sustained these injuries in connection with the assault and when his body was dragged along the ground."

"Can you say anything more about the time of death?"

"I can't fix the time any closer than to say he was most likely killed between midnight and five or six in the morning. That's all I have right now. I'll fax over a copy of the results right away."

Knutas thanked the ME for his call and put down the phone. Then he rang the main number for the National Criminal Police office and asked to be connected to Inspector Martin Kihlgård. The relationship between the two of them was complicated, but right now Knutas needed help from the National Police. Because Kihlgård was enormously popular with his Gotland colleagues, it would be foolish to ask for anyone else. Knutas listened to the phone ringing for a long time before Kihlgård answered. It was obvious that he was eating something.

"Hello?" he said, his voice muffled.

"Hi, it's Anders Knutas. How are things?"

"Knutie!" exclaimed his colleague with delight. "I was wondering when you were going to call. Wait just a minute, I need to finish what I'm eating."

A frantic chewing could be heard on the other end of the line, followed by a couple of gulps of some sort of liquid. That was finished off by a quick belch. Knutas grimaced. Kihlgård's insatiable appetite always got on his nerves, along with the fact that his Stockholm colleague insisted on calling him Knutie, even though Knutas had repeatedly asked him not to use that nickname.

"All right, I guess I'll live now. But I'm glad you called, because I was starting to think that nothing much was happening over here."

"You're lucky," said Knutas drily. "We need your assistance."

Briefly he explained the facts of the case as Kihlgård listened, murmuring his agreement now and then. Knutas could picture him sitting in his cluttered office in the NCP building in Stockholm, his huge body weighing down his chair, his long legs propped up on another chair. Kihlgård was six foot three and must have weighed well over 220 pounds.

"There's certainly a lot of action over in your neck of the woods. Sounds like the Wild West."

"Yes, I keep wondering where this is all heading," said Knutas with a sigh.

"I'll gather up a few colleagues, and we'll probably catch the first flight over tomorrow morning."

"Fine," said Knutas. "See you soon."

He'd gone past the place several times. At first he wanted to go inside, but decided to wait. Each time he went there, he put on a slight disguise. Just to be on the safe side. There was always a risk that he might run into somebody he knew. He'd decided to do everything in the proper order and take his time. Slowly but surely he would make his approach, so that when the time was right he could ruthlessly launch his attack. First he wanted to get to know his victim. Afterward it would be too late.

Right now he stood watching the man on the other side of the windowpane, trying to gather his courage to go inside. Not because he was afraid of the man; rather, he was afraid of himself. That he might not be able to stop himself from assaulting him. He took several deep breaths. Self-control was usually his strong point; at the moment he wasn't so sure.

He noticed that he was breathing hard and knew that wouldn't do. He took a walk around the block to calm his nerves. When he came back, the man was on his way out, carrying a big bag in his hand. He was headed for the subway.

He followed the man. After three stops the man got off and took the escalator up to the street level, then crossed the street and disappeared into the premises of one of the city's largest and most exclusive gyms. He followed, paying the fee at the check-in counter. It was shockingly expensive. They wanted 400 kronor for one visit.

The gym was almost deserted at this time of day. A few machines clattered, and music was thumping. A girl in leggings and a tight-fitting leotard was using a step machine while reading a book. After a while the man he was following came out of the locker room. He began running on a treadmill; it looked pathetic.

Since he hadn't brought any workout clothes, he couldn't join in, which was a shame. It would have been great to run right next to the man and provoke him in some way.

Even though he'd made the decision to proceed slowly in order to prolong the suffering as much as possible, he was seized by a strong desire to think up something right now, just to give the man a scare. He went into the toilet to make sure that his disguise was still in place.

When he came out, the man had moved over to the weight-training equipment. He was lying on a bench and lifting the weights overhead. From a distance he watched the man add more and more weight. Finally he lay there, gasping loudly with the effort. Each end of the barbell had 88 pounds on it.

Cautiously he glanced around before approaching. The man was lying on his back and didn't notice him. No one was near; the girl on the step machine was in a different room and had her back to them. The other guy who had been in the weight-training room had now left. But he needed to be careful.

At the last second he stopped himself. Something made him pause and then retreat a couple of paces. It wouldn't be good to get too eager right now. That would wreck everything. He had to restrain himself, not try anything that might ruin it all. What if he was arrested by the police before he was ready? That would be disastrous.

He went up the half flight of stairs to the gym's cafe, sank down on a chair, and tried to concentrate on breathing calmly.

After a while he stood up to get a glass of water, but was suddenly overcome by nausea. He had to rush to the nearest restroom, which happened to be in the weight-training room.

Strong convulsions surged through his body and he vomited into the toilet. He was mortified to discover tears running down his face. For a long time he sat on the floor, trying to gather his wits. Would he really be able to carry out the plan he had devised?

Suddenly someone knocked on the door. He froze and his heart began pounding fast.

He swiftly got to his feet, moved to the sink, and splashed water on his face. Then he flushed the toilet several times. When he opened the door he felt like he was having a heart attack. There stood the man, asking him with a worried look whether everything was all right.

For what seemed like an eternity but was actually only a few seconds, he stared into those gray-green eyes that showed both worry and sympathy. Then he muttered that he was okay and pushed his way past.

A t the meeting later in the day, Knutas informed the investigative team of Martin Kihlgård's imminent arrival. His announcement was met with scattered applause.

The cheerful, boisterous inspector from the NCP was not only a skilled officer but also a clown who had lightened the mood at many a dismal morning meeting when an investigation had seemed at its most hopeless. One person who was particularly fond of him was Karin Jacobsson, and right now she was beaming. Knutas hadn't seen her look so happy in a long time. Occasionally he thought the two of them might be sweethearts. At the same time, the very idea of those two as a couple was ridiculous. Karin probably weighed only half as much as Kihlgård, and she hardly reached up to his chest. He was also fifteen years older; not that the age difference would in itself be a hindrance. But Kihlgård seemed much older, as if he belonged to a different generation. Knutas thought he actually bore a strong resemblance to the old slapstick film star Thor Modéen from the forties. Sometimes they seemed even ludicrously alike. But Kihlgård's jovial exterior was deceptive. He was an incisive police detective: tough, analytical, and completely fearless.

When the excitement over the welcome news had died

down, the meeting continued with a discussion of what had been uncovered so far. Thomas Wittberg had been out knocking on doors and had gathered some interesting information from Snäckgårdsvägen, where the Wallins lived.

"First of all, it appears that Monika Wallin has a lover," Wittberg began.

"Is that right?" said Knutas in surprise.

He hadn't picked up any clue that something like this was going on when he had interviewed Egon Wallin's widow the previous day.

Everyone sitting at the table was paying close attention.

"She's sleeping with a neighbor, Rolf Sandén. He lives in the same row of terraced houses. He's been a widower for a number of years, and his children have all moved away. He's a construction worker who took early retirement. According to the neighbors they've been fooling around for years. Just about everyone said the same thing, except for an old woman who seemed almost blind and deaf, so it's not so strange that she hadn't noticed anything. If Egon Wallin knew nothing about their affair, then he was the only one in the neighborhood."

"The neighbor, Rolf Sandén—have you got hold of him?" Knutas asked Wittberg.

"You bet. He'd just come home from the mainland when I rang the bell, but he was on his way out again. I made an appointment to interview him tomorrow. At any rate, he was quite talkative and readily admitted to his affair with Monika Wallin. Considering the circumstances, I thought his behavior rather odd; he seemed almost exhilarated. It seems crazy to act so happy when your neighbor and the husband of your mistress has just been murdered. He should have at least pretended to show some sympathy."

"He probably sees his chance now," said Jacobsson. "Finally able to make their relationship public after all the sneaking around in secret. Maybe he's really in love with Monika Wallin and has been waiting to take her to the altar."

"Maybe he's the one who did it," Norrby interjected.

"Well, it's possible," said Wittberg. "Provided it wasn't the wife, of course."

"Or both of them," growled Sohlman in a ghoulish voice, holding up his hands like a vampire ready to attack.

Knutas stood up abruptly. Sometimes all the wild speculating about cases got on his nerves.

"The meeting is adjourned," he said and left the room.

Between interviews, Johan and Pia stopped by the Regional News office to pick up some batteries for the camera and check on the latest news. Just as Johan was about to switch on his computer he received a text message on his cell.

It said: "Yes, I will. Soon."

He sat in his chair, staring at the message with a silly smile on his face.

"What is it?" asked Pia, noticing that he had stopped what he was doing. Without saying a word, he handed her his phone

Pia read the words but merely looked puzzled. "What does it mean?"

"That Emma said yes." He turned to face Pia. "She said yes!" he shouted happily. "Don't you understand? She's ready—at last!"

He pulled an astonished Pia out of her chair, gave her a big hug, and then danced her around the room.

She laughed. "But 'yes' to what? What's this all about?" Then it finally dawned on her. "Wow. Do you mean it? She wants you to move in with her? Get hitched for real?"

"Yes!" shouted Johan. "YES!"

A few colleagues from the radio division stuck their heads in the door to see what was going on. Johan's joyous outburst had been heard in half the offices.

Pia grabbed his phone again. "And it says 'soon.' How soon? What does that mean?"

"No idea, but I'd marry her tomorrow if I could. This is fucking fantastic!"

In his mind Johan saw images flit past at breakneck speed. Standing next to Emma in a church, with all of their relatives and friends; the big wedding party afterward with Emma in a romantic white gown, cutting the wedding cake; Emma in overalls with a kerchief on her head and a big belly, expecting their second child; peacefully baking a cake in the kitchen while Elin played on the floor; with Emma and the children on a sun-filled holiday somewhere; parent meetings at the school; and buying a summerhouse so they could sit on the porch in their old age, each holding a cup of coffee while their grandchildren ran around on the lawn. Johan rushed over to his colleagues from the local radio station and gave each of them a hug before he picked up his phone to call Emma.

She sounded out of breath, and he could hear Elin gurgling and babbling in the background.

"Is it really true? You will?" he cried, his face radiant.

Emma laughed. "Yes, I will. I'm sure about that."

"That's crazy. I mean, it's wonderful, sweetheart! I'll go and get my things and move in today—is that okay with you?"

"Sure, do that," she said with a laugh. "Then we can start living together right away."

"I'll be there as soon as I can tonight."

"Call when you're on your way."

"I love you!"

"Love you too. Bye."

"Bye . . ."

Slowly he put down the phone, hardly daring to believe what he'd just heard. Had she really said yes after all the vacillating back and forth? He stared at Pia with tears in his eyes.

"You think she means it?" he asked.

"Yes, of course she does," said Pia, smiling. "She really means it, Johan."

Erik Mattson usually left his job at Bukowski's Auction House around five. On the way home he often stopped at the Grodan Restaurant on Grev Turegatan to have a drink. The bar had just opened when he stepped inside, but it wouldn't take long before it was filled with well-to-do residents from the Östermalm district, having a drink after work. People like himself. At least in appearance.

He and his closest friends met here as often as they could. On this particular evening Per Reutersköld, Otto Diesen, and Kalle Celling were having a beer when Erik came in. They'd all known each other for years, ever since they went to secondary school at Östra Real.

Now they were over forty, which was more obvious on some than others. The biggest difference nowadays was that most of his friends made do with a beer or two and then went home to their families. But a couple of evenings each week Erik would just stop by his apartment for a quick shower before he was back in the neighborhood around Stureplan.

He had children, too, but he was divorced and the kids had grown up living with their mother. The reason for this was Erik's abuse of alcohol and drugs. He managed to keep his habit relatively in check, but not entirely. After having several relapses while he was taking care of the children, he'd lost joint custody. The divorce had deeply affected him, and he'd landed in a terrible depression. At the time the three children had been very young, and presumably they hadn't noticed how chaotic his life had become or the bitterness that had welled up between their parents.

Over time things had improved. Erik succeeded in controlling his dependence enough that it wouldn't have an impact on the children, and after a while he was allowed to spend time with them every other weekend. Those days were priceless. Erik loved his children and would do anything for them. Almost. He couldn't completely give up drinking. That was asking too much. But he kept it to an acceptable level, at least that's what he told himself.

He did his job well except on those occasions when he partied too hard, which happened at regular intervals. His boss accepted that if he wanted to keep Erik on his staff, he'd have to tolerate those times when he simply didn't show up for work. Erik's expertise was well known and he was a definite asset to Bukowski's already excellent reputation. He also saved the company money because he was so fast. Yet he could never be promoted to curator because of his drinking problem. This was a fact Eric had accepted long ago.

Erik was a pleasant and sociable man, always impeccably dressed, quick-witted, and with a sly smile. He liked to joke, but never at anyone else's expense.

Outwardly he might be perceived as an outgoing person, but he actually possessed a strong sense of reserve that made it difficult to get to know him. He looked much younger than his forty-three years. He was tall, muscular, and elegant. His dark hair, combed smoothly back, his big gray-green eyes, and his regular features all contributed to his attractive appearance.

Occasionally he seemed distant, and those who knew him well interpreted this as a symptom of his alcohol use. In a strange way, he seemed untouched by things that went on around him, as if he were living in his own world, cut off from everything else.

In his social circle, most people knew everything about each other's families, but Erik was an exception. He was perfectly willing to talk about his childhood, but he never mentioned his parents by name or spoke of them at all.

Yet it was generally known that he was the son of a big shot in the business world. Certain people wondered how he could afford his extravagant lifestyle on the salary paid to an assistant at Bukowski's; he couldn't be earning very much. But such questions were promptly answered by Erik's friends. They explained that even though he had a poor relationship with his parents, he received a monthly allowance, which meant that he was able to throw around a lot of money. Apparently he was financially set up for life.

Now he stood there, nonchalantly leaning on the bar, dressed in a pinstriped suit, with a glass of beer in his hand. He looked around the place absent-mindedly as he listened to Otto Diesen's story about how he'd been lucky enough to crash head-first into a luscious brunette on the ski slopes while on a business trip to Davos. The episode had ended with them lying naked in a hotel suite, massaging each other's aching bodies. The fact that Otto was married didn't concern him in the least, or any of his friends either. Sometimes Erik was struck by how when they were together, his friends behaved as if they were suffering from arrested development.

They told the same old stories that they'd been telling for years. No matter how much their lives had changed with regard to new jobs, families, and so on, time seemed to stand still when they met. He told himself that there was actually something refreshing about that. It was somehow comforting that nothing ever changed between them, no matter what went on in their lives outside. It gave Erik a sense of security, and when they parted an hour later with the usual pats on the shoulder and thumps on the back, he was in a good mood. He stopped at the sushi bar on the corner and bought himself dinner to take home.

His apartment was on the top floor of a beautiful building on Karlavägen, with a view of Humlegården and the Royal Library. He went in; there was a large pile of mail in the hall. With a sigh he picked up the hodge-podge of advertisements and window envelopes, all of them bills. What his friends didn't know was that his monthly allowance had been stopped. He was living well beyond his means, and was seized by fear every time a new month rolled around and his bills had to be paid.

Without opening a single envelope, he tossed the mail aside and put on a CD of Maria Callas. His friends found it enormously amusing that he was so fond of her. Then he took a shower, shaved, and changed his clothes. For a long time he stood in front of the mirror, combing his hair.

His body felt relaxed and a bit tender; he had gone to the gym during his lunch hour and put himself through an extra long training session. The exercise served to counterbalance his vast alcohol intake. He was aware that he drank too much, but he didn't want to stop. Now and then he mixed alcohol with pills, but that was usually only when he lapsed into one of his depressed periods, which happened several times a year. Sometimes they lasted only a few days, but they could also go on for months. He had grown accustomed to these periods and dealt with them in his own way. The only thing that really bothered him about these depressions was that while they were going on, he preferred not to see his children.

Nowadays it was easier; they were all grown up and understood the problem. Emelie was nineteen, Karl was twenty, and David was twenty-three. Yet Erik still tried at all costs to avoid showing them that he was depressed. He didn't want to burden them or make them worried. Mostly he pretended that nothing was going on, merely saying he'd be away on a trip for a while or that he was extremely busy at work. They also had their own lives, with girlfriends and boyfriends, their studies and sports activities. Sometimes weeks would go by when he heard nothing from his children, except for David, whom he was particularly close to. Maybe it was because he was the oldest.

Erik Mattson lived two lives. One as a respected and es-teemed colleague at Bukowski's, with a social circle that in-cluded many friends, elegant parties, travels, and his role as a father, however sporadic that might be. His other life was completely different. Secret, hidden, and destructive. And yet it was essential.

An hour later, Erik Mattson left his apartment. He already knew that it was going to be a long night.

Knutas awoke with an aching head. He had slept badly. The image of the dead Egon Wallin had haunted his dreams, and he spent the hours he lay awake thinking about the murder investigation. During the day there was hardly any time to ponder matters, so it was at night that he worked through his impressions. The investigation was constantly being interrupted by so many other things that were a daily part of police work, and it was driving him crazy. The fact that the media seemed so well-informed was worrisome.

Sometimes he wondered how wise it had been to allow his deputy superintendent, Lars Norrby, to be the police spokesman. Maybe it would be better if he didn't know so much. The more involved a spokesman was in the actual investigative work, the greater the risk that he might reveal more than he should. It would really be best to take him off the investigative team, but that would undoubtedly meet resistance.

The famous photograph of the victim hanging from Dalman Gate had opened a can of worms. Not surprisingly, the picture had been taken by Pia Lilja. She and Johan Berg were a team that he preferred to avoid. Of course, he respected Johan; the reporter was aggressive but never asked irrelevant questions that led nowhere. And several times in the past he had offered help that had allowed the police to solve a case much faster. That inevitably meant that the officers at headquarters, including himself, were more inclined to accommodate Johan. To top it all off, during the last murder investigation, Johan had risked his own life, which only served to increase the goodwill of the police toward him. But in many ways that was not a good thing. Berg was a reporter to be avoided if Knutas wanted to do his job undisturbed.

Even worse was Johan's cameraperson, Pia Lilja. Humility and respect for police integrity were not exactly watchwords for her. She tramped about, never bothering to show any consideration for anyone else. Her looks alone were alarming, with her black hair sticking out like a scrubbing brush, the worst sort of war paint on her eyes, and then that ring in her nose, although he'd noticed that lately it had been replaced by a tiny gemstone. That at least was an improvement. Of course, Knutas understood the value of maintaining a good relationship with the press, but sometimes journalists encroached so much on his work that he wished they'd all go to hell.

Knutas reached for the alarm clock. It was only 5:45. Another few minutes before it went off. He lay on his side, facing Lina. She had on her pink nightgown with the big orange flowers. On the arm raised above her head, he could see thousands of freckles sprinkled over her pale skin. He loved every one of them. Her curly red hair was spread out over the pillow.

"Good morning," he whispered in her ear. She merely grunted in reply. Cautiously he pressed his hand on her waist to see how she would react.

Mari Jungstedt

"What are you doing?" she mumbled in Danish. When she was tired she sometimes spoke her native language.

She was from the Danish island of Fyn, but they had met in Copenhagen fifteen years earlier. It was often said that love changed over the years. That a relationship became something else, that the feeling of being in love disappeared and was replaced with something deeper, though not as passionate. Some people said that spouses became good friends, that the intensity died and was transformed into a feeling of security. That was not true of Knutas and his wife. They quarrelled and made love with the same frenzy as they had from the very beginning.

Lina loved her job as a midwife, although being surrounded all day long by blood and pain, both indescribable joy and the deepest despair, did take its toll. She cried often, but she was also quick to laugh; she spoke frankly, and nobody could claim that she didn't make her opinions and feelings clear. In many ways that made it easy to live with her. At the same time, Knutas occasionally tired of her emotional outbursts and stormy moods. Her "unprovoked ire," as he called it, which just made her even more angry whenever he made the mistake of saying it out loud.

But right now she lay here next to him, sleepy and relaxed. She turned to face him, looking at him with her green eyes. "Good morning, sweetheart. Is it already time to get up?"

He kissed her forehead. "We've got a while yet."

Fifteen minutes later he got up and put on the coffee. It was still dark outside. The cat rubbed against his leg, and he lifted her onto his lap, where she immediately curled up. He thought about the previous day's conversation with the victim's widow. Why didn't she say anything about her affair with Rolf Sandén? She must have realized that it was bound to come out sooner or later.

I need to call her again, he thought, reaching for his old

134

notebook. He used it for writing down ideas relating to his police work and reminders of things he didn't want to forget. He skimmed through his notes from their conversation, but could hardly make out what he'd written. And the book was getting so worn that several pages had already fallen out. He was going to have to buy another one.

He glanced at the kitchen clock on the wall. The daily meeting had been postponed from eight to nine because Knutas had agreed to participate in the live broadcast of Swedish Television's morning talk show. Now he wondered why he'd said yes. Being on TV made him nervous, and afterward he always thought that he looked awkward and indecisive. He had a hard time finding the right words when he stood there under the relentless spotlight, expected to spout perfectly formulated, well-balanced, and thoughtfully weighed replies that would satisfy both the TV reporter and his police superiors. The task was next to impossible: not to reveal too much, yet at the same time to say enough so that the police might get some tips.

The truth was that right now the police needed help from the general public. They had little concrete evidence to go on. So far not a single witness with anything substantial to say had come forward, and nothing in Egon Wallin's life had surfaced that might indicate a possible perp. There was no apparent motive. No one thought it was a robbery, even though both his wallet and phone had yet to be found.

Egon Wallin had tended to his gallery for all these years, working hard and with a purpose. He had good relationships with his employees and had never been in trouble with the law. And by all accounts he had never had any quarrel with anyone else.

The interview went better than expected. Knutas sat in a

small TV studio, with a direct hook-up to the host of the morning show. The interviewer was suitably cautious and didn't ask any probing questions. When the three-minute interview was over, Knutas was completely sweaty, but overall quite satisfied with how it had gone. The county police commissioner called him just a few minutes after the show, confirming that he had managed to successfully maneuver his way through the interview.

When Knutas got back to police headquarters, he rang the forensic psychologist that he'd consulted the previous year. He was hoping that she would be able to interpret the perpetrator's modus operandi and help them to move on. But she thought it was too early in the investigation and asked him to contact her again later. And no doubt she was right. Yet Knutas did manage to squeeze some information out of her.

She didn't rule out the possibility that it might be a first-time criminal. On the other hand, she didn't think it was a random murder; rather, a good deal of planning had been involved, perhaps undertaken over a long period of time. The killer was probably aware that Egon Wallin was thinking of leaving the house again, and that he would be alone. That meant that the perp had been keeping his victim under surveillance.

They needed to have another talk with everyone who knew him. Someone might have noticed something, maybe seen a new, unfamiliar face around Wallin. And the fact that he likely knew his killer—that definitely narrowed the field of interest. It was true that Egon Wallin's circle of acquaintances was unusually large, but it made things significantly easier knowing that the perp was probably somebody close to him.

The platform was crowded with patiently waiting travelers who had become inured over the years to commuter-train delays caused by frozen switches, snow-covered tracks, carriages that fogged up in the cold, and doors that refused to open. There was always something. Stockholmers had been forced to live with this commuter chaos for as long as anyone could remember.

With distaste he studied the people huddled around him. There they stood like helpless drudges, freezing in their woollen coats and down jackets, wearing jeans and gloves and moon boots, their noses running and their eyes watering in the cold. The temperature was 1°F. Disconsolately, they stared with vacant expressions at Swedish Rail's information boards reporting delayed and canceled trains. He stamped his feet impatiently on the ground in an attempt to stay warm. Damn this cold, how he hated it. And how he hated these poor fools all around him. What pitiful lives they led.

Leaving their homes in the dark of early morning, many of them stood in the biting wind of icy cold bus shelters and then sat jolting back and forth in buses, breathing in the smell of wet wool, exhaust fumes and mold, on their way to catch the commuter train. There they waited once again until the train finally showed up. When it arrived at last, the commuters were jammed together, station after station, until the train reached central Stockholm half an hour later.

After what seemed like an eternity, the train finally rolled into the station. He pushed his way on board to get a seat next to the window. His head ached, and even though the light was dim inside the carriage, he squinted to keep out as much of it as possible.

The train ride into town was a torment. He managed to squeeze in next to a fat woman who was sitting on the outer edge of the seat. He leaned his head against the window and looked out so as to avoid seeing the people around him. The train chugged past one suburb after another, each drearier than the last. He could have avoided this commute, could have been living an entirely different life. As usual, the thought made the acid rise up from his stomach. His body reacted instinctively, physically. He felt ill whenever he thought about how his life could have been. If only.

Impatience had begun to creep over him, and he could feel that something would have to happen soon. He couldn't wait much longer. It was getting more and more difficult to keep his expression calm. Sometimes he was scared that he had taken on more than he could handle.

He got out at Central Station and fell into step with the rushing crowds. He followed the flow of people through the swinging doors and headed for the subway. The train was already at the platform, and he sprinted the last few yards. Gamla Stan, the Old Town, was only one station away.

M onika Wallin got in touch with Knutas before he had a chance to contact her. He was on his way to work when she called. She sounded upset.

"I've found something. Will you please come over here."

"What is it?"

"I can't tell you on the phone. But I was going through our storage room last night, and I discovered something that I'm certain you'll want to see."

Knutas glanced at his watch. He was going to be late for the morning meeting, but it couldn't be helped. Fortunately he'd decided to drive to work this morning. Even though it wasn't far to Snäckgärdsvägen, which was on the other side of the hospital, it would be much faster by car. Instead of pulling into police headquarters, he drove past and turned onto Kung Magnus Road, circling the roundabout near the classic Norrgatt pastry shop before he headed toward the hospital. When he pulled up at the Wallin's home, Monika Wallin was standing outside waiting for him. She was wearing a pink down jacket, and he was surprised to see that she had also put on pink lipstick.

"Hi," she greeted him, her voice sounding a bit strained. She held her hand out to him. Even her gloves were pink.

Then she led the way to the terraced house. The storage room was at one end of the building, and the door was open. Monika Wallin stepped inside the poorly lit space, which was much larger than it seemed from outside. It was cluttered with all sorts of things. The Wallin's house was neat and tidy, but this was a whole different story. Jumbled together were clay pots, old skis, shovels, lampshades, bicycle tires, cardboard boxes, tools, and gardening equipment.

"The storage room was Egon's domain," said Monika Wallin apologetically. "I never came in here. I've always refused because it's so messy. I couldn't even change a light bulb because I never knew where to find one."

She sighed and looked around in resignation. They were standing close together in the only empty patch left on the floor. The walls were lined with shelves filled with all kinds of gadgets, and in the far corner was a table piled high with boxes.

"Over here," she mumbled, leading Knutas along the narrow passageway that she had apparently cleared in order to reach the very back of the storage room. There he saw a door, which was unlocked.

"It leads to the furnace room. It's connected to the laundry room, and there's a door from the inside, too. But we put a dryer in front of it, so now this is the only way to get in."

Knutas followed as they entered a smaller room. Here everything was very orderly. Cardboard boxes were neatly stacked along the walls. On one side stood a kitchen table, old-fashioned but nice. Monika Wallin moved aside a piece of particle board and lifted up a tarpaulin. Knutas's curiosity grew. He leaned forward eagerly to see what was underneath.

She pulled out a small box, placed it on the table and moved the tissue paper inside.

"Look," she said. "I have no idea where it came from."

Knutas looked down at the contents of the box.

There was a painting inside, no bigger than a sheet of

A4 paper. The scene showed part of the Royal Palace in Stockholm, and Riddarholm Church was visible in the background. Otherwise the painting was dominated by the waters of Stockholm's rapids. Judging by the golden color reflected in the palace windows, it was the light of the setting sun that the artist had captured. Knutas was no art connoisseur, but even he could tell that this was a fine painting. He didn't see any signature.

"Who painted this?"

"I'm not sure. I'm not really an art expert. I mostly took care of the administrative side of the business, but if I were to make an educated guess, I'd say it's a Zorn."

"Anders Zorn?" exclaimed Knutas with astonishment. "Then it must be worth a lot."

"If it's a real Zorn, yes. But there are more."

The next painting was a little bigger and had a beautiful gold frame. The motif was so recognizable that Knutas immediately knew who the artist was. Two plump, naked women, their skin white but their cheeks flushed red, on a shore that was undoubtedly Lake Siljan.

"Now this one has to be a Zorn, right?" he said excitedly. He looked for a signature and found it in the lower right corner of the painting.

He couldn't believe his eyes. Here he stood in this little storage room in Visby, looking at work by one of Sweden's most famous artists of all time. It was crazy.

Monika Wallin had more paintings to show him. There was one with a horse motif by Nils Kreuger, one with several sparrows in the snow by Bruno Liljefors, and another of two boys looking at an apple tree with a villa in the background. It was signed C.L.— Carl Larsson. All three were also Swedish artists whose work was acclaimed and very valuable.

Knutas had to sit down on a stool in the cramped space.

"You had no idea that these paintings were here?"

"Of course not. We've never had them in the gallery, we didn't buy them, and there's no documentation anywhere."

"They all appear to be by famous artists. What do you think they're worth?"

"A fortune," she said with a sigh. "Altogether we're probably looking at millions of kronor."

"Have you looked through any of the other boxes in here?"

"No. I can't handle it any more. You'll have to take over."

"We'll need to do a search of your house. Will that be okay?" She nodded and threw out her hands in a gesture of surrender.

While they waited for reinforcements from police head-quarters, Monika Wallin served Knutas coffee. That was when Knutas decided to take up the delicate issue. He chose to get right to the point.

"Why didn't you tell me when I was here before that you're having an affair with Rolf Sandén?"

Apparently Monika Wallin had been expecting the ques-tion. Her expression didn't change. "I thought it was of no relevance to the case whatsoever."

"Everything to do with you and your husband is relevant to the case. Did Egon know about it?"

She sighed heavily. "No, he didn't. He didn't notice a thing. He stopped paying any attention to me long ago."

"How can you be so sure?"

"Rolf and I had it all arranged so well. We met in the daytime, when Egon was at the gallery. I do a lot of my work at home. Usually I go to the gallery only on Mondays."

"Evidently your neighbors were aware of what was going on."

"I suppose that's unavoidable in this neighborhood. Not that I care. We don't socialize with anyone from around here."

"Except you and Rolf?"

"Yes, except for us."

The paintings found in the Wallin storage room were confiscated by the police and sent by the next plane to Bukowski's Auction House in Stockholm. There they would be identified and valued. Erik Mattson received them on Tuesday afternoon.

It took him less than an hour to identify them and confirm that they were genuine. All were originals. The larger Zorn painting with the Dalecarlian women on the shore of Lake Siljan was valued at between three and four million kronor. The others were worth several hundred thousand each. He calculated the total value to be between four and five million kronor. The works were registered, and after he looked them up in the databases, it turned out that they had all been stolen.

Both Zorn paintings were stolen three years earlier from a collector in Göteborg. The Carl Larsson painting had been taken from an exhibition in Falun the previous year, and the painting by Bruno Liljefors had disappeared during a move from an estate on Gotland just a few months earlier.

When he was finished with his appraisal, Mattson immediately called Knutas.

"Jesus!" exclaimed the superintendent. "Every one of them stolen? Are you sure?"

"Definitely. You can look them up yourself in your files."

"And you're sure that they're genuine?"

"Without a doubt."

"Thank you for your time." Knutas put down the phone and then punched in the direct number for the team at the NCP. He asked them to look into the facts of the thefts how they had been carried out, and whether there were any suspects.

He stared out of the window, but his thoughts were elsewhere.

So Egon Wallin had been involved in the theft of paintings on a national scale, or had at least acted as a fence, which was just as serious. Knutas was shocked. Was he such a poor judge of character? He had always regarded Egon as such a law-abiding man. What else didn't he know about him?

The search of the Wallin home was going to be conducted later that day. The gallery would also be searched. Knutas was looking forward to hearing the results.

The fact that the Wallin home was cordoned off and searched by the police did not go unnoticed by the media. The neighbors had seen the paintings being carried out of the storage room, and a rumor that they were stolen instantly began circulating.

"I had a hunch about this whole thing," said Pia eagerly as they drove toward Snäckgårdsvägen. "I knew there was something fishy about Egon Wallin."

When they arrived, the area around the house was swarming with activity. The site had been blocked off and several police cars were parked outside. A group of neighbors was boldly watching the police go about their work. Johan caught a glimpse of Monika Wallin through the kitchen window. He felt sorry for her.

He went over to one of the officers who was standing outside. "What's going on here?"

"I'm not answering that question. You'll have to talk to the police spokesman or the head of the investigation, Anders Knutas."

"Is either of them here?"

"No."

"Can't you at least explain why you've blocked off the area?"

"A discovery has been made on the property that is of interest to the police. That's all I can tell you."

"Does this have to do with stolen paintings?"

The officer's expression didn't change. "I'm not at liberty to say any more."

Johan and Pia tried talking to some of the neighbors, but they could say only that they'd had no idea the Wallins were hiding stolen paintings in their house. Several, however, told Johan to talk to the area's gossip queen, who lived at the very end of the block. If anyone knew anything about this, it was her.

The woman, who looked to be at least eighty, opened the door even before they rang the bell. She was tall and thin, with her silver hair pulled back in a chignon. The dress she wore was quite elegant, as if she were about to go out.

"What's this about?" she asked suspiciously. "Are you from the police? I've already told them everything I know."

The woman didn't seem to take in the fact that Pia was holding a big TV camera. They introduced themselves.

"You're from the television station? Well, I never." She laughed with embarrassment and automatically reached up to smooth her hair. "Ingrid Hasselblad," she introduced herself, stretching out her skinny arm to shake hands. Her fingernails were neatly manicured and painted red.

Suddenly she threw the door wide open. "Come in, come in. May I offer you a cup of coffee?"

"Yes, thanks." Johan and Pia exchanged looks. Coffee often meant that the interview would take longer than really necessary, but this time it might be worth it.

She showed them into the living room. There was a marvelous view, with the sea so close that it felt as if the waves might splash up against the window.

"Excuse me for a moment."

The woman disappeared. When she came back with the

coffee tray, Johan noticed that she'd touched up her lipstick and added a bit too much rouge to her cheeks.

The coffee was weak and the almond cakes dry, but both Pia and Johan said how good they tasted.

"Doesn't that hurt?" Ingrid Hasselblad asked Pia, pointing at the gemstone in her nostril.

"No, not at all. I can't even feel it." Pia smiled.

"That seems to be the fashion nowadays. It's not something that older folks like me can understand." She brushed away a crumb from her dress. "I was a model in my younger days. But that was a long time ago."

"We'd just like to ask you a few questions—about the Wallins," said Johan, thinking that he'd had enough of the chitchat. "Would it be all right if we filmed you while we talk?"

"Go ahead. That should be no problem." Ingrid Hasselblad straightened her back and smiled at the camera, as if she thought she was posing for a still photograph.

"Let's just pretend that the camera isn't here, and it's just you and me talking," said Johan.

"By all means." Ingrid Hasselblad didn't move from the pose she had taken, a rigid smile on her lips.

"Okay, if you wouldn't mind just turning to face me," Johan directed her, "and we'll do a little practice run before we turn on the camera. Just to get in the right frame of mind." He signaled to Pia to start filming. "What did you see at the home of Egon Wallin?"

"Earlier today I was out shopping and happened to walk past their house. That's when several policemen came out of the Wallin storage room carrying paintings."

"What did the officers do with the paintings?"

"They carried them over to a police car. The paintings were covered up, but when they placed one of them inside the car, the covering slipped off and I got a peek at it."

"Do you know what kind of painting it was?"

"I'm not sure, but it looked like a Zorn."

"Can you describe the painting?"

"It was of two plump women with white skin, the way they always look in a Zorn painting. There was green grass around them, and they were near a lake or a river. There was water, in any case."

"Have you ever noticed anything unusual going on at the Wallin house before?"

"I've seen him carrying paintings in and out, but I never thought anything of it. They own an art gallery, you know. So it's not so strange that he keeps works of art at home."

"Have you ever seen Monika Wallin carrying paintings?"

"No-o-o," she replied hesitantly. "I don't think I ever have."

"Is there anything else you can tell us?"

Now Ingrid Hasselblad blushed under her rouge. "Well, yes, there is something."

Johan perked up. "What is it?"

"That Monika, she's been having an affair. With Rolf Sandén, who lives right next door to me." She nodded furtively at the wall. "They've been carrying on for several years now, meeting in the daytime when Egon was at work."

"Can you describe Rolf Sandén? What sort of person is he?"

"He's been a widower for a number of years. Oh, his wife was so nice and kind, but unfortunately she died in a car accident. Their children moved out long ago."

"Doesn't he work in the daytime?"

"He's on a disability pension. Used to work in construction, but he injured his back. Even though he's still a young man, only fifty. He had a big fiftieth birthday party last summer." She leaned forward and lowered her voice. "He likes playing the horses, and I've heard that he's addicted to gambling."

"Who told you that?" Johan was listening with interest. This was getting better and better.

"People talk. It's common knowledge that Rolf Sandén is a notorious gambler. Everybody knows it."

With an effort Ingrid Hasselblad twisted around to look at Pia. "Should we get started now? I think I'd better go and touch up my lipstick."

As soon as Knutas returned from buying a sandwich for lunch, he could hear that Kihlgård and his colleagues from the National Criminal Police had arrived. Martin Kihlgård's bellowing laugh was unmistakable. Loud voices and bursts of laughter issued from the conference room; it sounded like happy hour in a cocktail bar. It was always the same. As soon as Kihlgård turned up, the mood in the criminal division lightened appreciably.

No one noticed Knutas as he pushed open the door. Kihlgård was standing with his broad back to the door, and he had clearly just finished telling one of his countless stories, since everybody seated at the table was doubled over with laughter.

"And then he went and crammed the whole thing in his mouth," Kihlgård went on, his voice excited as he threw out his arms. "Every damned crumb!"

This punchline evoked yet another burst of laughter that practically made the walls shake. Knutas deliberately surveyed the room and then discreetly tapped Kihlgård on the shoulder. When he turned around, the inspector's face expressed nothing but delight.

"Hey, there you are, Knutie, old boy. How's it going?"

Knutas almost disappeared in Kihlgård's wide embrace. He gave his colleague an awkward pat on the back.

"Fine. Just fine. You seem to be fitting in just fine."

"Yeah, that's what she said!" Kihlgård gave another roar of laughter, and the whole investigative team joined in. It wasn't merely Kihlgård's jokes that prompted laughter; everything about him was comical. His wild head of hair stuck out in all directions, as if he'd never owned a comb. He had a ruddy complexion, and he was slightly pop-eyed. He often wore brightly colored V-neck shirts that fit snugly around his paunch. The fact that he liked to wave his hands around when he talked and was almost always eating merely reinforced his clownish demeanor. It was hard to guess his age; he could be anywhere from forty to sixty. But Knutas happened to know that Kihlgård was three years older than himself, which made him fifty-five.

After Knutas had greeted the colleagues that Kihlgård had brought with him from Stockholm, the meeting could begin. Knutas gave his report and then cast an inquisitive glance at his colleagues from the mainland. "So, what do you think?"

"There are undeniably plenty of avenues to follow," began Kihlgård. "The part about the thefts is interesting. And they weren't just any old paintings. He wasn't exactly a small-time crook, was he?"

"I wonder how long he'd been a fence. If that was what he was doing," said Jacobsson.

"It could have been going on for a long time. But I think we would have got wind of what he was up to," said Knutas, sounding worried.

"To think that he just keep the paintings in a storage room," said Wittberg. "Doesn't that seem odd? The place could have burned down or something else might have happened. Somebody could even have broken in and stolen them."

"Maybe it was just a temporary hiding place for those particular paintings. An exception," said Norrby.

"But why did he still have them in his possession when he was so careful about all his other preparations? With the moving and everything else?" wondered Jacobsson aloud.

"He was probably planning to sell them in Stockholm,' Knutas suggested. "Presumably he had a contact over there."

"Have we looked at his computer?" asked Kihlgård.

"Of course," said Knutas. "Both at home and at the gallery. We searched his house today, so we'll be going through his computer files."

"The sale of the gallery must have stirred up a lot of emotions, both for his wife and the employees. How did they react? Not to mention the fact that he'd sold it to that Sixten Dahl."

"Monika Wallin seemed quite unmoved by the sale of the gallery when I talked to her," said Knutas. "But of course she could have been just putting on a show. We'll need to investigate the matter further. We'll have to ask for more help from Stockholm to find anyone else who was working with him. Plus we need to search the apartment that Wallin was planning to move into."

"Yes, he must have had good contacts in Stockholm," muttered Kihlgård. "Does his wife know anything about that?"

"Not according to what she's told us so far," said Knutas curtly. He was annoyed that he hadn't thought to ask the widow more questions when he interviewed her. "We'll need to talk to her again."

"What about the guests at the gallery opening?" Kihlgård went on. "Do you have a list of who was invited?"

"Yep, I've taken care of that," said Jacobsson, holding up a big piece of paper. "I've divided them into three groups. The first column lists all those who received an invitation. The second column shows the names of those who were invited and actually came. The third lists other guests, meaning those people the employees could remember coming to the opening without an invitation."

"Are there any interesting names?"

"Absolutely. A couple of well-known art dealers from Stockholm. And we know that Wallin had business dealings with both of them. Hugo Malmberg, who has a gallery in Gamla Stan, and of course Sixten Dahl, whom we already know," said Jacobsson. "He was supposed to be interviewed this morning, but we haven't yet heard from Stockholm how it went. Regardless, he's of particular interest because he was competing with Egon for the Lithuanian artist, and also because he bought the gallery here in Visby using a front man."

"I suppose you'll want to bring those two over here and interview them yourselves?" Kihlgård cast an inquiring glance at Knutas as he tore open a bag of sweets: Ahlgren's foam cars.

There was a pause before Knutas answered. "Not at the moment."

"Considering that Egon Wallin was secretly planning to move to Stockholm, and he was also dabbling in stolen paintings, don't you think it's highly interesting that two art dealers from Stockholm would come to the gallery on the very day that Wallin was murdered?" Kihlgård tossed a handful of foam cars into his mouth.

Knutas could feel himself growing more and more irritable. He couldn't be in the same room as Kihlgård for five minutes before the man began to infuriate him. "That's something we'll have to consider eventually. But right now I think it's important to hear back from Stockholm about the interview with Sixten Dahl."

He gathered up his papers and got to his feet, indicating that the meeting was over.

Knutas needed some fresh air.

His stomach was growling with hunger. It was late, well past lunchtime. The dry sandwich that Knutas had bought had done nothing to quell his hunger pangs, but right now he had no time to think about trivial matters like food. He needed to interview Mattis Kalvalis and his manager before they returned to Lithuania.

In the lavatory he splashed some water on his face and popped a mint in his mouth.

When he came down to the reception area, they were already waiting for him. He hadn't met the artist before, just seen a photo of him. Mattis Kalvalis looked out of place in police headquarters, to say the least.

The most extraordinary thing about him was his hair: it was black except for his bangs, which had been dyed neon-green. From one ear hung a long chain, and he was dressed in red leather trousers and a jacket of the same bright green as his bangs. With this peculiar attire he wore a pair of light-blue high-top sneakers that reminded Knutas of the kind he used to wear as a kid.

Mattis's manager, who was sitting next to him, was the polar opposite. He looked like a Russian miner with his burly body and rough features. He was dressed in a fur cap with ear flaps and a puffy, dark-blue down jacket. His palm felt sweaty when Knutas shook hands with him.

In stumbling English, Knutas offered a few words of greeting and then led the way up to the criminal division. Luckily the meeting of the investigative team was over, so he found Jacobsson and Kihlgård at the coffee machine. He motioned for Karin to join him.

Both of the Lithuanians declined a cup of coffee as they sat down on the visitors' sofa in Knutas's office. Knutas allowed Jacobsson, who spoke excellent English, to conduct the interview while he listened and observed the two men sitting opposite him. It was actually an advantage to play the role of observer. He'd be able to see every change of expression that the questions might produce and notice if the person being interviewed looked nervous or evasive.

Jacobsson began by switching on the audio recorder and giving the usual introductory information.

"Can I smoke?" asked the artist as he dug a cigarette out of a crumpled pack in his jacket pocket.

"I'm afraid not."

The gaunt, eccentric-looking man paused with the cigarette halfway to his lips. Then he stuffed it back into the pack without changing expression.

Jacobsson studied the handsome features of his young, pale face, which was marred by deep furrows. There were dark shadows under his eyes. Mattis Kalvalis looked as if he hadn't slept in several days. He seemed uncomfortable sitting on Knutas's sofa, crowded up next to his corpulent manager.

After asking the standard questions to establish the identity of the interviewees, Jacobsson turned to the artist.

"How well did you know Egon Wallin?'"

Kalvalis hesitated before answering.

"Hmm, not very well. He was easy to talk to, on a professional level, but we'd met only a few times."

"Where did you first meet?"

"It must have been a year ago," he said, glancing at his manager, who nodded in agreement. "Yes, that's right. It was last spring in Vilnius. He was attending some sort of conference, I think."

Again he looked at the man sitting next to him. His manager pursed his lips and nodded.

"How did you happen to meet?"

"We were seated at the same table at a dinner arranged by the Society for the Promotion of Lithuanian Artists. He'd seen my work. I had a show at a small gallery in Vilnius at the time, and he said that he liked what I did. The next day we met for lunch, and he offered to be my agent here in Scandinavia."

"And you accepted at once?"

"No, of course not. I was actually getting a lot of attention from that exhibition, which was my first, and there was a bunch of write-ups in the newspapers. I had offers from all over, but Egon Wallin's was the best."

That caught Knutas's attention. He wondered how Egon Wallin could have beaten the other agents so easily. He scribbled a few words in his notebook.

"What exactly did he offer you?" Jacobsson fixed her gaze on Mattis Kalvalis. Her eyes were just as dark as his.

"He wanted to sell my work over here, and he would take twenty percent."

"Why was that such a good deal?"

"Everybody else wanted to take twenty-five percent. And besides, he seemed to have good contacts."

Kalvalis smiled briefly. At the beginning of the interview he had acted very nervous, but now he seemed to be relaxing.

"That certainly seems to be the case, considering it was

156

your first show here," said Jacobsson. "As I understand it, nearly everything was sold."

"That's right."

"And the publicity has been great," his manager interjected, speaking for the first time. "Mattis has been in every major newspaper this weekend, and commissions for more paintings have been pouring in. Egon Wallin was a good man to work with; we could tell that right from the start. Now we don't know what's going to happen."

"No, we don't," Mattis agreed, shrugging his shoulders.

Judging by his expression, he wasn't particularly worried.

"We know that you had dinner at Donners Brunn after the opening on the night of the murder. What did you do after that?"

"I didn't go to the dinner," reported the manager. "I wasn't feeling well, so I went straight back to the hotel."

"Is that so?" Jacobsson frowned. She had assumed that Vigor Haukis was also at the dinner. "What did you do at the hotel?"

"Just went to bed. I was so tired after all the rushing around and nervousness before the opening." He laughed, as if embarrassed.

Jacobsson turned to Mattis Kalvalis. "Tell me about that evening."

"Okay. The opening went well, as I said. You could say it was a huge success. I had a great time, and it was interesting to talk to all the guests. People here are so open and enthusiastic," he said, looking pleased as he tugged at his green bangs. "There were lots of journalists, and I gave a bunch of interviews. Then afterward we all went to the restaurant, except for Vigor, and that was really nice."

"How long did you stay at the restaurant?"

"I left around eleven."

"What did you do then?"

"Went straight back to the hotel. I had to get up early the next morning."

"And you didn't see anyone on your way back?"

"No. The hotel is practically next door to the restaurant. I went up to my room and went to bed."

"Did anyone see you?"

"No. There's nobody at the front desk at night, so the lobby was deserted."

"So nobody can vouch for the fact that you're telling us the truth?"

"No," said the artist, surprised. "Am I a suspect?" His hand flew up to clutch at his chest.

"I'm just asking standard questions that we ask everybody," replied Jacobsson, as if to reassure him. "It's just routine."

"Okay. I understand." Kalvalis smiled uneasily and cast a quick glance at his manager.

"Why did the two of you go to Stockholm?"

"I might as well tell you the truth about that. I know that I'd promised Egon that he could be my agent in Scandinavia, but I hadn't signed the contract yet. During the opening, I was offered an even better agreement by another art dealer in Stockholm."

"Sixten Dahl?"

"Yes, that's right. He persuaded me to at least go and see his gallery and hear more about what he could do for me. So we decided during the opening that we'd go."

"Have you now signed a contract with Dahl?"

The artist threw out his hands. "As a matter of fact, I have. It's so much better. And it doesn't really matter anymore. Now that Egon is dead."

After the interview, Knutas and Jacobsson went to the pizzeria around the corner for a late lunch. They were the only customers. It was past two, and Knutas was faint with hunger. They each ordered a capricciosa pizza at the counter and then sat down at a table near the window with a view of the street. The sunshine was gone; they looked out at overcast skies and slushy snow.

"I didn't like having to let those two go," said Jacobsson, shaking her head. "There's still too much that's up in the air."

"I know," Knutas agreed. "But what could we do? We don't have any reason for arresting them."

Jacobsson took a sip of the light beer she had ordered. "This case just seems to get more and more complicated. First the murder of Egon Wallin; then we find out about his secretly planned move, the stolen paintings, and his wife's love affair. What a mess."

Their pizzas arrived, and they ate them in silence. Knutas gulped down his food so fast that he got the hiccups. He ordered a Ramlösa sparkling mineral water, which he swiftly downed to put a stop to the hiccuping.

"There are two points of intersection," he then said. "Art and Stockholm. Wallin was on his way there, and Kalvalis apparently has a number of contacts in the city. Is there anything else that comes to mind?"

"Secrets," said Jacobsson. "Both Wallin and his wife were keeping secrets from each other. Wallin managed to sell the gallery, buy an apartment in Stockholm, and virtually arrange for the whole divorce without his poor wife finding out a thing."

"What about Mattis Kalvalis?" murmured Knutas pensively. "What sort of secrets do you think he might have?"

He pushed aside his plate and gave his colleague a searching glance. *And what about you?* he thought. *Speaking of secrets.*

"How's it going?" he asked her.

"What do you mean? With me?" She looked worried.

"Yes."

"Fine. Everything's fine."

"You're a terrible liar."

"Now stop it," she said, although with a smile. But Knutas's expression was serious as he looked her in the eye.

"Haven't we known each other long enough for you to tell me what's going on?"

Jacobsson blushed. "Oh, Anders, nothing special is going on. Life just has its ups and downs, that's all. You know how it is."

"Do you have a boyfriend?" Karin gave a start. Even Knutas was startled by his boldness. He couldn't believe he'd asked her such a question.

She stared at the half-empty beer glass she was holding, slowly turning it round and round. "No, I don't," she said in a low voice.

"I'm sorry," he said. "I didn't mean to pry. It's just that I've noticed that something is bothering you. Am I right?"

She sighed. "Okay, I'm having some personal problems, but it's nothing I want to discuss. Not at the moment."

"So when?" he said crossly. All of a sudden he felt anger flaring up inside him. "When do you want to discuss things? Are you ever planning to tell me anything? We've worked together for fifteen years, Karin. If you have a problem, I want to help you. You should give me a chance to do something for you!"

Karin stood up abruptly, giving him a furious look. "Help me?" she snarled. "How the hell can you, of all people, help me?"

Without giving him a chance to respond, she left the table and walked out of the restaurant. Knutas stayed where he was, staring at the angry set of her back as she walked away.

He had no idea what had just happened.

When the investigative team met on Wednesday morning, only a few people had called the police to offer any tips about the case, in spite of requests made through the media.

"How could this happen? A man is murdered and hung from a gate in Visby's ring wall for all to see, yet not a single person noticed anything." Knutas was interrupted by a sneeze that sprayed out over half the conference table. For weeks he'd been dragging around with a cold that he couldn't shake. He quickly apologized to his colleagues and wiped the table with a handkerchief that he dug out of his pocket.

"If only we knew where the murder was actually committed," said Jacobsson with a sigh.

"That's bound to come out sooner or later," said Norrby soothingly. "At any rate, I can report that we've checked out the address in Stockholm where Egon Wallin was planning to move. Artillerigatan 38. It turns out that he bought the apartment two months ago, on November the seventeenth, to be precise. A newly refurbished two-bedroom apartment. It was almost fully furnished, with brand-new furniture, a new TV, and stereo. The kitchen was fully equipped with dishes and utensils. He bought the apartment through an advertisement, and paid 4.2 million kronor."

Wittberg whistled. "That's damned expensive. Did he have that kind of money?"

"Apparently Östermalm is a very pricey neighborhood. It's also a corner apartment with a balcony, on the sixth floor of the building. And it's not small by any means, at over 1,000 square feet." Norrby paused for dramatic effect, running his hand through his hair. "And to answer your question: yes, he did have the money. He'd just sold his gallery, and that's probably how he paid for the apartment. He also owned a number of stocks and bonds."

"Life insurance, too?" asked Jacobsson.

"Yup. Worth 15 million. At his death, the money goes to his wife."

"All right then," said Kihlgård, leaning back in his chair and clasping his hands over his stomach. "So now we've got another motive. Maybe we should bring in Monika Wallin for another chat. There seem to be some gaps in the previous interview." He cast a quick glance at Knutas, who stirred uneasily. "She had a lover, and her husband's death is going to make her rich. Two classic motives for murder."

"What about his children?" Jacobsson interjected. "What do they get?"

"It looks as if they're going to inherit quite a bundle, too. I can't tell you exactly how much at the moment, but he was presumably worth several million," said Norrby. "His wife and children will share the inheritance equally, so there's going to be plenty for each of them."

"So we have three people with plausible motives," said Jacobsson. "And we haven't talked to the children yet. As for Rolf Sandén, her lover, he had both a motive and the necessary physical strength. Unfortunately he also has an alibi for the night of the murder. He was visiting a good friend in Slite and stayed overnight. The friend has confirmed that they were together all night."

"I've done some checking up on Egon Wallin's business partners in Stockholm," Kihlgård went on. "First up, Sixten Dahl. We know he bought the gallery without revealing his identity. Dahl didn't say anything startling during the interview that was conducted in Stockholm. He also has an alibi for the night of the murder. He was sharing a hotel room here with a good friend from Stockholm, and they were together all evening and night. Well, I don't mean they were 'together' in that sense," Kihlgård quickly clarified. "We asked him about that. It turns out the hotel was fully booked, so there was only one room available. There was a convention in town at the same time, something to do with the Baltic Sea."

"Oh, that's right," said Jacobsson. "It was about the gas line between Russia and Germany that's supposed to run past Sweden on the bottom of the sea."

"Exactly," said Kihlgård. "And Dahl's story has been confirmed both by the restaurant staff at Donners Brunn and by the receptionist at the hotel. They were back before eleven and went straight up to their room."

"But that doesn't mean they didn't go out again, later on," Jacobsson pointed out.

"And it's an interesting coincidence that they had dinner at the same restaurant as Egon Wallin and his party," said Wittberg.

"Sure, but at the same time, there aren't that many places to choose from, and it happens to be the closest restaurant to the hotel," said Knutas.

"I think we'll need to come back to this again later," suggested Kihlgård. "All right. It turns out that Sixten Dahl is going to move over here on a trial basis for six months to get the business going, and his wife will be coming with him.

But that's actually beside the point," he muttered, leafing through his papers as if looking for something. Then his face brightened. "Ah yes, here it is."

With great deliberation he put on his glasses and took a bite of a cinnamon roll, which he washed down with some coffee. Everyone waited patiently as he brushed the crumbs from his lips, before he went on. "Egon Wallin bought a part ownership in an art gallery in Gamla Stan in Stockholm. It's owned by four partners, and he was to be the fifth."

"Who are the others?" asked Knutas, who by now had recovered from his resentment at Kihlgård's jab.

"I have a list of the names here." Kihlgård pushed his glasses into place and read the names from the list.

"Katarina Ljungberg, Ingrid Jönsson, Hugo Malmberg, and Peter Melander."

"I recognize the name Hugo Malmberg," said Jacobsson. "I think he might have been at the gallery opening." She looked through the lists lying on the table in front of her.

"Yes, I was right," she exclaimed happily. "He was interviewed in Stockholm. By someone named Stenstrom."

"Interesting. We'll get on that right away," said Knutas. "What stage had the business deal reached?"

"It was all set," said Kihlgård. "He'd paid his portion, and there don't seem to be any issues."

"We need to talk to this Mr. Malmberg as soon as possible," said Knutas. "And check up on the others, too. We need to find out whether any of them has been mixed up in dealing with stolen paintings."

"And we may have another possible motive," said Wittberg. "One of the other partners may not have liked the fact that Egon Wallin was invited to join them."

"But would somebody go so far as to murder him for that reason? I don't think so," said Norrby, shaking his head.

The cold was relentless, keeping everybody indoors. It was uncommonly quiet in Stockholm on this night in February. The temperature had dropped to minus 1°F, and everything seemed to have come to a standstill, frozen in place.

When Hugo Malmberg opened the door to Långholmsgatan, he was met by an icy wave of cold. He burrowed his face in his scarf and turned up his collar as he surveyed the deserted street. Still no taxi. It was close to three a.m. He lit a cigarette, stamping his feet on the ground as he waited, trying to keep warm. He considered going back inside until he realized that he'd forgotten the entry code. He glanced up at the fifth floor and the row of windows belonging to Ludvig and Alexia's apartment. No lights were on. They'd been quick to turn them off, no doubt glad that he'd finally left.

Yet another in a series of Friday night dinners with well-prepared food, excellent wine, and good friends. The waistband of his trousers felt tight; he needed to be careful not to put on more weight. He'd been the last guest to leave, which was often the case. This time he and the host, his good friend Ludvig, had got embroiled in a discussion about the lack of interest in art in the cultural pages of the major newspapers. Literature seemed to take up all the space. By the time all the arguments had been voiced and their indignation vented, it was two thirty in the morning. The rest of the dinner guests had dropped out, one by one, but that didn't prevent the two friends from continuing their lively debate. It was Ludvig's wife, Alexia, who had to see the other guests out with a kiss on the cheek.

Finally even Hugo realized that it was time to go home, and Ludvig rang for a taxi. The cabs always showed up promptly, so he thought he might as well take the lift down and wait outside as he smoked the cigarette he'd been longing for all evening. Smoking was not allowed in Ludvig and Alexia's apartment.

After Hugo had smoked a second cigarette and the cab still hadn't arrived, he glanced again at his watch. He'd now been waiting ten minutes, and he began to doubt that the taxi was going to show up at all. Unfortunately, he'd left his cell phone at home, and he wasn't thrilled about the idea of shouting or tossing pebbles at the windows so far overhead.

He turned to look toward Vasterbron. It really wasn't very far to go. Just across the bridge and then he could take the stairs down and walk through Ralambshov Park. After that it was a short distance along Norr Malarstrand to the corner of John Ericssonsgatan, where he lived. It shouldn't take him much more than twenty minutes, at most half an hour. The fact that it was so damned cold was the only thing that made him hesitate, but if he walked quickly, it shouldn't be too bad.

Hugo Malmberg was one of Stockholm's most respected art dealers. He was part owner of a large gallery in Gamla Stan. By making successful deals in the art world, he'd built up a small fortune during the eighties and it had only increased since.

He set off at a brisk pace for Västerbron, wanting to get his blood moving. The cold made every breath painful. Sweden isn't meant for human beings, he thought. If God does exist, He must have forgotten this corner in the northernmost part of Europe. The city had settled into a frozen torpor. The layer of ice covering the bridge railing glittered in the light from the street lamps. The bridge loomed up before him with its beautifully curved arch. Underneath it, solid ice stretched all the way to the heart of the city. He turned up his collar as far as it would go and stuffed his hands in his coat pockets.

He was annoyed to see the night bus drive past just as he stepped onto the bridge. It hadn't occurred to him that he might take the bus. Below lay the small island of Långholmen with its bare trees and rocks. The old prison island in the middle of town now consisted mostly of woods and moorage for boats around the perimeter. Up ahead, a short distance away, there was a staircase that led down from the bridge to the desolate island.

Suddenly Malmberg noticed a figure below, climbing the stairs. The man wore a dark down jacket and a knitted cap on his head.

At the very moment when he passed the stairs, their eyes met. The man in the dark clothes was tall and seemed to have a muscular body under his jacket. He had a boyish face, and curly blond hair stuck out from under his cap.

Malmberg couldn't think of a thing to say. It was a strange situation. The two of them were alone, out in the cold night, and perhaps they should have exchanged greetings. The younger man seemed wildly attractive. Never mind, thought Malmberg. Right now he just wanted to get home as quickly as possible. His cheeks felt frozen. He began walking faster.

Not a sound came from behind him. He didn't know whether the man on the stairs was following in his footsteps or had gone off in the other direction, toward Södermalm.

Finally Malmberg could no longer resist the temptation, and he turned around. He gave a start of surprise—the stranger was only a few yards behind him. He smiled and looked Hugo Malmberg right in the eyes.

Not knowing how to interpret that smile, Malmberg continued on his way.

As he approached the crest of the bridge, the wind picked up. The air was so raw and cold that he could hardly draw it into his lungs. Here he was, walking through central Stockholm, and he couldn't remember ever seeing the city so desolate. Everything around him was frozen, as if the life and noise of the city had suddenly turned to stone, arrested in midstream. It was the same feeling that he got from art. An expertly done painting that moved him made everything else around him freeze for a moment, like a photograph—time and space stopped and he was alone, except for the painting in front of him.

Now he caught sight of the stranger again: all of a sudden he was standing ahead of him. How had that happened? He was on the other side of the bridge, looking straight at Hugo.

A feeling of uneasiness suddenly came over him. There was definitely something not quite right about this young man's behavior. The next second Malmberg realized how exposed he was, in full view in the middle of the bridge, with not the slightest place to hide if he was about to be attacked. He could run, of course, but his pursuer would undoubtedly catch him before he even managed to get up to speed.

Over on Norr Malarstrand he saw a lone taxi driving toward the center of town. He continued walking, keeping his eyes on the man on the other side of the bridge. At the same time he heard the sound of an engine, which quickly rose to a deafening roar. An articulated truck came speeding across the bridge in the other direction. He caught a glimpse of the driver's face before the truck thundered by.

By the time the long expanse of the truck had passed, the young man on the bridge had vanished.

On Saturday, Knutas was woken by the phone ringing. He immediately recognized Sohlman's urgent
voice on the line.

"We've found what we think is the murder site."

"Really? Where is it?" Knutas was instantly wide awake.

"Near Kärleksporten. I think you'd better come over
here."

"Okay. I'll be there in fifteen minutes."

He jumped out of bed and into the shower.

Still wrapped in the sheets, Lina sleepily stretched out
her hands toward him. "What's going on?" she murmured,
sounding tired.

"Things are happening. I've got to go'" He kissed her on
the forehead.

"I'll call later," he called as he dashed down the stairs.
He threw together a sandwich, but his coffee would have to
wait. That was an almost unbearable sacrifice. Coffee was
his life's elixir and he needed it to function in the morning.

He drove down to the harbor as fast as he could and then
continued along the wall to the small opening on the west side
that was known as Kärleksporten—The Lovers Gate. By the
time he arrived, a large area had already been cordoned off.

"What's happening?" he asked Sohlman, who was peering through the gate when he got there.

"This morning a witness found this." Sohlman held up a plastic bag containing a black leather wallet. "Nothing seems to have been taken, so we can definitely rule out the robbery theory."

"Wallin's wallet?" Knutas ventured.

"Yes. He must have dropped it when he was attacked. There are other indications that this was the murder site. We found bloodstains on the wall and a cigarette butt that's the same brand as the one we found at Dalman Gate. Lucky Strike. It's a very unusual brand, at least here on Gotland."

"No trace of his phone?"

"No, unfortunately not."

"And it's possible to drive all the way up here by car," said Knutas, scanning the ground. "But I don't suppose there are any tire tracks to be found after all this time."

"Don't say that. It hasn't snowed since the night of the murder, and hardly any cars ever come through here. At least not in the winter. We might be in luck."

"It seems most likely that the perp followed him here from Snäckgårdsvägen. The question is, where was Egon Wallin going? Obviously into town, but then where?"

"He must have arranged to meet somebody. Either at one of the restaurants that are open late on Saturday night, or at a hotel. I can't imagine any other possibilities."

"Unless he was going to someone's house," said Knutas. "He could have been on his way to a secret rendezvous with someone who lives here."

"That's also possible, of course."

Knutas sighed. "In any case, it's good you found the murder site. Where's the witness?"

"Being interviewed," said Sohlman. "In the meantime, we'll keep working here."

"Okay. I'm going to call in everyone who can make it to a meeting this afternoon. I hope you can do your work here discreetly so that we won't have the press on our backs."

"That's going to be difficult," said Sohlman. "We need to keep a large area blocked off for most of the day. I'm hoping to map out the precise route that he took."

"I have a feeling that the killer was very familiar with the area," Knutas mused. "What if we're actually looking for a Gotlander?"

Back at police headquarters, he called Lina and explained that he was going to be busy most of the day.

Even though he'd been looking forward to having some time off, he was relieved that something was finally happening. Whenever an investigation came to a standstill for a number of days, he started getting worried. He'd become more impatient over the years.

It didn't take long before Sohlman called. He was also back at headquarters to do a technical examination of Egon Wallin's wallet.

"Can you come down here?" he asked Knutas.

"Of course." Knutas hurried downstairs to the tech division, which was located in the basement of the building. Sohlman had spread out the contents of the wallet on a table with strong lights overhead.

"Everything seems to be here: credit cards, cash, business cards. The wallet had fallen into a ditch and was completely covered with snow. It's not so strange that nobody found it until today."

"How much did the witness handle it, do you think?"

"It was an elderly man out walking his dog. The dog sniffed it out of the snow. The witness saw Egon Wallin's name and photo on the driver's license, so he had the good sense to drop the wallet on the ground and call the police. He was also wearing gloves, and he kept them on, because

173

he knew it was important not to leave his own prints. We can thank all the television crime shows for that. Unfortunately there are no fingerprints on the wallet because it was lying around outside so long."

"So what have you found?"

"Well, there's one thing that puzzles me."

With tweezers Sohlman picked up a scrap of paper from the table. A yellow Post-it note with four numbers scribbled on it.

"A code, apparently," said Knutas. "Could it be the PIN number for his bank card?"

"It seems a little stupid to keep it in plain view in his wallet along with the card," said Sohlman. "Of course, I know that people do dumb things like that all the time, but I don't think it fits with Wallin's personality."

"You're right," Knutas agreed. "It must mean something else. Is there a coded keypad on the door of the gallery? In case someone forgets their key and it's locked?"

Sohlman gave him a dubious look. "Wallin has run that art gallery for twenty-five years. He went there every day. Even if they'd recently changed the code, he would have had it memorized."

"We need to check out all possible options," said Knutas. "I'll put Kihlgård on it. That'll give him something to think about besides food."

Erik Mattson slowly regained consciousness. As if from far away, he could hear a shower running and other sounds that he didn't recognize. The roar of the traffic outside sounded different. It was louder than outside his own windows on Karlavägen. The air in the room was stale and stuffy, and the bed he was lying on was much softer and lumpier than the exclusive Dux mattress he was used to. His body felt bruised, and his groin ached. His head was pounding.

He opened his eyes and saw at once that he was in a hotel room. The events of the previous night came back to him, but before he had time to think any further, a big man appeared in the doorway to the bathroom. He dried off his shaved head as he stared at Erik lying on the bed.

He was completely naked and without embarrassment dried off his penis, now hanging limply. The muscles bulged on his athletic body. His skin was exceptionally white, and he had almost no hair, not even around his dick. On one arm was a small tattoo shaped like a turtle. It looked ridiculous.

They had met at one of the city's more decadent gay clubs, which Erik often frequented on Fridays. All it took was half a drink and a few long looks for the burly man to make his move. He was in a hurry; they had only had a few drinks before he wanted to leave. When Erik explained that he charged a fee, the other man had looked surprised and then left. But it wasn't long before he was back, asking the price. Apparently the fee was acceptable, because they had left the club together and taken a cab to his hotel.

He'd been rough and determined, almost to the point of violence. A few times Erik had felt scared, but the big man never crossed the line. Though he did come close. When he took a break and went out to use the toilet, Erik had quickly downed two of the little yellow pills, to deaden the pain and be able to last the night. His customer showed no sign of being finished; he seemed insatiable.

Erik felt that this episode had been tougher than usual. Sometimes he enjoyed himself, both sexually and mentally. It was as if he was escaping, as if he took pleasure in the destructive aspect of the whole thing. His life was headed downhill, and there was no other path to take. He might as well just let things happen. The pain sometimes even made him feel more content the next day. And the element of excitement was an added spice that couldn't be underestimated.

Whenever he entered a club, he knew that within a few hours he'd be involved in an extremely intimate scene with another human being. But he had no idea who in that club it would be.

Of course there were pleasures in this double life of his, and it also kept him going financially. At the same time it was exhausting, both mentally and physically. Occasionally he would be struck by panic attacks, despair, and an overwhelming sense of emptiness. He quelled those feelings by popping pills and drinking excessively. A momentary escape, of course, but he didn't see any other option. There was no other life for him. He was like a goldfish in a bowl of water, with no chance of ever getting out.

The man smiled at Erik, bringing him back to the present. With a triumphant gesture, he tossed aside the bath towel. One look at his swelling cock made Erik realize that he was still not satisfied.

All of the officers from the NCP had gone back to Stockholm for the weekend, except for Martin Kihlgård. Sometimes Knutas wondered whether Kihlgård had a life outside of his police work. At any rate, he knew very little about his colleague. Kihlgård never talked about his family, and he didn't wear a wedding ring, so Knutas assumed he wasn't married. But he had no idea what his colleague did in his free time, except eat, of course. Even today, when Knutas dropped by the office temporarily assigned to Kihlgård, he found him munching on a baguette with salami and brie.

"How are things going?"

"Great. I've checked up on that mysterious code. I started by asking myself a very simple question."

As usual, Kihlgård was talking with food in his mouth. Knutas waited for him to finish chewing.

"You see, I wondered how the killer happened to know that Wallin was going to leave the house again."

Knutas shrugged. "It's possible that it was pure chance. Maybe he was tailing Wallin and waited outside his house until the lights were turned off."

"Or maybe he knew that Wallin was going out to meet

178

somebody!" Kihlgård sounded triumphant, as if he'd come up with something new and revolutionary.

"Yes, well, we've already discussed that possibility at least a hundred times," said Knutas impatiently. He had no intention of standing there, wasting valuable time on such drivel.

"The perp must have known that Wallin was planning to go out later in the evening to meet someone," Kihlgård went on, unperturbed. "He probably also knew that the person was staying at the Wisby Hotel."

"At the Wisby?" Knutas raised his eyebrows. "How do you know that the woman he went out to meet was staying there?"

Kihlgård held out the code that Knutas had copied from the Post-it note earlier in the morning. "Why else would he be walking around with the hotel's nighttime code in his wallet?"

"How did you figure that out?"

"First I checked the bank to see if it might be his PIN number. Then I asked his wife if it was a code for the security alarm at their house. They have lots of valuable stuff, after all. But both were dead ends. So I started thinking about the fact that he was on his way to meet someone, possibly at a hotel. I checked to see which hotels had receptionists on duty at night. It so happens that after the female night manager at the Wisby was murdered, the hotel changed their system. If you arrive at the hotel after midnight and before six in the morning, you have to ring the bell and the receptionist will unlock the door for you. So anybody who doesn't belong there can't just come in. But if a hotel guest doesn't want to call the receptionist, possibly because he or she wants to smuggle someone up to their room . . ." Kihlgård winked at Knutas with a you-know-what-I-mean look on his face, ". . . all of the guests are given a code they can use instead of ringing the bell. I checked the hotel code, and it turned out to be a match. For security reasons, they change the number every day, and this was the code that was valid between Saturday the nineteenth and Sunday the twentieth of February."

Knutas whistled. "Not bad," he said with admiration. "Very impressive. So now we've narrowed it down to the Wisby Hotel. There can't be many guests to choose from. Brilliant, Martin."

He gave his colleague a friendly pat on the back.

"Thank you."

They were interrupted by Karin Jacobsson, who poked her head in the door. "Lunch, anybody?"

Kihlgård's face lit up. "That sounds like a splendid idea," he said, stuffing the last bit of baguette into his mouth. "There's just one more thing. I compared the list of hotel guests on the night in question to the list of people invited to the gallery opening."

"Yes?"

"Not a single woman is on both lists. All of the individuals who went to the opening and also stayed at the hotel are men."

On Saturday morning Johan woke early. He lay on his side, staring at Emma's face as he thought about what plans they should make for the wedding. Considering how turbulent their relationship had been up until now, he wanted to comply with Emma's wishes that they get married soon. He didn't want to risk having something else happen that might upset their plans.

He might have to give up his dream of getting married in a church, even though that would be wonderful.

It was now the end of February, and they would need at least two months to send out the invitations and make the arrangements. Having friends and family members present at the wedding was a minimum requirement. He refused to budge on that issue. But where could they hold the ceremony if not in a church? The instant he asked himself that question, an idea popped into his head—why not at the Roma cloister ruins here on Gotland? And then they could have the party at home. It might get a little crowded, but the house was a spacious 2,000 square feet, and if the guests spread out into all the rooms, it should be manageable. They didn't have to serve a formal dinner; maybe it would be enough to offer a light snack and champagne, followed, of course, by coffee and wedding cake. And that would obviate the need for seating arrangements and embarrassing speeches. Just laughter and conversation, fun and celebration.

He got so wrapped up in the whole idea that he got out of bed to find a pen and paper. He wanted to make a list of people to invite, to see if it would even be possible to hold the party at home. Though if they were going to get married outdoors, maybe they should postpone the ceremony until a little later. Wait until May or June, when it was warmer and everything was green and in bloom. Of course, they would have a honeymoon. It shouldn't be any problem finding someone to babysit. It would be best if they could leave Elin at home; either his mother or Emma's parents, who lived on the island of Fårö, could take care of her. And Sara and Filip could stay with them too.

Maybe they should go to Paris, he daydreamed. He couldn't imagine a more romantic city. In the springtime or early summer. That would be perfect.

He was just about to wake Emma when something occurred to him. Shouldn't they make their engagement official, now that he had proposed? Should he buy her an engagement ring or should they do it together? He didn't know how such things were done. He would have to ask somebody. He ran his finger along Emma's bare back. He had no doubt whatsoever that he loved her deeply, so it really made no difference what sort of wedding they had. The only thing that mattered was that they got married.

The emptiness that always followed one of those nights washed over him. Erik Mattson had gone home and spent a couple of hours recovering. Later in the afternoon he left his apartment and took a bus to the Waldemarsudde Art Museum in the Kungliga Djurgården, the Royal Deer Park.

He got off at the museum bus stop, which was close to the shore. He walked the last stretch of the way up to what had once been Prince Eugen's home during the first half of the twentieth century. The painter prince who never became king. He was a great artist and an especially good landscape painter. During his lifetime the prince put together an enormous art collection, which he donated, along with his beautiful villa, to the Swedish nation at his death in 1947.

The building with its yellow facade was located on a hill and seemed to be rising out of the rock. It stood on the shore at the very end of a peninsula facing the Baltic Sea, which reached all the way to Stockholm on this side. The main building in which the prince had lived was called the castle, although it looked more like a mansion on a small country estate.

At the moment the museum was showing an exhibition of Swedish art from the early 1900s. Erik went inside and paid the entrance fee. He wasn't interested in going into the beautiful gallery; instead, he headed for what had once been the prince's private residence, the castle. There, too, artworks were on display, and hanging in one of the drawing rooms was the painting he was looking for.

He saw it from far away. The large oil painting took up an entire wall. It was the mood depicted in the painting that attracted him—the colors, the soft and gentle movements, the tragedy and the coquettishness. Reverently he sank down on a bench that had been placed in front of Nils Dardel's masterpiece, "The Dying Dandy."

The motif was bewitching, and Erik hardly noticed the other visitors. Contradictory emotions welled up inside him.

He felt so close to Dardel, as if there were some kind of secret bond between them, a connection not limited by time or space. The fact that they'd never met was of no importance. He knew that they were twin souls. That was something he'd felt ever since he saw "The Dying Dandy" for the first time when he was visiting the home of a fellow student many years ago.

He was seventeen at the time, insecure and searching. The painting seemed to speak directly to him. The pale, handsome dandy was in the center of the scene and immediately drew the eye of the viewer. The same mystery and enigma hovered over the dandy as over Dardel himself. How young he is, Erik thought as he sat there. So fragile and attractive. Those closed eyes with the thick dark lashes against the pale cheek. The slender body in the semi-reclining position on the floor with his legs apart, almost erotic in the midst of tragedy. The dandy had one hand pressed to his heart, as if it hurt. And judging by the pallor of his face, the life force had already left his body.

Erik was fascinated by the figure's appearance: the sensitive face, the elegant clothing, one hand coquettishly stretched out on the floor with the long, slender fingers holding a hand-mirror. What did it mean? Was he fleeing from his own image? Was he weary of his life, his alcoholism and his homosexuality? Was he trying to escape his decadent life, just as Erik wanted to do but didn't dare?

Erik's gaze took in the three loving women surrounding the dandy, their soft figures, their tenderness. One of them was about to place a blanket over the slender, elegant young man, as if putting a piano cover over an exquisite instrument that was no longer played.

There was another man in the scene as well. Standing in the background, partially turned away from the small group. The young man seemed desperate with grief as he pressed a handkerchief to one eye, like a monocle. There was something theatrical about him, with his dark eyes and red lips. He was also dressed like a dandy in vibrant colors: purple jacket, orange shirt, and a red-and-green tie. Erik was positive that the man in the background represented Dardel's most important lover, Rolf de Maré. Dardel had carried on many homosexual affairs, although he'd had relationships with women at the same time.

Erik's eyes moved back to the dandy's hand over his heart. Was the pain purely physical? Was he killed by a heart attack? Dardel had suffered from heart disease after a serious case of scarlet fever when he was a child, but was it really that simple? Maybe the painting was about a broken heart from a love affair. Did the artist want to show that he was on his way to leaving Rolf de Mare and his own homosexuality behind in order to enter into marriage with a woman? When Dardel painted the work in the summer of 1918 he was secretly engaged to Nita Wallenberg, the daughter of a cabinet minister. Was that why the man in the background was grieving?

The painting moved him on so many levels; it touched his innermost soul and reflected the tragedy of his own life. If only we could have met, he sometimes thought in despair. If only we had lived in the same era. How he would have loved Dardel. How many times had he wondered what the artist had in mind when he created that painting?

Maybe he can see me right now, thought Erik, glancing automatically up at the ceiling. Then his eyes returned to the painting.

The way the three women had gathered around the dying dandy reminded him of Christ's death, with the dandy as Jesus. Erik thought that the woman placing the blanket over him resembled an angel, with the green palm leaves like wings behind her. Another of the women could have been Mary, with her dress the strong blue traditionally used for her. And the younger girl holding the pillow under his head might symbolize Mary Magdalene with her red hair and red and purple clothing. The man in the background had the features of Christ's favorite apostle, John. Sure, why not?

There was no mistaking the sense of tragedy, no matter what it might symbolize. It might have something to do with the war. When Dardel painted the scene, Europe was in the grip of the First World War. Sweden had remained neutral, but Finland had just entered the conflict, which was getting closer to Sweden and having a tremendous impact on the country. Not even in the wealthy salons frequented by Nils Dardel could anyone continue to close their eyes to the horrors being inflicted on people all around them. Maybe the artist wanted to portray the changes taking place in society during that time. The luxuries and amusements of the exclusive salons enjoyed by him and his friends must have begun to seem absurd—the self-absorbed dandy had become conscious of what was happening around him.

Erik thought that Dardel was an idealist, but a complicated

and multi-layered man, in many ways a tragic person who wanted to flee from himself. He did so through alcohol, but also through art.

Exactly like Erik.

Knutas and Kihlgård spent the rest of Saturday preoccupied with the question of whether Egon Wallin might have been homosexual. Knutas had rung Monika Wallin to ask her about the matter, but she rejected the idea. Not because there was any passion between them anymore; she simply had a hard time believing that her husband could have been gay. During the many years of their marriage she had never noticed any such tendency in him.

But Kihlgård talked to the two women who worked at the art gallery and got an entirely different response. They had both suspected that Egon Wallin was interested in men.

Finally Kihlgård started from a different angle. He wanted to find out if any of the men who attended the gallery opening and also stayed at the Wisby Hotel on the night of the murder were homosexual. He came up with two names. Hugo Malmberg, one of the owners of the art gallery in which Egon Wallin planned to invest, and Mattis Kalvalis.

Kihlgård knocked on Knutas's door and found him absorbed in his own work. He told the superintendent what he had discovered.

"Interesting," said Knutas. "Kalvalis and Malmberg. So

Egon Wallin may have been on his way to meet one of them."

"Or why not both?" suggested Kihlgård, fluttering his lashes. "Maybe they were having a ménage à trois!"

"Oh, come on," said Knutas. "Let's not get carried away. Who do you think is the most likely?"

"Malmberg is closer in age. Kalvalis is at least twenty years younger than Wallin. Although I don't suppose that really makes any difference."

"No, but Wallin was going to be Hugo Malmberg's business partner," said Knutas. "And he was planning to move to Stockholm. It's also possible that Malmberg could be dealing in stolen artwork. Maybe they were both mixed up in it together."

"I've checked out Malmberg," said Kihlgård. "He doesn't have a police record, and his professional life is spotless. I also talked to him on the phone. He flatly denies having had a relationship with Egon Wallin, and he said he didn't think Wallin was gay. He claims he would have noticed if he was."

"So what about Mattis Kalvalis? Have you talked to him?"

"Yes, and his reaction seemed genuine. He burst out laughing when I asked if they'd had a homosexual relationship. 'That old guy?' were his exact words. 'Not on your life!' On the other hand, Mattis was convinced that Wallin was gay. He said he gave off that kind of vibe, even though Wallin had never said anything overt."

Kihlgård looked at his watch. "Well, I've got to run. I have a dinner date," he said with delight.

"Really? With whom?"

"I'm not telling." Kihlgård gave him a wink, laughed heartily, and left the room.

When Knutas was alone, he began filling his pipe again.

As far as Wallin's involvement with stolen paintings was concerned, they'd hit a brick wall and at the moment couldn't seem to find out anything more. The search of his Stockholm apartment had produced absolutely nothing. The hard drives of his computers were missing. Wallin's bookkeeping and records of his bank accounts were all immaculate. There was nothing to indicate any sort of irregularity. Monika Wallin had done her work perfectly.

Knutas was feeling extremely frustrated about the fact that they had no idea how to proceed in terms of Wallin's art galleries. They had checked out his prospective business partners in Stockholm but again had found nothing of interest.

He began making another careful study of the guest list for the gallery opening. He gave a start when he noticed the name of Erik Mattson from Bukowski's Auction House on the list. He had not received a personal invitation; instead, a general invitation had been sent to the auction house. The firm had sent two representatives, and one of them was Erik Mattson. How strange, thought Knutas. Mattson had valued the stolen paintings found in Egon Wallin's home, but he hadn't said a word about attending the opening when Knutas talked to him on the phone.

He punched in the number for Bukowski's and spoke to the head curator, who was in the midst of preparing for the big spring auction taking place the following week. The curator confirmed that they had sent two colleagues to Gotland on the weekend in question. They had a valuation to do in Burgsvik on Friday, and then they were supposed to attend the gallery opening on Saturday. Since both men were experts in modern art, it was important for them to keep up-to-date with what was happening in the art world. And all indications were that Mattis Kalvalis was going to be a big name.

Knutas asked to speak to Erik Mattson, but he wasn't in. The curator gave him Mattson's cell number. No one answered, so Knutas left a message on his voicemail.

It was now past six, and it was Saturday. Knutas searched for Mattson's home phone number on the internet, but without any luck. Apparently he had an unlisted number. He tried the cell number again, but without success. Well, it would just have to wait. But Knutas felt an uneasiness gnawing at him as he drove home.

It was almost dusk, and the sky was tinged with crimson. That was one of the things that people who visited Gotland always talked about. The light. That it was different on Gotland. They were probably right. Even though he was so used to it, occasionally he still stopped to look at the special glow that settled over the island.

Knutas's heart belonged to Gotland, without question. He had deep roots here; his family had lived on the island as far back as anyone cared to research his genealogy. His parents still lived on a farm in Kappelshamn in the northwest. They were now past retirement age, but they continued to bake flatbread, which they delivered to island restaurants and shops. The bread was famous. Some tourists even claimed that they went to Gotland just to buy that bread. It wasn't available anywhere else.

Knutas had a good relationship with his parents, but he preferred to keep them at a safe distance. When he and Lina decided to buy a summerhouse, his father tried to convince him to find one in Kappelshamn. They decided instead to buy a place in nearby Lickershamn. If his parents needed help with something in the summertime, it wouldn't take him long to get to their house, but he didn't really want them stopping by all the time.

Knutas had an older sister who lived in Färjestaden on the neighboring island of Öland. He also had a twin brother, who was in the military and lived on Fårö. The brothers saw each other mostly at family gatherings. Knutas usually saw his sister Lena only at Christmas and Midsummer; she was seven years older than him, and they'd never been close. But he spoke to his brother on the phone from time to time, and occasionally they went out for a bite to eat or a beer. Even though they saw each other so seldom, their relationship was easygoing and uncomplicated. Knutas thought that was probably because they were twins. They always knew where they stood with each other, without constantly needing to re-establish contact. When his brother came to Visby for a visit, he would stay overnight. The children were very fond of their uncle. Petra and Nils enjoyed listening to his tall tales about military life, and he could always keep them laughing.

When Knutas turned into his driveway, he caught sight of Lina through the kitchen window and was suddenly seized with melancholy. To think that people could live side by side and keep such secrets from each other, the way Egon and Monika had done. He was appalled by the idea that a woman could go around believing that she had a good marriage when the exact opposite was true. And then to find out that her spouse was cold-heartedly planning to move away and start a new life in a completely different place without saying a word. For Knutas it was incomprehensible that a person could be capable of such betrayal. He felt sorry for Monika Wallin. Even though she herself had taken a lover, she had still been thoroughly deceived by her husband.

With a deep sigh Johan dropped his suitcase on the floor of his apartment. Soon he would have only one address, and the idea certainly appealed to him.

Max Grenfors had called him on Sunday afternoon, just as he and Emma had decided to order Thai food and rent a movie for the evening. Typical. For a week he'd enjoyed living with Emma and Elin, but now he'd been forced to return to Stockholm. Yet it was perfectly understandable that he'd been summoned back by head office. At the moment there was nothing more to report about the murder, and half of the Stockholm reporters were off with flu. So in the meantime, Pia would have to hold the fort on Gotland.

He started by opening the windows to air his apartment. The two potted plants that he owned were drooping badly. He gave them a good watering and then went through his mail. The substantial pile that he'd found in the hall consisted mostly of bills, as well as a number of advertising brochures, and a postcard showing a tropical paradise; it was from Andreas, who was on holiday in Brazil.

Johan sank onto the sofa and looked around. His ground-floor, one-bedroom apartment in the Södermalm district wasn't especially spacious or remarkable, but the location meant that it would be easy to sublet. He just had to get permission from the building owner.

He looked at his worn leather sofa, the oak coffee table that his mother had given him, and the Billy bookshelf from Ikea. He wouldn't miss any of his furniture. On the other hand, he would take his CD collection and player with him to Gotland. Not surprisingly, Emma's ex-husband Olle had laid claim to the stereo after their divorce.

He went over to the kitchen and stood there a moment, leaning against the doorpost. How spartan everything looked compared to Emma's large fully furnished house in Roma. The kitchen held nothing more than a small drop-leaf table and two chairs next to the window. He saw nothing he wanted to take with him, except possibly the toaster oven, which in his bachelor existence he had used constantly. Actually, it might be a relief not to see it again. Nor did the bedroom contain much to talk about. The bed was covered with an ugly old spread, and it lacked a headboard. It dawned on him that he'd made no real effort to furnish a home for himself. He'd had this apartment for over ten years and was comfortable here, but it was as if he'd been using it as some sort of way station. Not a real home. It now seemed anonymous and inhospitable, somehow empty and lifeless. It would be great to move out.

He listened to his phone messages. His mother had called several times; she seemed to have forgotten that he was working on Gotland. Two of his three brothers had also left messages. He missed them and hoped that he'd have a chance to see them while he was back in Stockholm. Johan was the oldest and had consciously taken on the role of paterfamilias when his father died several years earlier. Luckily, his mother had now found a new love interest. She still lived in her own house, but she seemed to get on splendidly with her sweetheart, and that made Johan happy. Not just for her sake, but also for his own. She didn't need him in the same way as she had in the past. He thought about how things would go now that he and Emma had decided to move in together and get married. Johan would be the first of his brothers to take a wife. It was a big step, a serious decision. He didn't want to tell anyone about it. Not just yet.

Anxiety crept over him toward evening. Erik had always thought there was something unpleasant about Sunday nights. The weekend was almost over, and the working week was just around the corner, with its responsibilities, routines, commitments—and he had to be able to function. That alone could fill him with panic. He was lying on the sofa in the living room, staring at the ceiling. A whisky would deaden the feeling of emptiness, but he wasn't going to drink today. He never did on Sundays.

Instead he got up and took out a few old photo albums from his childhood. He put on a CD of Maria Callas and began turning the pages. A picture of himself at the age of seven on the Möja boat dock. Hoisting the sail on the boat with his father, a friend in the dinghy. As a child he had loved the Stockholm archipelago. His family always went sailing for several weeks in the summer. They would go out to Möja, Sandhamn, and Utö, attend the dances on the wharves, and eat dinner at the elegant inns. His father would come along, and that always made his mother happier and more relaxed. With her husband at her side she would forget about the irritation she felt toward Erik, although she made no attempt to hide her feelings when the two of them were at home alone and his father was traveling. She liked to sunbathe on holiday, and her thin, taut body acquired a deep tan; she even put on a little weight. It was as if the tension in her face eased, and she became more like the cheerful girl she may once have been; the one Erik thought was still there under that stern exterior.

Erik grew up as an only child, living with his parents in a luxurious house in the fashionable suburb of Djursholm. He attended private schools and then majored in economics at Östra Real secondary school. His future was decided in advance. He was going to follow in his father's footsteps and go to business school, get top marks, and then start working for the family business. No other alternatives were ever discussed.

Erik managed fairly well during his school years, in spite of his coldhearted mother and absent father. He'd always had an easy time making friends, and the socializing he did outside the house made it possible for him to survive, year after year. He longed fervently for the day when he could pack his bags and leave home.

It was when he was a teenager that the change happened. There was a new boy in class who was interested in art; he went to all the gallery openings in town, and he also painted in his spare time. He was so enthusiastic and captivating that several of his classmates joined him on the weekends when he would go to Liljevalch Art Centre and the National Museum, Waldemarsudde and small, obscure art galleries. Erik showed the most interest of any of the boys. He was particularly taken with Swedish art from the early twentieth century. It was then that he discovered "The Dying Dandy" and became utterly overwhelmed by it. Back then he didn't understand why the painting had such a strong effect on him; he just knew that it resonated with something in him that was deep and hidden and over which he had no control. He started reading everything he could find about Dardel and the paintings of the early 1900s in general. He even went so far as to begin studying art history along with his other subjects. He was planning to keep his interest secret from his parents for as long as possible.

But it wasn't just his interest in art that complicated his life during those years. He began feeling himself drawn more and more to his own gender; he was totally uninterested in women. Whenever his friends talked about girls and sex, he would laugh along with them and contribute some tall tales about his own advanced sexual experiences. In reality, Erik was furtively looking at men. On the bus, on the street, and in the showers at the gym. It was the male body, not the female, that interested him. Since he was painfully aware of his parents' old-fashioned and narrow-minded view of homosexuality, he did everything he could to suppress his attraction to men. But then one day he his feelings were confirmed.

His family was supposed to spend a weekend on Gotska Sandön, staying overnight in a cabin. On the ferry ride over, they met a pleasant family from Göteborg whose son was the same age as Erik. Late that night, while the adults were still up drinking wine, the two youths left the party and set off for a walk along the sandy beaches that surrounded the small island. It was just before Midsummer, and the night was bright and warm. They lay down next to each other on a sand dune and gazed up at the sky while they talked. Erik liked Joel, as the boy was called, and they had a lot in common. They soon began confiding in each other, and Erik told his new friend about his problems at home. Joel was kind and understanding, and all of a sudden they were lying in each other's arms. Erik would never forget that night. They exchanged addresses and phone numbers, but they never contacted each other again.

Erik had gone back to his life in Stockholm truly shaken by his first homosexual experience. He was so terrified by his feelings that at university he began going out with a girl who had been giving him long looks during classes.

Her name was Lydia. They soon became a couple and in due course got married. At first their marriage was relatively happy, and they had three children in quick succession. Erik's excessive drinking had begun much earlier, but it escalated with each year that passed.

His parents found nothing unusual about the fact that he was so self-absorbed, and they gave Erik and Lydia money so that they could live comfortably in a large, fancy apartment in the Östermalm district. Lydia was from a middle-class family in Leksand. She trained to be an art restorer and eventually found a job at the National Museum.

Erik got into the habit of not coming home until two in the morning, still under the influence of alcohol and drugs. One Saturday, Lydia decided that she'd finally had enough. She took the children and went to stay with her parents-in-law.

Erik's parents were furious, of course, and they threatened to stop sending the money that they usually provided each month. Lydia wanted a divorce, and naturally his parents took her side. It was Erik who had behaved badly and broken his promises.

Erik didn't care what his mother thought or felt; she had destroyed any love he might have felt for her through years of psychological tyranny and indifference while he was young. He thought about all the times that she had insulted and criticized him in front of teachers, neighbors, relatives, and friends. He felt absolutely nothing for her, and was convinced that the feeling was mutual. If there was any emotion left to speak of, it might almost be described as deep contempt.

But he still had warm feelings for his father. Mr. Mattson had never been actually unkind to Erik, yet he had always meekly submitted to his wife's wishes, in spite of the fact that he was so successful in the business world. She was the one who ruled the roost for all those years. He had seldom questioned her authority, letting her do as she liked. It was the best thing for domestic harmony, as Erik's father would say with a good-natured smile before he fled the scene and left on yet another business trip.

Erik saw his parents only once after his divorce, when Emelie turned five. Sitting at the table to celebrate his daughter's birthday, Erik saw the pain and disappointment in his father's eyes, and that upset him. A feeling of sorrow and deceit hovered over the party, despite all the balloons, daycare friends, gifts, and plates of cake. Erik had been forced to go out on the balcony to get some air.

Even though Lydia felt deeply disappointed in Erik after the divorce, she still understood him better than anyone else ever had. He had told her about his miserable childhood, about the complicated relationship he had with his mother, and how he'd become aware of his homosexuality. Lydia accepted him as he was, and after all the agitation connected with the divorce had faded, they were able to remain friends. He thought that Lydia realized he'd tried to do the best he could. They decided that the children should live with her, since they were still so young, but they would stay with their father every other weekend.

This arrangement worked well for six months. Erik did his job in an exemplary fashion and remained sober on the days when he had the children. His parents continued to deposit a sizeable sum into his bank account every month, although his mother made it clear that the money was for her grandchildren and not for him.

Then one Saturday after Erik had picked up the children from Lydia's house, an old boyfriend of his turned up and stayed for dinner. After the children went to bed, the former lover started getting friendly, and they had sex. Then they began drinking some of the excellent whisky that he'd brought along. And, as usual, once Erik started he couldn't stop.

The next day he woke up on the living room sofa around noon when the doorbell wouldn't stop ringing. It was Lydia. She came storming into the apartment and found the three children sitting in the bedroom in front of the TV, munching on crisps, cake, and raw spaghetti.

They were all supposed to have gone to Skansen amusement park that Sunday. That was the last weekend that Erik was allowed to have the children stay with him, and his parents stopped the monthly payments.

He hadn't seen his parents since.

By chance he once caught sight of his mother in the hat section of the NK department store. For a long time he stood behind a pillar and watched her laugh as she tried on hats along with a woman friend of hers. He couldn't understand how this person he was looking at could be his mother. That she could have carried him inside her body, given birth to him, and nursed him when he was a baby. It was incomprehensible. Just as difficult to understand was the fact that she had ever chosen to have children at all.

The night was black and cold. When he turned his car onto Valhallavägen, he didn't see a soul around. The temperature was 10°F. He pulled into an empty parking slot outside the 7-Eleven, almost all the way down to the open space at Gärdet. It was far enough away that his car wouldn't be immediately linked to the crime scene if anyone, contrary to all expectations, happened to notice him parking here.

The backpack stored in the trunk was lightweight and well packed. He fastened the sling with the cardboard tube to his shoulder so he'd be able to move his arms freely. He headed quickly across the street, choosing a path along the edge of the fields of Gärdet so as to avoid being seen.

At the Källhagen Hotel and restaurant, he cut across the parking lot and continued down the slope toward the Djurgårdsbrunn canal. A short distance away he saw that the magnificent white facade of the Maritime History Museum was illuminated, as always at night. The area around him was quiet and deserted. He could just make out the rocks of Skansen's hill on the other side of the canal, outlined against the dark night sky. Farther off in the distance he glimpsed the lights of the city. The center of town seemed

202

so far away, even though he was only a mile away from the main shopping district.

Down at the dock he put on his skates. The thin layer of snow covering the ice had now been blown away, making it easier to skate. Several times over the past few days he had tested the ice along this stretch; he knew it would hold if he stayed close to shore.

It was extremely unusual for anyone to take this route on skates. Normally the ice was either too thin and uneven, or the snow cover was too thick. But right now it was possible. As a means of transportation it was perfect. No one would see or hear him coming.

The ice crackled and whistled under his feet as he set off. He skated at a good speed along the canal and then rounded the point of Biskopsudden out near the Thiel Gallery. There the ice opened up in front of him like an expanse of polished floor. He hoped that it would hold. Farther out in the waterway, near the sea approach to Stockholm, a channel had been broken in the ice so that boats could pass through.

At the Waldemarsudde dock everything was dark. He skated past and didn't stop until he was right below the castle. It was pitch dark, and his fingers were stiff with cold. Quickly he took off his skates, leaving them on the ice. He picked up his backpack and crept up toward the building, which stood on a hill in solitary majesty. Fortunately there were no other buildings nearby; the closest neighbor's house couldn't be seen from the sea.

There were no lights on in the building. He was dressed in dark clothes with a knitted cap on his head. He had all the necessary tools in his backpack. Nothing was going to stop him now.

Climbing up the fire escape at the back of the building, he reached a small landing and then continued up to the part of the roof facing the sea. That's where he knew he would find a hatch to a ventilation shaft. In old blueprints of Waldemarsudde, he'd seen that the ventilation shaft led straight down to a storage room near the stairwell.

He opened the hatch and went in, wriggling down through the narrow duct by pressing his elbows and knees against the walls. It took only a minute for him to reach the grating, which he quickly unscrewed. He was inside.

He found himself in a cramped, dark space with no windows. The light of his flashlight helped him to find the door. For a brief moment he stood still, hesitating, with his fingers gripping the door handle.

The instant he opened the door, it was highly likely that the alarm would go off, and he prepared himself mentally for the racket. Then the question was how long it would take before the police made it out to Waldemarsudde. Since the museum was located at the very end of Djurgården, he figured it would take at least ten minutes. Unless a patrol car just happened to be in the vicinity, but that would be the ultimate bad luck. He had calculated that the operation would take six or seven minutes, which gave him a certain margin. Very slowly he pressed down the handle and opened the door.

The sound was deafening, screaming from every direction. His eardrums felt as if they would burst as he raced across the floor, through the dark rooms, and over to the salon where the painting he wanted hung on the wall. Moonlight was shining through the tall windows, making it easier for him to find his way.

The painting was bigger than he remembered, and the scene looked ghostlike in the dim light. He steeled himself to maintain his focus, even though the noise was driving him crazy. From his backpack he took out a collapsible ladder. It teetered a bit as he climbed up, and for a second he was afraid that it would topple over.

The painting was so big that the only solution was to cut the canvas out of the frame. He stuck his upholstery knife in one corner and drew it along the edge as carefully as he could. He finished the top without mishap and continued around the canvas until it fell to the floor. Swiftly he rolled up the painting and stuffed it into the cardboard tube. It fit perfectly.

There was one more thing he had to do. He glanced at his watch and saw that so far he'd used up four minutes. At most three minutes remained. He dug inside his backpack and took out the object that would complete his mission. He set it on the table that stood in front of the frame where the painting had hung.

Then he dashed back through the rooms. It should have been easy to exit through a window or a balcony door, but they were all equipped with steel frames and bulletproof glass. Impossible to force open without a bulldozer.

His only option was to return the same way he had come, through the ventilation shaft. He carried the tube containing the painting in the sling on his back. When he emerged on the roof again, he stopped to catch his breath. He looked in all directions but couldn't see a single person or police vehicle.

Focusing all his attention on a swift escape, his heart pounding in his chest, he jumped down to the ground, rushed around the corner to the back of the building, and stumbled down the steep steps toward the ice. With fumbling fingers he strapped on his skates. As he took off he came within a hair's breadth of falling, but he quickly regained his balance and disappeared as fast as he could, taking long, gliding strokes on the ice.

Far in the distance he heard the wail of police sirens; the sound was getting closer. When he reached the canal he could see police cars speeding across Djurgård Bridge, on their way to Waldemarsudde.

He listened to his own gasping breath. His lungs ached from the cold and the exertion. At the same time, he felt a seed of happiness sprouting within him. Finally the debt would be repaid. The painting was on its way to its rightful owner, and knowing that gave him a sense of peace.

The tracks he had left behind would end on the rocks below the castle. They would never catch him. Not this time either.

For the first time in the history of the museum, someone had broken in during the night. When the museum director, Per-Erik Sommer, arrived at three a.m. on Monday he felt as if someone had barged into his own living room. He'd been the museum's director and chief curator for fifteen years. Waldemarsudde was like his second home, his beloved child. No one had ever imagined that a thief might get in during the night. The security measures were rigorous. Stockholm had experienced several big art thefts over the past few years. An armed robbery at the National Museum had taken place in broad daylight while it was open to the public, and a raid had been made on the Museum of Modern Art when the thieves got in through the roof. Naturally these events had affected what security precautions were subsequently taken in every museum in the city. At Waldemarsudde, millions had been spent to protect the prince's home and his enormous art collection.

The police were on the scene with a canine patrol when Sommer arrived. The area had been cordoned off and the grounds were being searched. At the main entrance Sommer was met by police inspector Kurt Fogestam, who was in charge of the case and showed him how the thief had got in. After all the security measures that had been taken, he had brazenly entered through the ventilation shaft.

Sommer just shook his head.

Then he and the inspector walked through the museum to see what was missing.

All of the rooms were now brightly lit. They started with the library. Nothing was missing there or in the conservatory. Sommer breathed a sigh of relief when he saw that the living room was also untouched. A portrait by Anders Zorn of the prince's mother, Queen Sofia, hung on the wall in that room. It was one of the prince's favorite paintings, and it would have been disastrous if that particular work of art had been stolen. The other exceptionally valuable painting, titled "Strömkarlen," by Ernst Josephson, was set into the wall itself, making it impossible to steal.

But then the museum director discovered what had been taken. Due to its size, the painting had dominated the entire dining room during the exhibition. Now that it no longer hung in its place, the wall seemed terribly naked. "The Dying Dandy" was gone. Cut out of its frame, which gaped at them, empty and ominous, like a mute witness to what had happened.

The director needed to sit down, but the police officer stopped him from doing so, as he might disturb possible evidence. Sommer felt numb with shock, but he turned away to see if anything else had been stolen.

That was when he discovered an object that he hadn't noticed at first.

On a table in front of the missing painting stood a small sculpture. It did not belong in Prince Eugen's home. Sommer didn't recognize it at all. Slowly he leaned forward to get a better look.

"What is it?" asked Kurt Fogestam.

"This isn't part of the collection," said Sommer. He reached out his hand to pick it up, but the inspector stopped him.

"What do you mean?"

"This statue doesn't belong to the museum. The thief must have put it here."

They both stared in surprise at the little statue that had been carved from stone. It was a nude bust with a long neck; the head was turned to the side and tipped back slightly. The facial features had been carved with simplicity; the eyes were closed, the lips pressed together, the expression one of melancholy or yearning. It was hard to tell whether it was a man or a woman. Its androgynous image actually seemed well suited to the motif of the stolen painting.

"What in the world does this mean?" asked Fogestam.

Per-Erik Sommer could only gawk with astonishment. It was one thing for thieves to steal something, but he'd never heard of a thief leaving behind a work of art at the scene of the crime.

When Johan arrived at the Stockholm editorial offices of Regional News, he found his boss Max Grenfors in a frenzied state. He was sitting at his desk with his hair sticking out in all directions, his shirt wrinkled, and a wild look in his eyes. He held a phone to each ear and had a pen gripped between his teeth, and there were four half-empty coffee mugs in front of him. All signs that he was totally swamped. The fact that half of the reporters were off sick just as a big news story was breaking was a nightmare for the editor-in-chief. The bold theft at Waldemarsudde was going to dominate the broadcast. It was clear even from a distance that the situation was straining Grenfors's nerves. His haggard face lit up when he caught sight of Johan.

"Great that you're here," he shouted, even though he was in the middle of two different conversations. "You need to get out there right away. Emil is waiting for you."

Emil Jansson was a young, ambitious cameraman who worked mostly in hotspots like the Gaza Strip and Iraq. He gave Johan a friendly handshake, and then they hurried downstairs to his car in the SVT garage. It took them only five minutes to get out to Waldemarsudde. The headquarters of Swedish TV was just down the road from the bridge to Djurgården.

The police had blocked off the entire park surrounding the castle, the gallery, and the old house. The grounds were still being searched. Johan got hold of a police officer who was willing to be interviewed. The conversation he'd had with the officer in charge during the brief car ride to the museum had produced nothing that Johan didn't already know.

It was a good backdrop for the interview, showing the police tape cordoning off the castle and officers walking around with police dogs.

"So what happened here?" Johan began. The simplest question was often the most effective.

"At 2:10 a.m. we were alerted that the museum had been broken into. A painting had been stolen," said the policeman. "It was a painting that happened to be on loan. 'The Dying Dandy' by the artist Nils Dardel."

"How did the thieves manage to do it?"

"Or thief," the officer corrected him. "Although clearly it would be difficult to carry out this type of crime alone. There were probably at least two individuals involved."

He turned to glance toward the museum building. Emil kept his camera fixed on the man. For a moment it almost seemed as if the officer was unaware that he was taking part in a filmed interview. He was behaving in an unusually natural manner and seemed genuinely distressed about what had happened. Johan also had the impression that he was actually interested in art.

"How did they get in?"

"Apparently through a ventilation duct at the back of the main building." He motioned with his head in that direction.

"Aren't there any security alarms?"

"Of course there are, but the thieves just let the alarms go off, took what they'd come for, and then disappeared."

"Sounds like they had nerves of steel."

"Yes, it does. But since the museum is in an isolated location, it takes time for the police to get here."

"How long did it take?"

"They say it was about ten minutes. And that's rather a long time. Enough for a thief to make off with what he wanted and disappear. Which is precisely what happened."

Johan felt his cheeks burning. It was extremely unusual for a police officer to criticize his own colleagues.

"How long would be reasonable, in your opinion?"

"I think it should be possible to get here in five minutes. If the alarms go off, it's obviously an emergency."

Johan was caught off guard by the officer's candor. This guy must be a real beginner, he thought as he studied the young officer. He was probably no more than twenty-five, and he spoke with a strong Värmland accent. *He's going to catch hell for this,* thought Johan, *but who cares? It's to our advantage that the guy's so clueless.*

"So how did they do it? If I remember correctly, that painting is really big."

Johan was very familiar with Dardel's painting. He'd seen it several times when his mother had dragged him along to the Museum of Modern Art in some of her countless attempts to interest him in culture.

"The thief or thieves cut the canvas out of the frame."

"And nothing else is missing?"

"Apparently not."

"But doesn't that seem strange? Shouldn't the thieves have taken other paintings? I assume that there are many valuable works of art inside."

"Yes, it does seem odd. But evidently that was the only painting they were interested in."

"Do you think it was a contract job?"

"There seem to be clear indications pointing in that direction."

The young officer now started to look nervous, as if he realized that he'd said too much.

The next second an older officer in uniform came over and pulled his colleague away from the camera.

"What's going on here? The police never give interviews in this kind of situation. You're going to have to wait for the press conference this afternoon." Johan recognized the man as the newly appointed spokesman for the county police force.

The young policeman looked scared out of his wits and quickly took his leave, along with his older colleague.

Johan glanced at Emil, who had let the camera roll. "Did you get all that?"

On Monday morning Knutas had a phone conversation with the Stockholm police. It was his old friend and colleague Kurt Fogestam who called. They'd met at a conference shortly after they'd both joined the force, and their friendship had remained strong ever since. They always tried to meet whenever Knutas was in Stockholm. Since both of them were devoted AIK fans, they usually went to a match together during the soccer season. Afterward they would go to a pub for malt whisky, their favorite drink. Kurt had also come to Gotland a few times.

"Hi," said Knutas happily. "It's been a while. How are things?"

"Can't complain," replied Kurt Fogestam. "Thanks for asking. But right now I'm calling because I've got news that seems to have something to do with the case you're working on."

"Is that right?" said Knutas, suddenly alert. New information was exactly what they needed at the moment.

"Someone broke into Waldemarsudde during the night, and a very valuable painting was stolen. It's 'The Dying Dandy' by Nils Dardel. Do you know it?"

"'The Dying Dandy'," Knutas repeated. In his mind's eye

he saw a vague image of a pale, recumbent young man with his eyes closed. "Well, sort of," he replied. "But what does the theft have to do with my investigation?"

"The thief cut the canvas out of the frame. It's an enormous painting, you know."

"Is that so?"

Knutas still didn't know where his colleague was going with this account.

"But he happened to leave something behind. A little sculpture that he set on a table right in front of the empty frame. We checked up on it this morning. It's the same sculpture that was stolen from the gallery in Visby owned by the murdered man. Egon Wallin."

Hugo Malmberg woke early on Monday morning. He got up, went into the bathroom, and splashed water over his face and torso. Then he went back to bed. His two American cocker spaniels, Elvis and Marilyn, were asleep in their basket and didn't seem to notice that he was awake. He absentmindedly studied the detailed stucco work on the ceiling. He was in no hurry—he didn't have to be at the gallery until just before ten. He always took his dogs with him to work, so they were used to having their morning walk on the way there. Hugo let his gaze slide over the brocade of the canopy bed, the dark tapestries of red and gold, the ostentatious mirror on the opposite wall. Amused, he reached for the remote control to have a look at the morning news.

A bold robbery had taken place in the early hours at Waldemarsudde. The famous painting "The Dying Dandy" had been stolen. It was incomprehensible. A journalist was filing a live report from the scene at the museum. In the background Hugo caught a glimpse of the police and the blue-and-white tape cordoning off the area.

He made himself a breakfast of eggs Benedict and a pot of strong coffee as he listened to the news on both the radio and TV. An incredibly brazen theft. The police suspected that the thief had made his getaway on ice skates.

He was late leaving. The fresh air felt exhilarating as he opened the door to the street. John Ericssonsgatan linked Hantverkargatan to the exclusive shoreline boulevard of Norr Mälarstrand, which ran from Rålambshov Park all the way to City Hall. Malmberg owned a corner apartment with a view of both the water and the beautiful boulevard with its trees, wide pavements, and lawns in the courtyard of every building.

There was a thick layer of ice on the water, but he still chose to take the route along the marina, where the old boats were lined up even in the wintertime. When he glanced over toward Västerbron, he recalled the man he'd seen on the bridge on Friday night. How strange that had been.

He turned his back to the bridge and briskly continued on, passing the proud City Hall, designed in the National Romantic style and built near the shore of Kungsholmen from 1911 to 1923. In his opinion, that had been the most exciting period in the history of Swedish art. His dogs frolicked in the snow. For their sake he cut across the ice toward Gamla Stan. They loved to race over the open expanses created by the ice.

Several times that day Malmberg thought he caught sight of the man from Västerbron. Once a young guy happened to stop outside the gallery. He wore a down jacket and the same type of cap. The next second he was gone. Was that the same man who had followed him on Friday night? Malmberg brushed the thought aside. He was probably just imagining things. Maybe he was subconsciously hoping to meet the handsome man with the intense gaze again. It was possible that the youth had, in fact, been interested in Hugo, but then changed his mind.

Just before lunch, Hugo Malmberg received a phone call.

The gallery was deserted at the time. When he picked up the receiver, there seemed to be nobody on the line.

"Hello?" he repeated, but got no response.

"Who is this?" he tried again, as he stared out at the street.

Silence.

All he heard was the sound of someone breathing.

There was an air of tension when the investigative team gathered for their meeting on Monday afternoon. Everyone had heard about the Gotland sculpture that was left at Waldemarsudde, and they were all eager to hear more. Even Kihlgård was silent as he fixed his eyes on Knutas taking his seat at the head of the table.

"All right now, listen to this," Knutas began. "This case just seems to get more and more mysterious. Apparently there's a connection between the murder and the theft that took place at Waldemarsudde in the middle of the night."

He told them what Kurt Fogestam had reported.

"Plus we have the stolen paintings found in Egon Wallin's home," said Jacobsson. "So there must be some sort of link. Is there some disgruntled gangster who had dealings with the victim? Maybe Wallin neglected to pay him, so the guy ended up killing him. And now for some reason he wants to talk about it, so to speak."

"What else could it be? It's obvious that this has something to do with stolen artworks," said Wittberg.

"But why did the thief take only one painting?" Kihlgård looked at his colleagues. "If the art thieves were willing to take the risk to carry out a coup against one of Sweden's most well-protected museums, why steal only one painting? And not even the most valuable one. I can't figure it out," he said as he unwrapped a piece of chocolate cake he'd brought along.

No one said a word.

"We actually know nothing about what Egon Wallin was doing with those stolen paintings," Jacobsson then said. "How extensive was his involvement? And how long had it been going on? None of the interviews done here on Gotland has proved productive, and he seems to have been totally unknown among the art thieves and fences in Stockholm. Good Lord, surely we should be able to flush out at least one person who knows something about his shady art dealings. Those paintings hidden in his house weren't just trifles."

"We should actually be glad that Waldemarsudde was burgled," said Norrby tersely. "At least we have something new to investigate, and we really needed that."

"Yes," agreed Knutas, rubbing his chin. "But why would the thief make such a point of linking the two crimes? I just don't understand it."

No one had any response to that.

"Another question is why he chose to take 'The Dying Dandy.' He made no attempt to hide the purpose of his actions by stealing at least one other painting."

"He probably didn't have time," Jacobsson objected. "Because the alarms went off."

"That may be true, but the question still remains: why the Dardel? Why that particular painting?"

"It could have been a contract job," suggested Wittberg. "A fanatic collector who hired somebody to steal the painting. It won't be possible to sell it, at least not in Sweden. What do we know about the painting?"

Lars Norrby looked through his papers. "I've done a little

research. It was painted in 1918 by Nils von Dardel, or rather just plain Nils Dardel. He came from a noble family, but he dropped the 'von' from his name after he grew up. I've actually found out all sorts of titbits about him."

He smiled with satisfaction. His colleagues looked at him, uncomprehending.

"Dardel began painting in early 1900 and had his heyday in the twenties and thirties. His painting 'The Dying Dandy' has been owned by various private individuals, but in the early nineties the Museum of Modern Art bought it from the financier Tomas Fischer. It was also once sold at an auction run by Bukowski's firm for a record amount. You may remember the sale; there were plenty of articles about it in the newspapers at the time."

Bukowski's, thought Knutas. *How strange that the firm keeps cropping up.* Erik Mattson's name flitted through his mind. He still hadn't received any explanation for why Mattson hadn't mentioned going to Egon Wallin's gallery opening. Something wasn't right. He needed to talk to Mattson again. He wrote himself a reminder in his notebook.

"Who in Sweden has a strong interest in Nils Dardel? Should we be looking at that angle?" Jacobsson suggested.

"Yes, but what did Egon Wallin have to do with Nils Dardel? There must be some kind of link," said Wittberg.

"We don't know, but that's one of the threads we'll follow," said Knutas. "I want one of you to go to Stockholm immediately to meet the police, visit Waldemarsudde, and try to do some more digging into the whole art business. It might also be a good idea to meet Sixten Dahl and Hugo Malmberg on their home turf."

"I'll go," offered Kihlgård.

"In that case, I'd like someone from our team to go with you," said Knutas.

"I can do it," said Jacobsson. "I'd like to go."

"Fine. That's settled then," said Knutas, giving her a rather disapproving look. Why her? And why him?

The long, narrow hall of Bukowski's Auction House had a thick, patterned rug covering the oak parquet floor. Rows of chairs made of steel and black plastic had been arranged to fill the space all the way to the entrance, where the reception area and cloakroom were located. At the front, above the podium, hung a big white banner with a portrait of Henryk Bukowski, a serious looking man with a high forehead, beard and mustache, wearing glasses. His eyes were looking upward, as if he were peering into an uncertain future. The exiled Polish nobleman had founded the auction house in 1870, and over the years it had become Scandinavia's largest enterprise auctioning quality artworks.

He studied the podium, which was made of gleaming white wood with a gilded "B" in the middle. His disguise was in place. No one would recognize him. He was on the lookout for a particular man, but he didn't see him anywhere.

The scent of expensive perfume and aftershave wafted through the room. Everyone took off their coats and furs and hung them in the cloakroom.

Programs were sold and auction paddles were handed out. There was an air of tense anticipation. A longing and a need to spend money.

It made him feel sick.

He was sitting in the last row on the left side of the room; from there he had a good view of the entrance. A woman in her forties came in and sat down next to him. She was wearing a brown fur coat and glasses with thin gold frames. Her skin was lightly tanned. Maybe from a Christmas holiday spent at some idyllic beach on the other side of the globe, he thought enviously. She reeked of money. Her brown hair was pulled back in a classic chignon. She wore a shawl, leather boots, and black trousers; a heavy diamond ring glittered on one finger.

Otherwise the average age in the hall was over fifty. There were just as many women as men present, all well dressed, well groomed, and radiating the same calm and self-confidence. An innate sense of assurance and self-esteem that was largely based on money.

He glanced at his watch. Ten minutes left before the auction began. Again he looked for the man who was the reason why he was here. The hall was almost full now; a soft murmur passed through the crowd and a few phrases in English were heard. At the very back of the room groups of people had gathered, conversing in low voices; the whole scene had the air of a cocktail party. They all seemed to know each other, and scattered greetings of "Hi" and "Hello" and "Nice to see you" could be heard.

Now the husband of the woman seated next to him also arrived. He was gray-haired and suntanned, wearing a tailored jacket, a canary-yellow sweater, and a bright blue shirt. The colors of the Swedish flag. *Give me a break*. He looked like a typical big shot in the business world.

An acquaintance greeted the couple. "You'd better

keep her under control. Ha, ha. Make sure she doesn't spend a bundle. Watch out for that."

He felt nausea come creeping over him. He had to force himself to stay seated on the uncomfortable chair.

Up at the front the auctioneer had taken his place on the podium. He was in his fifties, austere and elegant. A bit haughty-looking, tall and thin, with a crooked nose and his hair combed back. He pounded the gavel three times on the lectern to silence the murmuring in the room.

The first work was brought out by two rosy-cheeked boys who looked no older than sixteen or seventeen. They were well dressed in newly pressed dark trousers and crisp white shirts, with dark blue ties under leather aprons wrapped around their boyishly slim figures. Their eyes followed the bids with interest as they kept a light grip on the work of art that rested on an easel as it was offered for sale.

With growing contempt mixed with the deepest envy, he watched what went on in the hall. The auctioneer efficiently guided the bidding; he seemed to enjoy the tension and energy. The bidding went back and forth like a ping-pong ball between those seated in the room and the invisible customers on the phones. He knew that in the balcony above, Bukowski's experts had customers on the line. They couldn't see him, and he couldn't see them. The price rose quickly as bidders either nodded or shook their heads, lifted their bidding paddles, blinked, or raised their hands. Energy and anticipation, hopes dashed or fulfilled. Binoculars were raised in order to better examine the smaller objects. The auctioneer stood in the spotlight the whole time, striking like a cobra at the various bids, and allowing himself a pleased little smile whenever the price went up. The auctioneer held all the bidders in a tight grip.

"The lady in the third row . . . A bid from Göteborg. . .

Going, going, gone." And then finally the little crack of the gavel.

A painting titled "Indolence" by Robert Thegerström started off at 80,000 kronor. The final price was 295,000.

Close to the back of the hall sat an elderly couple. The man kept bidding for various works with an inscrutable expression on his face while his wife sat next to him, giving him admiring glances.

A woman in an ankle-length mink bid 100,000 kronor without batting an eye and without saying a word to her husband.

Up by the podium, a silver-haired woman carefully announced the name of the artist and motif of each painting. Only once did she hesitate. "It says 'peregrines', but we suspect that they're really goshawks." An amused murmur spread through the rows.

This is a game for the rich, he thought as he sat there, watching the spectacle. As far removed from the daily life of ordinary people as possible.

Sometimes the crowd got too noisy, and the auctioneer had to hush them.

When the two handsome boys with the ruddy cheeks brought in a magnificent oil painting by Anders Zorn, a respectful silence settled over the room. The opening bid was three million kronor. There were fewer bidders as the price skyrocketed. Everyone was attentively following the bidding. An entirely new sense of focus came over the room when the bidding went over 10 million. Finally it stopped at 12,700,000 kronor. The auctioneer announced the amount with exaggerated drama, as if relishing every syllable. Before he let the gavel fall, he paused with his hand over the table for a few extra seconds, prolonging the moment and giving the interested competitors one last chance. When the gavel finally fell, everyone heaved a sigh of relief.

This is pure bullshit, he thought.

He got up and left; he couldn't bear to wait any longer. The man he was looking for had never turned up. Something must have gone wrong.

K arin Jacobsson arrived at Waldemarsudde accompanied by Kurt Fogestam from the Stockholm police. In the meantime, Kihlgård was taking care of the interviews with Sixten Dahl and Hugo Malmberg.

They started by walking around the cordoned-off park area surrounding the museum building. The garden was completely covered with snow, and the water outside had frozen over. It was exquisitely beautiful.

"We suspect that the perpetrator got away across the ice," said Fogestam.

He and Jacobsson had met several times before when she had visited police headquarters in Stockholm.

"I know. But aren't there boats that go through here even in the winter?"

"Yes, but it has been exceedingly cold this year, so there's ice all along the Djurgården shore, and it extends out for several yards. Close to shore the ice is four inches thick and solid enough to walk or skate on. It's also unusually smooth. We think he made his getaway on long-distance skates."

"An art thief who comes in the middle of the night to steal a famous painting from a museum, and then takes off wearing long-distance skates. It sounds like pure James Bond."

Kurt Fogestam laughed. "I suppose it does. But that's how he did it."

The inspector led the way down the steep steps to the rocks at the icy shore. He stopped and pointed. "This is where he came ashore. He left the same way."

"How far were you able to follow his tracks?"

"We got here ten minutes after the alarms went off, but it took another fifteen or twenty minutes before the dogs arrived. And unfortunately that cost us a lot. They were only able to track him down to this spot. Nothing after that. And it's impossible to see the marks of his skates because there's hardly any snow on the ice."

"How did he get inside the building?"

"This guy knew what he was doing. He entered through the ventilation shaft at the back and climbed down so that he landed in the hallway. After that he didn't care about the alarm sounding; he just took what he came for and got out."

"A real cool customer," said Jacobsson. "And speaking of cool, it's freezing out here. Let's go inside."

In the entrance they found the museum director, Per-Erik Sommer, who insisted on offering them coffee so the two frozen police officers could thaw out a bit first. He was a tall, vigorous-looking man with kind eyes behind his horn-rimmed glasses.

They sat down in the café, which was located in what had once been the prince's kitchen. Coffee and warm apple cake with vanilla sauce was served. It tasted delicious after their cold walk outdoors.

Kurt Fogestam had explained to Jacobsson that he was simply there to keep her company. The Stockholm police had already interviewed Sommer, so now it was Jacobsson's turn to ask any other questions that she wanted answered.

"This is so terrible, just terrible," said Sommer with a sigh as he stirred his coffee. "We've never had a burglary here before. Well, not from inside the building," he quickly corrected himself. "Several sculptures have been stolen from the garden, and that was serious enough. But this . . . this is a whole different matter. The alarm system was on, but what good did it do? The police didn't get here in time."

"Do you have security cameras?"

"In a few places, but unfortunately we didn't get any pictures of the thief."

"How many people work here?"

"Let me see now . . ." The museum director mumbled to himself, counting on his fingers. "There are nine full-time employees, if you count grounds and building maintenance. We have our own gardener and caretaker. There are also a number of temporary staff that we bring in now and then."

"How many altogether?"

"Hmm . . . probably ten or fifteen, I'd think."

"Do any of them have ties to Gotland?"

"Not as far as I know."

"Did you or anyone else here know Egon Wallin?"

"I didn't, but I can't speak for the others. Although I think I would have heard about it if they did, considering the horrible thing that happened to him."

"Have you ever had any sort of collaboration with his gallery in Visby?"

"Not since I've been the director here."

"Do you know if anyone has been in contact with Muramaris, the gallery in Visby, or any other enterprise on Gotland?"

"I don't think so."

Jacobsson turned to Fogestam. "Have you interviewed all the staff?"

"The interviews are still being conducted. I don't think they're finished yet."

"I'd like a list of the employees."

"Of course. I'll take care of it. But there are no indications that this was an inside job."

"The thief was very familiar with the site," Jacobsson pointed out.

"Yes, but the blueprints of the building are available to anybody who bothers to look for them."

"By the way, what else is on display in the current exhibition?" she asked Sommer.

"Swedish art from the early 1900s to 1930s. And of course we have paintings from the prince's personal collection. Some of them are on permanent display and are never moved. Many of the works of art are much more valuable than the Dardel painting. We have works by Liljefors and Munch that could raise a significantly higher price than 'The Dying Dandy.' Why was that the only painting that the thieves took? It's incomprehensible."

On their way to the room where the painting had hung, Sommer took the opportunity to tell Jacobsson about Waldemarsudde, since this was her first visit.

"The prince was a broad-minded person who supported the Swedish artists of his day," he explained. "His home was finished in 1905, and it became a gathering place for free-thinking people; the social life flourished out here. He was personal friends with many of the artists. And he himself became a great landscape painter. His collection contains more than two thousand works," Sommer went on enthusiastically, as if forgetting why Fogestam and Jacobsson were there.

"Do you have other paintings by Nils Dardel here?"

"We've borrowed three other paintings for this exhibition. And Dardel did a pencil sketch of Prince Eugen that is part of his collection. No other paintings were stolen.'

They entered the bright, beautiful areas that were the former living quarters of the prince. They immediately noticed a strong floral scent. The rooms were furnished in a style typical of Sweden in the early 1900s. Fresh flowers filled all the rooms, in accordance with the prince's wishes. There were scarlet amaryllis, shimmering blue hyacinths, and great bouquets of tulips in assorted colors.

Jacobsson knew that Prince Eugen had never married, and he'd had no children. She wondered whether he might have been homosexual, but didn't dare ask.

The dominant room was the prince's drawing room. Light flooded in through the tall French windows and onto the yellow silk wallpaper. Most eye-catching was the large painting titled "Strömkarlen" by Ernst Josephson, with the motif of the fiddle-playing Näcken spirit sitting on the rocks by a roaring river. Sommer stopped there.

"This painting has been set into the wall and can't be moved. It was the prince's favorite."

The naked young man who was the central figure was handsome and sensitive looking; there was something both tragic and tender about the scene. The position of the painting was well chosen. It was highly visible, and the gilded fiddle of the river sprite harmonized with the yellow silk wallpaper in the room.

The floor creaked under their feet as they passed through the rooms: the conservatory, with its marvelous view of the city and Stockholm's estuary; the dark-green library, its shelves filled with art-history books and its ostentatious fireplace.

Finally the museum director ushered them toward the dining room, where "The Dying Dandy" had hung. The room was still cordoned off, so they had to make do with looking inside from the doorway. The dining room had light-green walls, an impressive crystal chandelier, and elegant Rococo furniture typical of the eighteenth century. One of the walls was noticeably bare. The frame had been removed in order to be examined by police technicians.

"Yes, well," sighed Sommer, "that's where it was."

"Isn't the painting quite large?" asked Jacobsson.

"Yes, it is. Almost six feet wide and four feet tall."

"So he must have stood on something to cut it out of the frame."

"Yes, that's right. We found one of those ultra-light aluminum ladders in the room. He didn't bother to take it with him."

"And the sculpture? Where did you find it?"

"Right in front, on that little table."

"Where is it now?"

"The police have taken it."

Jacobsson stared at the bare wall and then at the table in front. A triangular pattern was emerging. Egon Wallin—Muramaris—"The Dying Dandy." At the moment it seemed impossible to figure out how everything fit together. By stealing the sculpture from Wallin's gallery and placing it here, the thief obviously wanted to tell them something. Was the painting thief the same person who had killed Egon Wallin?

It suddenly seemed highly likely.

The theft at Waldemarsudde was of course the top story on all the TV news programs, and Johan received much praise for his efforts at the morning meeting the following day. Regional News had been the first to report that the perpetrator had entered the museum and then made his escape across the ice. Of course, the other news editors at Swedish TV got their hands on some of Johan's material and used it in their own reports. As soon as a reporter returned to television headquarters, he was supposed to share his material with everyone there. That way all of the reporters could make use of the interviews and pictures that were available. But Johan had begun to resist this way of operating. He didn't want to run the risk of not being able to edit his own story just because he had to spend all his time providing material and information for everybody else. He also thought it was wrong that he and the cameraperson, who worked hard to obtain unique images and exclusive interviews, should have to dole these out like free sweets to children and then see them be chopped into pieces for different broadcasts. That was no fun, nor did it do anything for his professional pride. Both he and the cameraperson suffered.

Of course, his resistance had provoked reactions from both management and his colleagues. It was certainly not a good strategy for anyone angling for a rise in salary, or who had ambitions about climbing the career ladder. On the other hand, he thought it might make it easier for him to be transferred to Gotland, if a permanent position was ever established on the island. Then the Stockholm office would be rid of a difficult reporter.

Even though he was now back in Stockholm, he couldn't help wondering what was happening with the murder investigation on Gotland. When the morning meeting was over, he spent a few hours trying to get information. He tried calling both Knutas and Jacobsson, but without any luck. Pia Lilja was at home in bed with the flu, so she had nothing useful to tell him. Finally he had to settle for talking to Lars Norrby. Johan asked him if anything new had happened in the investigation.

"Well, nothing that I can really discuss at the moment."

"But there must be something you can tell me. We have to keep the viewers interested in the story, and that's to your benefit too. So that anyone who happens to have information will contact the police."

"Don't try any of your tricks on me. I've been in this job too long."

Johan could hear that Norrby was smiling. He was still in the good graces of Visby's police force after the drama of the previous year, so he decided to keep trying to get more information. After fifteen minutes trying to pry something out of the police spokesman, he finally had the man where he wanted him. When Johan asked if Jacobsson was away, since he hadn't been able to get hold of her on the phone, Norrby replied that she'd gone to Stockholm on police business.

"Why's that?" asked Johan.

"Because of the robbery, of course."

That stopped Johan short, and he wasn't quite sure how to continue. "What do you mean?" he asked.

"The robbery at Waldemarsudde. We're investigating a connection to the murder of Egon Wallin." Johan gave a start. What on earth was the man talking about? He waited for a few seconds, hoping that Norrby would let slip something more.

The police spokesman apparently found the silence bothersome because he then went on. "All right, let's keep this between us, but the sculpture that was left behind at the crime scene at Waldemarsudde was the same one that was stolen from Egon Wallin's gallery."

Johan hadn't known that a sculpture had been stolen from the gallery in Visby, but he decided to play along.

"Oh, I see. Hmm. Well, thanks for the info."

M ax Grenfors was tipping back the chair at his desk, which was the focal point of the editorial offices. As usual, he held a phone to each ear. Next to him sat the newscaster, her eyes fixed on the computer monitor. She had earphones on and was watching a news story. So it would be best not to disturb them. The news producer was busy trying to find images for a report on domestic violence, which was always difficult to illustrate. There was a risk that the same old images would crop up over and over again.

All of the reporters were preoccupied with editing their stories; it was obvious from the pulse of the editorial offices that only a few hours remained before the news broadcast.

Johan felt as if he would burst if he didn't tell someone the incredible news he'd just heard. He tapped Grenfors on the shoulder and motioned that he had something important to report. For once the editor acknowledged the urgency and ended his phone conversations.

He ran a hand through his hair and sighed. "Certain re-porters seem to need help with everything. It's crazy! Soon I'll be doing their interviews for them, too!'

Johan was well aware of how much the editor liked to

get involved in a story, so he didn't take his complaints too seriously.

"Listen to this," he said, pulling up a chair and sitting down next to Grenfors. "The robbery at Waldemarsudde wasn't just an ordinary art theft."

"No?" A glimmer of interest appeared in Grenfors's eyes.

"No. The thief didn't just steal a painting. He also left something behind."

"What was it?"

"He put a sculpture near the empty frame where the painting used to hang."

"Is that right?"

"Yes. And it wasn't just any sculpture. It's the one that was stolen during Egon Wallin's gallery opening on the day of his murder."

"So what does it mean? That the person who killed Egon Wallin also stole the painting?"

"Very possibly," said Johan.

"How reliable is your source for this?"

"Got it straight from the police."

Grenfors took off the glasses that he'd begun to wear lately. He'd chosen designer frames, of course. "So there's a connection between the theft and the murder. But how the hell does it fit together?"

He cast a quick glance at his watch.

"Damn it all, we've got to have this. Get over to editing—you've got to put together a spot about this right away."

The news that there was a clear link between the daring burglary at Waldemarsudde and the murder of Egon Wallin—and that the perpetrator wanted the police to be aware of it—headed every news program on Tuesday evening.

Johan was pleased, and not just because he was responsible for the hottest news story two days in a row. Before he went home, he was told to take the first plane back to Visby the next morning.

Karin Jacobsson looked her boss in the eye as he sat down at the table opposite her. And then she said the words that he didn't want to hear.

"I'm resigning, Anders."

Everything started spinning around in his head. He couldn't seem to grasp the meaning of the words; they just kept bouncing off one another and disappearing in the distance.

Knutas slowly lowered his fork. He had just speared a big piece of boiled cod with egg sauce. "What did you say? You can't be serious."

He cast a glance at the clock on the wall, as if he wanted to document the moment when his closest colleague stated that she was leaving him.

Jacobsson gave Knutas a sympathetic look. "Yes, I am, Anders. Quite serious. I've been offered a position in Stockholm. With the NCP."

"What?"

His fully loaded fork was still hovering in the air as if his arm were frozen, paralyzed by Karin's statement. She looked down and began poking at her food as she went on. All of a sudden it seemed to Knutas that the whole cafeteria stank of egg sauce, and the smell made him feel sick.

"It's actually Kihlgård's boss at the NCP who offered me the job. I'll be working with the same team as Martin. It'll be a challenge for me, Anders. You need to understand that. And there's nothing holding me here."

Knutas stared at her in astonishment. Her words were ringing in his ears. Martin Kihlgård again. Of course he would be the one behind the job offer. Knutas had never really been taken in by that jovial demeanor of his. The man was a snake. Slippery and untrustworthy underneath that inoffensive facade.

From the very beginning there had been a real chemistry between Kihlgård and Jacobsson, and that had upset Knutas although he would never admit it.

"But what about us?"

Karin sighed. "Come on, Anders, it's not like we're a couple. We work really well together, but I want to try something new. And besides, I'm tired of sitting here molding. Of course I like my job and working with you and all the others, but nothing else is happening in my life. I'm going to turn forty soon. I want to grow, both in my professional and my personal life."

Red patches had appeared on Jacobsson's throat, always a sure sign that she was upset or was finding the situation uncomfortable.

Neither of them spoke for a moment. Knutas didn't know what to say. He was at a complete loss as he stared at the petite, dark-eyed woman sitting across from him.

Then she sighed and stood up. "That's how it's going to be, at any rate. I've made up my mind."

"But . . ."

That was as far as he got. She picked up her tray and walked away.

He was left sitting at the table alone. He stared out of the window at the gray parking lot barely visible through a snowy haze. He was mortified to feel tears filling his eyes. He cast a furtive glance around. The cafeteria was packed with colleagues talking and laughing as they ate.

He didn't know how he was going to do his job without Karin. She gave him so much. At the same time he could understand why she'd made this decision. Of course Karin wanted the chance to develop in her job, and maybe meet someone and have a family. Like everybody else.

Feeling dejected, Knutas went back to his office, closed the door, and took his pipe out of the top drawer of his desk. He filled the pipe with tobacco, but this time he didn't leave it unlit, as usual. Instead, he lit the pipe and then opened the window and stood there in the breeze. Was she really serious about this? Where would she live? She and Kihlgård may have hit it off, but in the long run would she be able to stand him and his eternal obsession with food? Of course he was pleasant enough in small doses, but what about on a daily basis?

The moment he had that thought, he was struck by an awful insight. Maybe he wasn't so much fun himself. Here she was, working with him every day, and he thought they had a great working relationship. He was fond of Karin; he appreciated her lively manner and her temperament, which sometimes manifested itself in surprising ways. Karin brightened up his life, made him feel alive at work. Because of her, he felt better about himself. But what about her? What did she think about him? All his complaints and grumbling about cutbacks in the police force. He searched his memory. What exactly did he give Karin in return? What did she get from him? Apparently not much.

The question was whether it was too late to do anything about the matter. Karin hadn't yet submitted her resignation. Maybe she was planning to take a leave of absence first—to try it out. Her parents and all of her friends lived

here on Gotland. Would she be happy on the mainland—
and in the big city? Knutas felt panic-stricken at the mere
thought of showing up for work every day without her.

He had to find a solution. Anything at all.

L ate on Friday afternoon Knutas had something else to preoccupy his thoughts. The Stockholm police emailed him a list of individuals in Sweden who were considered to have a special interest in Nils Dardel.

He scanned the list, at first not recognizing a single name. But when he reached the middle, he stopped abruptly. The letters practically jumped off the page as they formed a name that he'd already encountered several times during the investigation. Erik Mattson.

Knutas slowly exhaled through his nostrils. Why on earth did this man's name keep cropping up?

He got up and looked out of the window, trying to keep his excitement in check. Erik Mattson, the man who valued works of art at Bukowski's and who had also attended the gallery opening here in Visby. He had assessed the stolen paintings found at Egon Wallin's home without mentioning that he'd been on Gotland on the day of the murder. Knutas was ashamed to admit to himself that he'd actually forgotten to ring Mattson and question him about that. The theft at Waldemarsudde had taken precedence.

Just before receiving the email, Knutas had been about to leave for the day. He'd planned to buy a couple of bottles of wine and some flowers for Lina on his way home. He'd been neglecting his family far too much lately.

Now he was going to be late again. He called home. Lina didn't sound as understanding as usual. And that wasn't surprising. Even she had her limits. Knutas felt guilty, but he pushed that aside for now. He had to focus on Erik Mattson. He would have liked to call Bukowski's Auction House at once, but he stopped himself. If Mattson was the perpetrator, or one of them, Knutas needed to proceed with caution. He felt a strong urge to talk to Karin and went out into the corridor. The door to her office was closed. He knocked. No answer. He waited a moment before he cautiously opened the door. The office was empty. She'd gone home without saying goodbye to him, he realized, feeling hurt. He couldn't recall her ever doing that before. With his tail between his legs he slunk back to his own office. He had to do something, so he punched in the number for Bukowski's, even though he knew their offices would be closed by now. The phone rang for a long time before someone finally answered.

"Erik Mattson."

Knutas nearly fell out of his chair. "Er, yes. This is Anders Knutas from Visby police. I'm sorry for calling on a Friday evening like this, but I have a few important questions I need to ask you."

"Yes?" replied Mattson, his voice expressionless.

"When we discussed the paintings that were found at Egon Wallin's home, you didn't say that you were actually at his opening on the day before he was murdered."

A brief pause. The silence on the phone was palpable.

"There's a simple explanation for that. I didn't go to the opening."

"But according to your boss, you had an invitation. You and a colleague stayed overnight in Visby so that you could both attend the opening."

"Actually Bukowski's received a general invitation, and my colleague Stefan Ekerot and I were thinking of going since we were going to be on Gotland anyway. But neither of us ended up attending the opening. Stefan's baby daughter got sick during the night, so he caught the first plane home on Saturday. She's only a month old, you see. And I wasn't feeling well on Saturday afternoon, so I stayed in my hotel room to rest. So I didn't go to the gallery either. That's why I didn't happen to mention it."

"I see," said Knutas, deciding for the time being to accept Mattson's explanation. "I understand that you're an expert on the work of Nils Dardel. What do you think about the theft of 'The Dying Dandy'?"

Again there was silence on the phone. Knutas heard Mattson take a breath before he replied.

"It's terrible, a sacrilege. And a tragedy if the painting's not recovered. 'The Dying Dandy' is without a doubt one of the most important paintings in the history of Swedish art."

"Who do you think might have stolen it, and why?"

"It must have been a contract job, so that it can be sold to a collector. The painting is so well known, both in Sweden and the rest of Europe, that trying to sell it on the open market would be impossible."

"Are there any big collectors of Dardel's work here in Sweden?"

"His paintings are scattered among different collections. His art has been controversial. Some people even think his work isn't important; don't ask me why. I'm sorry, but I actually have to go now."

"Of course. I'm sorry to have bothered you."

Knutas thanked Mattson for his time and said goodbye.

After he hung up, he felt even more confused. The surge of hope that he'd felt a few minutes earlier was already gone.

Erik Mattson didn't sound like a murderer.

He decided to put the investigation aside for the weekend. Maybe he just needed to let things percolate for a while. He hoped that he'd be able to view the case with fresh eyes on Monday.

Right now he just wanted to go home and spend time with his family.

The next step in his plan was now decided, and his head was filled with all sorts of ideas. Earlier in the day he had called the funeral director to find out when Egon Wallin was going to be buried. The funeral wouldn't be for another two weeks, which gave him plenty of time to make his preparations. He was thinking of attending; wearing a disguise, naturally, so that nobody would recognize him. He was longing for that day. To see everyone without anyone seeing him. He felt a flutter of anticipation in his stomach as he pictured the whole scene in his mind.

Right now he was alone, and there was something he had to do today. He went down to the cellar storage room and took out the canvas that he'd hidden there. Luckily he didn't run into any of his neighbors. He quickly returned to his apartment and then carefully unrolled the canvas on the living-room floor. Several weeks before the theft, he had ordered a custom-made frame that would be the right size.

Just as he was about to put the first nail in the frame, the phone rang. Annoyed at being interrupted, he glanced up and let it ring a few more times, thinking he might not answer. But then he dropped the hammer and stood up.

After the conversation was over he couldn't help marveling that he'd called at that exact moment. It had to be fate.

Then he spent a long time carefully attaching the canvas to its new frame. When he was done, he leaned the painting against the wall, took a few steps back, and regarded his handiwork.

He was more than satisfied.

S aturday started off with the pale and hesitant light of winter sunshine.

Johan served Emma breakfast in bed. He placed a red rose on the tray. They ate warm croissants with raspberry jam, drank coffee, and read the newspaper as Elin slept sweetly in her crib. Emma's parents would arrive around eleven to take care of Elin and then they'd have the rest of the weekend all to themselves. They'd gone to the jeweler's together to select their rings. Emma had decided on a ring of white gold with five diamonds. Johan felt dizzy when he saw the price, but then how often in life did a person get engaged?

Over and over they'd discussed how they should exchange rings, yet both of them had agreed that they should do it soon. Of course they wanted to have some peace and quiet and time alone after the engagement ceremony, free from a crying baby and dirty diapers, but they didn't want to be away from Elin for too long.

Finally they had decided to have a private ceremony at Emma's favorite place: the beach at Norsta Auren, at the northernmost tip of Fårö. Her parents owned an old limestone house there, and Emma and Johan could have it all to themselves. They wouldn't be able to have dinner in a restaurant because none was open on Fårö in the wintertime. Instead, they would have a cozy time at home alone. The house stood right by the sea, and it had a fireplace, so it should be fine.

They left Roma before lunch and drove north. At Fårösund they took the ferry across the channel and over to the small island. The landscape was more desolate and barren there, although in the winter the difference didn't seem as great as in the summer.

Beautiful Fårö church stood high on a hill. The Konsum grocery store was open, although only one car was parked in front. Johan wondered how the shop managed to stay in business during the winter. They had done all of their grocery shopping in Visby, just in case. They didn't want to run the risk of the small shop not stocking steaks, tiger prawns, and Belgian chocolates.

Johan enjoyed looking at the landscape as he drove. The snow was unusually deep, a thick white layer covering the island's lovely stone fences, windmills, and pasture lands. Here and there they passed a farm, its stone buildings built to withstand the wind and severe weather.

When they turned off the main highway that cut across Fårö, the road got narrower. They passed the beach at Ajkesvik, where seagulls bobbed on the crests of the waves, and continued on toward Skär and Norsta Auren. The road became a bumpy cow track for the last stretch of the way, and here the snowdrifts were even higher. They almost couldn't drive all the way up to the house, in spite of the fact that Emma's father had been out to shovel off the snow that morning.

The white limestone house stood all alone, surrounded by low stone walls, with only the sea as its neighbor. When they got out of the car, they were struck by the magnificence of nature. And for once the wind was hardly blowing at all.

The first thing they did was go down to the shore, which extended for more than a mile and was wider than most beaches that Johan had seen. It stretched beyond the bay's furthest promontory, preventing them from seeing the Fårö lighthouse, which stood on the other side.

This was a special place, for several reasons. Not just because of its natural grandeur but also because of the memories it evoked. Here Emma had run for her life as she was chased by a serial killer a couple of years earlier. The memory was still strong for both of them. Johan had joined the chase and was closing on them. But the perp was too fast for him, and he had disappeared in a car with Emma as his hostage.

Maybe they both wanted to replace those awful memories with something as positive as their engagement. Regardless of what had happened, Emma loved this shoreline more than any other place on earth.

They decided to carry in their belongings, have lunch, and then take a walk along the shore. The rings were in a little box in Johan's pocket. He felt as if the box were on fire.

They ate fish soup with prawns and fresh basil. They had brought along fresh-baked bread, which they warmed up in the oven. Johan felt strangely solemn as he sat there at the big drop-leaf table in the kitchen. Emma was wearing a turtleneck sweater, and she had pulled her hair back into a ponytail. He found himself wondering how she would look as an old woman. The next second he felt a surge of happiness come over him. Were they really going to grow old together? Spend the rest of their lives together? Sometimes that realization seemed so obvious, like a door thrown open with him standing outside, looking at himself from a distance.

Emma was his family now. Emma and Elin. And that felt amazing.

They bundled up in warm clothes and a bit reluctantly left the warmth of the house to take their walk along the beach. Johan took Emma's hand and led the way, trudging through the snow.

"Take it easy," she said with a laugh. "I'm about to fall over."

"The question is, how are we going to exchange rings without freezing our fingers off? I'm already frozen," he shouted happily.

Out on the beach it was bitterly cold and the wind cut right through their clothes, making their eyes fill with tears. The sea was a steel gray and the water struck the shore in rhythmic waves. Johan had never seen a longer horizon. The sky and sea merged—it was hard to tell where one began and the other ended. There were no buildings in sight except for the house owned by Emma's parents. They were enveloped by the sky, the sea, and the snowy white shore. Its wide expanse rose up to an embankment, and on the other side were the woods, so typical of Fårö with their stunted pines, the branches twisted by storms that had come and gone over the years. It was all so magnificent that Johan shouted with joy, reaching out for the wind.

"I love Emma! I love Emma!"

His words vanished over the sea, drowned out by the shrieks of seagulls. Emma's eyes were filled with laughter as she looked at him, and he felt more strongly than ever before that it was true. So true. He didn't want to wait a second longer. He pulled out of his pocket the box holding the rings and then drew Emma close. He pressed his lips against her hair, damp with cold, as he put the ring on her finger. She did the same for him.

All of a sudden she cried, "Look, Johan! What's that?"

Something big and gray was lying at the water's edge a short distance away. It looked like a big boulder, but how had it ended up there? Everywhere else the beach was flat and white as far as the eye could see.

Cautiously they approached. When they were about twenty yards away, the shape began to move. Emma instantly pulled out her camera. She snapped a picture just as the gray seal dived back into the water.

For a long time they stood there in silence, watching as it disappeared into the waves.

On Monday morning, Knutas arrived at police head-quarters early; it was only six thirty. The weekend had provided a much-needed respite from the investigative work. On the other hand, he hadn't been able to stop thinking about Karin, so he had discussed the matter with Lina. She thought he needed to do something dramatic if he wanted to keep Karin on the force. Over a few glasses of wine on Saturday evening, while the children were watching a song contest on TV, they had come up with a solution. It wasn't going to be popular, but that couldn't be helped. He felt confident about his decision, and he was prepared to weather whatever storm would come. He'd discussed the idea with the county police commissioner on Sunday, and she had accepted the reasons for his proposal.

One thing that Jacobsson and Knutas had in common was that they were both morning people. He'd been at work only half an hour and was putting together a draft for his plan when he heard Karin's light footsteps in the corridor. He asked her to come into his office.

"Sure," she said happily. "I've found out some really interesting things over the weekend, and I can't wait to tell you about them."

"All right, but that can wait," he said dismissively as she sat down in his visitor's chair. "There's something else we need to talk about first."

"Okay." Jacobsson gave him an inquisitive look.

"I don't want you to resign, Karin. You know that. So I have an offer to make. You don't have to answer right now; take some time to think about it, and then let me know sometime this week whether you accept my proposal or not. Okay?"

"Of course." Jacobsson looked both nervous and full of anticipation.

"I want you to be the assistant superintendent for the criminal division. Meaning my deputy. One day, when I retire, I want you to take my place. This police station has never had a woman detective superintendent, and it's certainly about time."

"But—"

"No, no, I have no plans to retire. But I'm at an age when ten more years on the job will be the maximum. And besides, Lina has been telling me that she wants to try working on the mainland in a few years, and I'm open to the idea. If she decides to do that, I'll move over there with her. We have more freedom now the children are older. I want a deputy I can trust completely. And you're the only one, Karin."

She gave him a bewildered look. Her expression had changed from nervousness to surprise to astonishment. The telltale red spots had appeared on her throat. She opened her mouth as if to speak.

"No, Karin, please don't say anything right now. The only thing I ask is that you think it over. And let me also say something about the salary. Of course you'll receive a significant pay increase, and we can discuss that in greater detail if you decide to accept the offer. But just so you have some idea what you're looking at, it would be at least seven thousand kronor more per month, plus you'd be attending a number of courses in management skills, and so on. And you should know that I have the full support of the county police commissioner. She would like to see you as assistant superintendent."

"But Lars . . ."

"Lars Norrby is my problem, not yours, Karin. So I hope you'll consider the offer."

Karin nodded mutely.

"Good," said Knutas, relieved to have the conversation out of the way. He got up and went over to stand at the window, not daring to look at her. Neither of them spoke for a moment.

"Shall I tell you what I found out?" she asked.

"Yes, tell me."

"This weekend I checked out the connection between Nils Dardel and Muramaris. The original of the sculpture that was found at Waldemarsudde after the theft happens to stand in the garden at Muramaris, and I wanted to find out whether Dardel had any links to the place."

"Smart thinking," murmured Knutas.

"But I found out something else. Listen to this," said Jacobsson eagerly. She leaned forward and gave him an intent look. "Did you know that Dardel was homosexual?"

"I'd heard that mentioned, yes. But wasn't he married?"

"Yes, he married Thora Klinckowström, and they had a daughter, Ingrid. Dardel had several serious relationships with women. For example, he was secretly engaged to Nita Wallenberg before he met Thora. But their engagement was broken off because her father didn't think Dardel would make a proper son-in-law. Even back then rumors were raging about his alcoholism, homosexuality, and decadent tendencies. That was in 1917, when he was twenty-nine years old. But at the same time that he fell in love with women, he was in love with men. Dardel had a long-lasting and relatively open homosexual relationship with his friend and patron Rolf de Maré, the only son of Duchess Wilhelmina von Hallwyl's daughter Ellen."

"Is that right? But what do Dardel's sexual inclinations have to do with Gotland?" Knutas sounded tired. This news was not as exciting as he had hoped.

Jacobsson's eyes were shining. It wasn't hard to see that she was interested in the artist's life. "Well, there's more. Do you know anything about Wilhelmina von Hallwyl—the archduchess with the Hallwyl palace in Stockholm?"

"No, I've never heard of her before."

"The palace is on Hamngatan, right across from Bern's Restaurant and Berzelii Park—you know, next to Norrmalmstorg. A fantastic place. Duchess Wilhelmina von Hallwyl was fabulously wealthy, and she devoted her life to collecting things that are now on display there: art, silver, oriental porcelain, and ceramics. I think there are close to five thousand objects, and she donated both her home and the collection to the state. You really should go there the next time you're in Stockholm," said Jacobsson enthusiastically.

"But this is where the story gets really unbelievable. Duchess von Hallwyl had four daughters, and one of them was Ellen, who married a top military officer, Henrik de Maré. They had a son, Rolf, and they moved to Berlin because Henrik was the military attaché there. The son needed a tutor, and so Ellen hired a young man named Johnny Roosval. Now it so happened that Ellen and Johnny fell in love. He was twelve years younger than her and a complete nobody, while she was part of high society and from a noble family. All the elements for a classic drama. Ellen defied convention; she got divorced from her military husband and married the young Johnny Roosval!"

Jacobsson clapped her hands in delight, while Knutas still looked puzzled.

"Okay, but what about Gotland?" he said wearily.

"Yes, I know. We're getting to that. Naturally the whole thing caused a big scandal—bear in mind that this was around 1910! The archduchess Wilhelmina von Hallwyl broke off all contact with her daughter and took her grandson, Rolf de Maré, away from Ellen. But Ellen and Johnny were still very much in love, and they had their dream house built—on Gotland. It was called Muramaris, of course. It was finished in 1915, and Ellen also had a small summerhouse built for her son. It still exists today, and it's known as Rolf de Maré's cottage. Ellen was an artist and sculptor, and Muramaris became her studio. She was the one who made most of the sculptures in the garden. Johnny Roosval later made a name for himself, and he became Sweden's first professor of art history. That gave him access to the more exclusive homes, and do you know what happened next? Well, the sour old Duchess von Hallwyl took Ellen back into her favor, and she was allowed to resume contact with her son. So Rolf de Maré spent a lot of time at Muramaris during the summers. And guess who he often brought along? Nils Dardel. He even ended up designing the garden at Muramaris. There's a lovely baroque garden in the grounds, you know. And the estate is in such a beautiful location, right near the sea. Isn't that a romantic story?'

Jacobsson leaned back in her chair with a pleased look on her face. She took another sip of her coffee, which was now cold.

"It's a good story, all right," said Knutas, relieved that it was finally over. "So there is a link between Nils von Dardel and Muramaris, after all. But what on earth does all of this have to do with Egon Wallin?"

"Well, I'm not really sure, but it was so interesting to read about him—Dardel, I mean. He was a fascinating person, such a complex personality," said Jacobsson dreamily.

Knutas seemed to have had enough of Nils Dardel for the morning. He drained the last of his coffee and stood up. "Good work, Karin. It's time for our meeting. Afterward I think I'll head out to Muramaris."

He didn't dare admit to Jacobsson that he'd never set foot in the place before, even though he'd driven past the sign a thousand times on the way out to his summerhouse.

When Hugo Malmberg picked up the morning newspaper under the mailbox, he discovered a folded slip of paper that had landed partway under his extravagant wooden shoe rack from Norrgavel. It was a nice little piece of red paper. He thought it might be an unusually small advertisement, yet he had an eerie sense of foreboding as he opened it. Only a single word was printed inside: "Soon." He went into the kitchen and sat down. The dogs were yapping at his feet, as if they too felt there was something menacing about the mysterious message.

He automatically wrapped his robe more tightly around him before he looked at the word again. It had been written with a black marker in bold letters—the same sort of print that might be used for an invitation to a party. *Soon.* What on earth could that mean? He felt a cold sweat come over him at the thought of its intent. This was clear evidence that he was actually being stalked. He hadn't been imagining things, after all.

Ever since he'd seen the man on Västerbron on that Friday night, he'd had a feeling that someone was spying on him. He'd also started to wonder whether he might be losing his mind.

But now there was no question. Somebody was after him. He suddenly felt vulnerable even in his own home, and he nervously glanced around the apartment. This person knew where he lived, had come into the building and stood in front of his door. With trembling hands, Malmberg reached for the phone and punched in the number for the police. He had to wait a long time before he was transferred to someone who told him that if he wished to file a report, he would have to come down to the police station in person. Impatiently Malmberg hung up.

He sank down onto an armchair in the living room and tried to collect his thoughts. The only sound was the antique clock on the wall, ticking nervously. He needed to think clearly and objectively. Did this have anything to do with Egon's murder?

In his mind he went over recent events, the people he'd met and what he'd done, but he couldn't recall anything out of the ordinary.

Then he happened to think about the young man standing outside the gallery. There was something about his expression.

After he'd pulled himself together, Malmberg did go over to police headquarters on Kungsholmen and filed a report. The inspector who took the details seemed moderately interested. Malmberg was advised to come back if he received any further threats.

When he left the police station, he didn't feel a bit reassured.

K nutas began the morning meeting with a question that had been nagging at him all weekend, although he'd pushed it aside out of sheer self-preservation. He had wanted to be able to devote himself to his family in peace and quiet.

He dropped a pile of weekend newspapers on the table. The headlines screamed: "MURDERER BEHIND ART THEFT," "HUNT FOR KILLER AT ART MUSEUM," and "PANIC IN THE ART WORLD." All of the newspapers made reference to the TV news programs on Friday evening, when Johan Berg had reported that a sculpture stolen from a gallery in Visby owned by the murdered Egon Wallin had been left in front of the empty frame in Waldemarsudde.

"What's the meaning of this?" asked Knutas.

Everyone seated around the table looked worried, but the question prompted only muted murmuring as a few people shook their heads.

"Who leaked this to the press?" Knutas fixed his eyes on his colleagues.

"Maybe you need to stop for a moment and calm down," said Wittberg crossly. "It didn't necessarily come from here. Maybe somebody in Stockholm leaked the news. So many people are involved in this case that it makes the risk of a leak even greater."

"So none of you has talked to anyone outside of this room about the sculpture?"

Before anybody had time to answer, the door opened and Lars Norrby came in. "I'm sorry I'm late," he mumbled. "My car wouldn't start. I'm really getting tired of this freezing weather."

His eyes fell on the evening paper with the big headline that Knutas was holding up, and then he caught sight of the rest of the papers spread out on the table.

"That was unfortunate," he said, shaking his head.

"That's putting it mildly," growled Knutas. "Do you have any idea how this got out?"

"Absolutely not. I've only given out the bare essentials to the press. As usual."

"The county police commissioner is on my back, demanding an explanation. What do all of you think I should do about it?"

There was utter silence in the room until Kihlgård spoke.

"Come on now, Anders. What makes you think the leak came from here? Plenty of people might know about the sculpture being found at Waldemarsudde. The museum employees, for example. Can you really trust them not to talk?"

His colleagues seated at the table immediately agreed with him.

"All right, we're not going to waste time trying to find out who leaked the information. But let me emphasize again how important it is for all of you to show discretion," said Knutas. "Things like this can harm the investigation, and we can't afford to have that happen. Lars, could you send out an internal memo about this?"

Norrby nodded without changing expression.

Knutas decided not to wait any longer and went out to Muramaris right after lunch. He'd called the owner after the morning meeting and explained briefly why he'd like to see the place, although without going into detail. He didn't need to. She'd seen the newspapers and understood perfectly the reason for his visit.

As he turned off the main road and headed toward Muramaris, he thought it was strange that he'd never been here before. The road meandered down toward the sea with stands of stunted pines and spruce trees on either estate came into view. It stood on a plateau with woods all around and the sea far below the steep cliff. The big, sand-colored main building looked like a Mediterranean villa with large mullioned windows. The house was enclosed by a wall, and the garden was austerely laid out with low hedges and shrubs that were now covered with snow. Sculptures had been placed here and there, looking ghostlike in the desolate grounds. In one corner stood a small structure built in the same style as the main house. It looked as if it might be a gallery or an artist's studio. In the distance stood a cluster of small wooden cabins. He parked in front of the main building and got out to look around. The owner was nowhere in sight. He glanced at his watch and realized that he was a little early. He breathed in the fresh air. What a peculiar place. The building looked abandoned, like a decaying beauty. It seemed to have been unoccupied for years. The sculptures were like mementoes of a bygone era. Art and love had both flourished here at one time, but that was clearly long ago. Now the owner came walking toward him along the gravel path from the cabin area. She was a stylish woman in her fifties; her blonde hair was drawn into a knot on top of her head. She was wearing bright red lipstick but no other makeup. Even though they were about the same age, Knutas didn't know Anita Thorén. They'd gone to different primary schools before starting secondary school, but even then they hadn't frequented the same circles.

She gave him a friendly but slightly wary look as they shook hands.

"Well, truth be told, I'm not sure exactly why I'm here," he explained. "But I wanted to see the original of the sculpture that was found at Waldemarsudde."

"Of course."

They went around the corner, and there it stood, against a wall.

"It's called 'Yearning,' and I think you can see that emotion in her eyes, can't you?"

"Is it a woman? I can't really tell."

"Yes, I agree that there's something rather sexless about her. And that fits in well with Dardel . . . the androgynous, slightly indeterminate . . ."

Anita Thorén looked as if she were seeing the sculpture for the first time. A genuine enthusiast, thought Knutas. Imagine taking over a place like this. It would undoubtedly require a real commitment, and he admired that sort of person, someone who had a genuine passion for something.

"The sculptor's name was Anna Petrus. She and Dardel were contemporaries, and she was also good friends with Ellen Roosval."

"Yes, I've heard the whole story about how he often came here. And that he was the one who designed the garden," said Knutas, feeling like a real expert.

"And that wasn't all," said Anita Thorén. "That art thief really knew what he was doing when he placed a sculpture from Muramaris under the empty frame. It was actually here that Nils Dardel painted 'The Dying Dandy.'"

Knutas raised his eyebrows. "Is that so?"

"That's what people say, at any rate. Come on, I'll show you."

She led the way through a creaking wooden gate. The house had certainly been grand and imposing in its day, but now it looked dilapidated and run-down. The walls were crumbling in places, the paint was peeling off, and the windows were in dire need of repair. They used the side entrance and entered an old-fashioned kitchen.

"There," she said, pointing to a room next to the kitchen. "It was in there that Dardel painted 'The Dying Dandy' during the same summer that he designed the garden. He walked around the property with the head gardeners, explaining how everything should look. It's all described in letters and other documents from that period. But Dardel also worked on his painting. First he did a watercolor with a similar motif, but using other colors, and with three men standing around the dandy. In that version he was holding a fan in his hand instead of a mirror. The first painting had a much more blatant homosexual theme."

Knutas listened dutifully, but he wasn't particularly interested in art history.

Next they went into the drawing room, where a magnificent fireplace made of Gotland sandstone dominated the space.

"Ellen was both a painter and a musician, but her primary interest was sculpture," said Anita Thorén. "She studied with Carl Milles, among others. She sculpted this enormous fireplace. It's almost nine feet high, and it was the centerpiece around which the rest of the house was built. Those reliefs symbolize the four elements—earth, fire, air, and water. The others represent human love, suffering, and work. That figure over there is the goddess of love," she added, pointing to one of the beautiful reliefs etched into the stone. "On the twenty-first of June, the summer solstice, the last rays of the setting sun strike her face. That's the shortest night of the year. Well, actually, there's practically no night at all."

They walked through the music room and the library, then went upstairs to have a look at the bedrooms while Anita Thorén told him the history of the house. Outside they stopped by Ellen's studio as well as beside a large house for the caretaker who looked after the garden.

"He's really the only one here in the wintertime," said Anita. "My husband and I live in the city and just come out once in a while to check on things."

"But what about the cabins over there? What are they used for?" asked Knutas, pointing to the identical wooden cabins near the edge of the woods. They looked newly built.

"We rent them out in the summertime. I'll show you."

Anita Thorén led the way over to the group of cabins, which stood a good distance away from Muramaris and close to the woods. She unlocked the door to one of the cabins and showed him inside. It was plainly furnished but with the requisite comforts. Directly below the plateau where they stood were some steps leading down to the beach. Standing by itself was a red-painted cottage that seemed older than the others.

"That's Rolf de Maré's cottage," said Anita. "Ellen had it

built for her son so that he could have some privacy when he spent his summers here."

They went inside. There was a simple kitchen with a wood stove, a big bedroom with two twin beds, and a small toilet and shower room. That was all.

"So this is where he lived," said Knutas, nodding as he surveyed the bright floral wallpaper on the walls. "And Dardel also came here?"

"Yes, he came here often over a period of several years. As I said, they were quite open about their homosexuality, at least as much as was possible in those days. Rolf de Maré was also Dardel's benefactor; he helped him financially and gave him a great deal of support emotionally. Dardel's life wasn't exactly carefree. They also stayed in touch through letters. Later they spent a lot of time together in Paris. Rolf de Maré was the founder of the avant-garde Swedish Ballet in Paris, you know. And Dardel created the set designs and costumes for several performances. They also traveled together, going to Africa, South America, and all over Europe. Rolf de Maré was probably the person who was closest to Dardel, except maybe for Thora, whom he later married. And his daughter, Ingrid, of course."

As Knutas listened to Anita Thorén's account, an idea started to take shape in his mind. He stood there in the cottage, now smelling of damp in the winter, with its low ceiling, and listened to the sound of the sea outside. He suddenly felt that he was standing at the very hub of what this investigation was all about.

"Do you rent this cottage out too?" he asked.

"Yes," said Anita Thorén. "But only in the summer. The water is turned off in the winter, and besides, there's no demand for it. Except in a few cases."

Knutas was instantly alert. "What sort of cases?"

"Well, sometimes I make an exception. For instance,

there was a researcher here not too long ago. He wanted to rent it in connection with the work he was doing on some project."

Knutas felt his mouth go dry. "When was this?"

"A few weeks ago. I'd have to check my notes to be more precise about the date. I think I wrote it down."

She opened her bag and took out a little pocket calendar. Knutas held his breath as she looked through it.

"Let's see now . . . He rented it from the sixteenth until the twenty-third of February."

Knutas closed his eyes and then opened them again. Egon Wallin was killed on the nineteenth. The dates matched.

"Who was this person? What was his name?"

"Alexander Ek. From Stockholm."

"How old was he? What did he look like?" Anita Thorén looked at Knutas in surprise. "He was young, maybe twenty-five or so. Tall and well-built. Not over-weight but very muscular. Like a bodybuilder."

"Did you ask him for ID?"

"No, I didn't think that was necessary. And besides, he seemed so nice. I also had the feeling that he'd been here before, but he said he hadn't when I asked."

That was enough for Knutas. He cast a quick glance around the cottage. Then he took Anita Thorén by the arm and practically pushed her outdoors.

"We'll talk more about this later. We need to cordon off the cottage and bring in the techs to go over the whole place. No one is allowed to set foot inside until that's been done."

"What? What do you mean?"

"Wait just a minute." Knutas called Prosecutor Smitten-berg on his cell phone to obtain a search warrant. Then he rang Jacobsson and asked her to make arrangements to have the area blocked off and to bring in the police dogs.

"What's this all about?" Anita Thorén eyed Knutas nervously as he finished his phone conversation.

"The dates when the cottage was rented out match the timing of the murder of the art dealer Egon Wallin. The theft of 'The Dying Dandy' may be connected to his murder. And it's possible that the researcher who rented the place is involved."

It took twenty-four hours before the media got wind of the fact that the police had blocked off Muramaris and were searching Rolf de Maré's cottage. On Tuesday afternoon someone was out taking a walk in the area and happened to see the blue-and-white police tape around the cottage. That's when the rumors started to fly. The police refused to comment on their actions, citing the need for keeping the preliminary investigation under wraps.

Johan was about to burst with frustration because no one would tell him anything. He and Pia were back at the editorial offices after going out to shoot whatever they could get at Muramaris. They'd been forced to plod through the woods to take pictures. Even then they only got partial shots of the grounds. The police had blocked off the parking lot.

As usual, Grenfors had rung Johan to demand a story to headline the news broadcast. Johan had been unable to contact either Anita Thorén or anyone else willing to make a statement. He was tearing his hair out, staring vacantly into space as Pia edited the footage they had shot.

"I've got no text," he said. "The only thing I can report is that we have nothing to report! The police aren't talking.

Nor is the owner, and there aren't any neighbors in the area. What the hell are we going to do?"

Pia stopped typing on the computer keyboard and took her eyes off the screen, with its sweeping image of the woods and the imposing building just visible in the background. She took out a small tin of snuff and took a pinch.

"Hmm . . . who the hell might know something? Wait a minute, there's a restaurant out there that's open in the summertime. And I know a girl who usually works there. It's a long shot, but I can try calling her."

Ten minutes later they were on their way to Muramaris again to do a piece-to-camera. Johan was going to report on the latest news on-site with the house in the background, even though it was barely visible because the grounds had been blocked off by the police. But it would be much more effective on TV. Pia Lilja's friend turned out to be the girl-friend of Anita Thorén's son, and she was surprisingly well informed. She knew about the police searching the place, and she told them about Nils Dardel's connection to Muramaris. She also said that it was presumably there that he had painted the stolen work of art. She said she'd heard that the police suspected that the perpetrator had rented Rolf de Maré's cottage just before Egon Wallin was murdered.

The story on the TV news startled him so badly that he nearly spilled his coffee. Of course he had expected it. The connection was bound to come out eventually; he knew that. But not so soon. He studied the reporter standing there with Muramaris in the background; he recognized the man from earlier reports. He was annoyed by the reporter's manner of speaking. So self-confident, even though he didn't have a clue as to what this was all about.

It was bad enough that he had the police on his heels; now he also had to worry about journalists. There was something about the reporter's face that he found especially irritating. Who the hell did he think he was, anyway? Then his name appeared on the screen. Oh, that's right, it was Johan Berg.

Tonight he wasn't sitting in front of the TV alone, and he had to make a real effort not to reveal how upset he was. He had to maintain a neutral expression. That was almost worse than anything else. Pretending that nothing was going on, that everything was the same as usual. He would have liked to shout to the whole world about what he had done and why. Those two seconds had been burned into his soul, and the evil wouldn't go away until he'd carried out everything he had planned. Only then would he be free. After he had washed away the shit. Done a thorough clean. Then they could start over again, and everything would be fine.

Today he'd done an extra-long workout at the gym. The more he worked out, the better control he felt he had over himself. It somehow provided a release for his frustration, nervousness, and doubt. When he studied his body in the countless mirrors in the weight-training room, he felt strong. His reflection spoke loud and clear—he'd be able to carry it out. No one was going to catch him. Not the police, not some cocky reporter who thought he was hot stuff because he was on TV. Fucking idiot. Just let that guy try and stop him.

The man who rented the cottage at Muramaris had used a false name. There was no Alexander Ek with the address he had given. He had paid cash, and the van he'd been driving was traced to a car-rental company in Visby. The police spent a long time interviewing the gardener, even though he had been away most of the week in question. But on the day when the guest arrived, he'd seen the man's vehicle and even noticed on the back window the name of the rental agency, which he was able to recall. The van had been rented for the same period as the cottage, also under a false name. All indications were that the perpetrator was indeed the man who had rented the cottage at Muramaris. Rolf de Maré's cottage was combed for evidence.

Both blonde and pitch-black strands of hair were found in the bed and bathroom. Cigarette butts, the Lucky Strike brand, were scattered outside on the ground. In a bag of rubbish forgotten behind the cottage, the police found a used bottle of foundation make-up and disposable colored contact lenses that were bright blue.

The fact that the police had cordoned off Muramaris attracted a lot of attention, and when representatives from the local media arrived on the scene, they began asking the usual questions. Knutas had instructed Norrby not to say anything about the link between Muramaris and Egon Wallin's murderer. Yet strangely enough, Johan Berg included that information in his report on the evening news. Knutas was at least grateful that the journalist didn't know more of the details. The passenger lists from the ferries had been examined, and Alexander Ek was found to be one of the passengers who arrived from Nynäshamn on the morning of Wednesday, February 16. He returned on Sunday, February 20. He did not take a car aboard the ferry.

"So at least we now know when the killer arrived and departed," said Jacobsson when the investigative team gathered for a meeting at police headquarters late that night.

"He rented a car from Avis in Östercentrum," Sohlman went on as he motioned for Jacobsson to turn off the lights. "It was a white van like this one." Sohlman pointed to the screen. "The van is being searched at the moment. The tracks in the snow at Norra Murgatan match the tire tread on this vehicle, so there's no longer any doubt. The van was definitely used by the perp."

On Wednesday morning, only a few minutes after Knutas had arrived at work, Karin Jacobsson knocked on the door of his office.

"Come in."

He could tell from her expression what she wanted to discuss. He felt a lump rise in his throat. It was as if his own fate were about to be determined. It was crazy that Karin could have such a strong effect on him. Ever since he presented his proposal to her on Monday, he'd tried not to think about the matter, but he'd been having nightmares about Karin vanishing and leaving him all alone. Their fifteen years together on the job had made a big impression on him. It wasn't so easy just to let it all go. He would never find anyone else like Karin.

Without giving away what she was thinking, Jacobsson sat down opposite him. Knutas didn't say a word, awaiting the verdict.

With each second that passed, he felt more discouraged.

"I accept, Anders. I'll stay. But on one condition. I don't want to have anything to do with the press."

Then she gave him a big smile, revealing the gap between her front teeth that had always delighted him. Knutas was so relieved that he felt dizzy. This was too good to be true.

He jumped up from his chair, rushed around the desk, and pulled his dear colleague to her feet to give her a hug.

"Thank you, Karin! Wonderful. I'm so happy! You won't regret it. I promise!"

For a brief moment she stood motionless in his embrace. Then she gently pulled away.

"You're welcome, Anders. I think it's going to be both fun and exciting for me."

"When this investigation is over, I want to take you out for a fancy dinner. We have to celebrate!"

He glanced at his watch. He would have just enough time to talk to Norrby before the meeting started. He wanted to announce the news that Karin was going to be his deputy as soon as possible. Then a thought occurred to him.

"Does Martin know about this?"

"Yes, I told him yesterday evening."

"How did he take it?"

"It was no problem. You know how he is. Don't worry about it."

Knutas had assumed that Lars Norrby would have a strong reaction, but not this strong.

"What the hell are you telling me? Is that the thanks I get after all these years? We've worked together for twenty-five years. Twenty-five years!"

His colleague had straightened up to his full height and was angrily staring down at Knutas as he sat in his old chair, feeling more uncomfortable than he'd ever felt before.

Norrby spat out his words. "And what the fuck were you planning for me to do? Sit and twiddle my thumbs behind a desk, waiting to retire? What did I do wrong?"

"Lars, please, calm down," Knutas admonished him. "Sit down."

He'd never seen his soft-spoken and amiable colleague react so forcefully. He'd explained to him that he'd had to offer Karin something dramatic in order to keep her on the force, but Norrby wasn't buying that argument.

"So is that what you have to do to get ahead in this place? Threaten to quit? Damn it, how low can you get?"

"But Lars," said Knutas, "please, let's be realistic. You and I are the same age, and I have no intention of throwing in the towel for a long time yet. I suspect that I'll be sitting here until they literally chuck me out. That's ten more years if I retire before I turn sixty-five, which is what I'm planning to do. Then somebody else will have to take over. Karin is fifteen years younger than we are. By then she'll have the experience and the influence. Besides, you're an excellent spokesman for the department, and that's what I want you to consider your primary concern from now on. Nobody is better at it than you are. And of course you'll keep the same salary."

"How decent of you," Norrby hissed. "I wouldn't have believed this of you, Anders."

He slammed the door when he left the office.

Knutas stayed sitting at his desk, unhappy with the conversation and with himself. He hadn't even managed to mention the most sensitive issue. That he'd decided to take Lars Norrby off the investigative team.

The tolling bells of the cathedral could be heard in every lane and alleyway in Visby.

Inside, the pews gradually filled up. A restrained air of gloom hovered over the mourners. Everyone seemed to be thinking about how brutally Egon Wallin had ended his days. No one deserved such a fate, and a controlled anger was evident even on the pastor's face. The art dealer had been highly popular, with a warm demeanor and a good sense of humor. His family had enriched the city with art for more than a century, and he himself had made major contributions to see that art flourished. Many people would be coming to the service to honor him today.

Knutas had positioned himself next to the imposing church doors and was discreetly studying the guests. A black-clad Monika Wallin arrived, escorted by her son on one side and her daughter on the other. *The investigation has really come to a standstill*, Knutas thought.

Lately they'd made no progress whatsoever. All the evidence and new information still hadn't produced anything concrete that would move the investigation forward. In his darkest moments, Knutas had begun to think they might never solve the murder. When the theft took place at Waldemarsudde, he thought they were close to finding the killer. But that hadn't happened. Not yet, at any rate.

He sighed to himself as he caught sight of Karin Jacobsson among the crowd. It hadn't taken long for everyone to react to the news that she was going to take over the role of assistant superintendent as of June 1. The criminal division quickly became divided into two camps—one in favor of the decision, the other against it. Knutas was astonished that the appointment had created such a deep divide. Those opposed to it were primarily his older male colleagues, while those applauding the appointment were the women and the younger members of staff.

One person who had truly surprised Knutas was Thomas Wittberg. He and Karin had always been good friends at work, but he was among those who had reacted most strongly to the news that she was going to be promoted. A chill had set in between the two of them as soon as the news was announced. Outwardly Karin didn't show any sign that it bothered her, but Knutas knew that she was hurt.

It was amazing what happened to people when conditions changed and something unexpected occurred. Then everybody's relationships came into play, and it became very obvious who your real friends were.

Knutas scanned the crowd of mourners. Many seemed to have close ties to the family. They offered warm greetings to Monika Wallin, who still hadn't taken her seat. She was standing in the entrance, just inside the church doors along with her son. The man looked tense and resolute and seemed visibly upset by the whole situation.

There were a number of people that Knutas didn't recognize. Several middle-aged men arrived as a group, and he assumed that they must be business associates from the art world. He wondered whether Egon Wallin's prospective partner in Stockholm, Hugo Malmberg, would show up. To his dismay, Knutas realized that he wouldn't recognize the man if he did appear. How stupid of him. He'd seen Malmberg only in a photograph that was ten years old, and it was a long time since he'd looked at the picture. He should have brushed up on everything about the case before the funeral. He didn't understand how he could have been so dense.

The group of men had their heads together, and they were talking in low voices, as if they didn't want any outsiders to hear what they were saying. Could Malmberg be one of them?

Knutas's thoughts were interrupted as he caught sight of the artist Mattis Kalvalis. It wasn't hard to pick him out in the crowd. He was wearing a long, pink-and-black-checked tweed coat and a bright yellow scarf. Today his hair was red and sticking out in all directions. His face was as white as chalk, and he had outlined his eyes with kohl.

To think that he came all the way from Lithuania for Egon Wallin's funeral, thought Knutas. They hadn't really known each other very long. But maybe they'd had a closer relationship than they'd let on. Knutas's suspicions were instantly aroused; he hadn't been able to let go of the idea that there may have been something going on between those two.

Knutas waved at the artist, and Mattis Kalvalis came over to say hello.

"Are you here just for the funeral?" Knutas ventured to ask in stumbling English.

He thought he saw Mattis's eyebrow twitch slightly.

"Actually I'm on my way to Stockholm, but I wanted to be here today. Egon Wallin meant a lot to me. We hadn't worked together very long, but in that short time he accomplished a lot on my behalf. And besides, he was a good friend. I really respected him."

Mattis Kalvalis seemed to mean what he said. Knutas hadn't noticed before how slender he was. He had sloping shoulders, and his coat looked too big for his thin body. He wondered if Kalvalis was on drugs. His movements were abrupt, and what he said always sounded so disjointed. Even Knutas, with his lousy English, could hear that.

It was a lovely service. Almost every seat in the cathedral was taken. The only awkward moment was when Egon Wallin's son stumbled as he approached the coffin and almost fell onto an enormous marble vase that was filled with white lilies. He dropped the rose he was holding, and the stem broke. Knutas felt truly sorry for the man. He murmured something inaudible; then with a tormented expression he placed the rose on top of the gleaming black coffin.

There was nothing to do but admit it. The police investigation of Egon Wallin's murder had come to a standstill. Knutas was becoming increasingly convinced that the guilty party was not a Gotlander, maybe not even Swedish.

The investigation involved so many theories, hints, and leads that had taken them in all sorts of different directions, and it seemed impossible to pull them together into a coherent whole. When it came down to it, Knutas wasn't even sure anymore that the murder and the theft at Waldemarsudde were connected. Maybe the sculpture had been left there simply to confuse the police.

Knutas had been in contact with Kurt Fogestam in Stockholm, but even there the police had reached an impasse.

One positive thing was that the media frenzy had gradually died down, and the investigative team was now able to do its work undisturbed. Again and again they had gone over all the information that had come in and all the witness statements, but nothing had moved the case forward. Knutas was disappointed that they'd made no progress with the paintings that were found in Egon Wallin's home, or with the mysterious renter at Muramaris. They still hadn't identified or located the man.

The Agricultural Ministry hadn't commissioned any sort of report on the future of the sugar industry, and no one there knew anyone by the name of Alexander Ek. The analysis of the strands of hair found in the hired van showed that they belonged to Egon Wallin. So it was now crystal clear: the man who had rented the cottage was the perpetrator. But where was he?

Hugo Malmberg lay in bed in his suite at the Wisby Hotel, unable to sleep. The funeral had been a torment. He'd been foolish enough to believe that he'd feel better after attending. But the sight of Egon's family, relatives, and friends had merely made him realize how alone he was.

It was absurd to think that a person could mean more after his death. When Egon was alive, they'd had a relationship, of course. It had been passionate and exciting in many ways, but Hugo hadn't been in love. There was a certain infatuation in the beginning, but that had cooled after a while. After the first thrill was gone, he usually tired very quickly of his lovers. He and Egon had met whenever possible, without demands or expectations. They had both thoroughly enjoyed the hours they spent together, but afterward they each returned to their own lives, almost forgetting about one another until the next time they met. At least that had been Hugo's experience.

Now, after Egon's tragic and violent death, he suddenly felt a much greater longing for him than when his Gotlander lover had been alive.

Maybe he was getting old. He would turn sixty-three at

his next birthday. There was something about the funeral that made him start thinking about the past. His solitude frightened him. An emptiness had crept in, and he thought a lot about the decision he had made long ago, which he now regretted. Of course, he had a large circle of acquaintances, but there was no one who truly cared about him. It was somehow such a basic assumption that somebody would be there to take care of a person when he reached old age. Someone close, with whom he had a deep connection.

Yet he'd had a good life; he couldn't complain about that. He'd had a successful career and made plenty of money. That gave him a freedom that he'd always enjoyed. He'd been able to buy whatever he liked, done things that interested him. And he'd traveled to all parts of the world. He'd been able to satisfy his needs, and his work was both interesting and stimulating. The only thing his life was really missing was a deeper love relationship. Maybe that would have been possible with Egon. If he had lived.

Egon had had a marvelous attitude toward art. He could talk about a work of art for hours, or focus on one small detail in a painting, or speculate endlessly about what an artist's intention might have been with a specific work. Maybe that was precisely what Hugo was lacking. There was a genuine quality about Egon, an unfeigned joy and a curiosity about life.

It would be a long time before Hugo Malmberg returned to Gotland. If ever. For him, the island would always be too strongly associated with Egon. He wanted to forget about everything, the whole heinous story. He no longer cared who the murderer might be. The first thing he was going to do when he got home was to book a trip to somewhere sunny and warm. Maybe Brazil, or Thailand. He deserved a few weeks' holiday after everything he'd been through.

He gave up trying to sleep and got out of bed. He stuck his feet into the slippers provided by the hotel and put on his robe. From the minibar he took out a little bottle of whisky, which he emptied into a glass, then went over to the sofa. He lit a cigarette and slowly exhaled the smoke.

It would be damned nice to get home.

At that moment he heard a clattering sound outside the window. The suite was on the second floor, but there was a roof right outside. It was an old building that had been constructed with multiple terraces and levels.

He went over to the window, pulled aside the curtains and looked out, feeling uneasy. A faint light issued from a streetlamp below, but it didn't reach far in the dark. There was nothing to see. It was probably just a cat. He closed the curtains and went back to the sofa, taking a gulp of the whisky, which warmed his throat wonderfully as he swallowed. He remembered that on Friday he was invited to a major social event at Riddarhuset, the House of the Nobility. That would be nice. He had many friends of noble birth. Another clattering sound. He gave a start and glanced at his watch. It was 2:15 in the morning. Quickly he stubbed out his cigarette, got up, and switched off the lights. The room was suddenly pitch dark. Then he crept over to the window, took up a position against the wall, and waited. The next second he heard a rattling noise followed by a thud. It sounded as if someone were right above him. He wasn't sure what to do; he didn't dare look out, for fear of being seen, in spite of the darkness. Then a light flickered outside. Through a gap in the curtains he saw the beam of a flashlight directed straight at his window.

With every muscle on full alert, he waited another minute.

Then he obeyed an impulse and picked up a table lamp with a heavy porcelain base. He took off the lampshade and carefully set it on the floor. Then he firmly gripped the base of the lamp. It was the best weapon he could find. He stood to one side of the window in a corner of the room; he'd managed to slip behind the heavy curtain to hide. The only thing he could think about was Egon's terrible fate. And the threats that he'd received himself: the note in his mailbox and the mysterious phone calls.

An ice-cold sensation settled in the pit of his stomach. Someone was out for revenge, and now it was his turn.

Just as he had predicted, it wasn't long before a creaking sound broke the silence, as if somebody were trying to pry open the window. Apparently using a crowbar. The wood gave way. Gloved fingers appeared, groping in the meager light. They unlatched the second window.

Then a leg appeared, followed by another. A tall, large man dressed in dark clothing leaned in through the window and then landed on the floor only a few feet from Hugo. The man's face was covered by a black knitted ski mask pulled over his head, with holes for his eyes.

Hugo pressed his body against the wall as best he could, hoping that this uninvited guest would move past without noticing him.

The suite was located in a corner of the hotel building, and the rooms within it were arranged in a circle. They were in the living room—the intruder could choose to turn left into the bedroom or go right into a smaller sitting room. For several moments the masked man stood motionless, and Hugo could hear his rapid breathing.

The darkness was intense. Silently he prayed that the man wouldn't be able to smell his presence. Presumably he stank of both whisky and cigarette smoke. The man turned and for several terrifying seconds Hugo was convinced that his hiding place had been discovered. But then the stranger crept toward the bedroom doorway and was swallowed up by the dark.

Hugo backed away from the curtains, keeping his eyes fixed on the bedroom. Behind him was the sitting room, the entrance hall, and then the door to the hotel corridor. He could still make his escape. It seemed unreasonable to try overpowering such a beefy intruder. He wouldn't have a chance. Thoughts whirled through his mind—he had no sense of time, he couldn't even guess how many seconds had passed.

Just as he was considering throwing himself at the door, he felt someone grab his wrist. The lamp he was holding fell to the floor with a crash. He tried to yell, but no sound came out. As if he realized that it would do no good.

An air of listless dejection hovered over the morning meeting on Wednesday. Knutas thought it was ridiculous what a difference his announcement of Karin Jacobsson's promotion had made to the general morale. Now Wittberg refused to sit next to her, and Norrby seemed to have developed an antipathy to everyone and everything. Earlier that morning Jacobsson had complained of the matter to Knutas when they had coffee together, wondering if it was really worth all the trouble. He understood how she felt, but he urged her to be patient. Given time, Norrby was bound to mellow, and even Wittberg would come round. Knutas assumed that Wittberg had ambitions and might even have expected the position himself.

It was impossible to satisfy everyone.

Right now Wittberg sat at the conference table looking sullen, even though Knutas happened to know that he was actually doing quite well. His girlfriend, who was no longer new, had moved in with him, and she seemed to be having a good influence on him. He was more alert and lively than Knutas had ever seen him before. So it was especially annoying that he should begrudge Jacobsson the promotion.

"I've done some more checking on Rolf Sandén. You know, Monika's lover," Wittberg began. "He does have an alibi for the night of the murder, but it's not exactly watertight. His friend who says that they were together might be lying. Rolf Sandén likes to play the horses, and it turns out that he has big gambling debts. He owes a lot of people money."

"Is that so?" Knutas frowned.

"On the other hand, Monika Wallin claims not to have known anything about his gambling problem or the fact that he's up to his ears in debt."

"Okay, then that's a possible motive. He's also a former construction worker. With strong muscles, in other words."

"But isn't he on disability leave?" objected Jacobsson.

"For a bad back, yes," Wittberg rebuffed her. "That doesn't mean that he's not strong."

"Even so," Jacobsson persisted, "do you really think he could hoist a body so high up if he's having back problems?"

"For God's sake," said Wittberg with a sigh. "Surely you don't think we should rule him out, do you?" He shook his head as if that was the stupidest thing he'd heard in a long time.

"Of course not," said Norrby. "Maybe he's been faking the back problems to get on sick leave. That happens all the time. Or doesn't anybody ever try to cheat the welfare system in your world?" His voice was dripping with sarcasm. Norrby and Wittberg exchanged looks.

Without warning Jacobsson stood up so abruptly that her chair fell over. She stared at Wittberg with such fury that he looked both surprised and alarmed.

"That's enough!'" she exclaimed, fixing her eyes on her colleague. "What a petty, jealous, conceited idiot you are. Do you have such a big ego that you actually begrudge me my promotion? We've worked together for years, Thomas—and I've been on the force twice as long as you have. Why are you so against me being the deputy superintendent? Tell me your reason right here and now—come on!"

Without waiting for an answer, she turned to Lars Norrby. "And you're no better. Going around sulking as if I was the one who made this decision! If you have anything to complain about, talk to Anders, but stop whining and snapping at me like a child. I'm sick of both of you, and I refuse to put up with it any longer. So let's drop it—do you understand?"

Jacobsson ended her furious outburst by picking up her chair and slamming it against the wall. Then she left the room. The door banged shut behind her.

Before anyone managed to say another word, Knutas's cell phone rang. By the time he'd finished the conversation, he looked even more somber.

"That was the Wisby Hotel. Hugo Malmberg checked in yesterday morning. He attended Egon Wallin's funeral and was going to spend the night at the hotel. But he didn't check out today, and he wasn't on the plane back to Stockholm. When the hotel staff went into his room, they found all of his belongings still there. The window had been pried open, and there were traces of blood on the floor."

"And Malmberg?" asked Kihlgård.

"Gone," said Knutas, reaching for his jacket, which was draped over the back of his chair. "Disappeared. They can't find him anywhere."

The Wisby Hotel was located on Strandgatan near Donners Square, close to the harbor. It was a beautiful and venerable luxury hotel.

There was a noticeably uneasy mood in the lobby when Knutas, Kihlgård, Sohlman, and Jacobsson all came through the door just fifteen minutes after the front-desk manager had notified the police that Hugo Malmberg was missing. After a brief greeting, the officers asked to see the room.

The suite was on the second floor. To the manager's horror, Sohlman immediately fastened police tape to the door.

"Is that really necessary?" the man asked, sounding worried. "That makes it quite clear that this is a crime scene, and it will make our guests nervous."

"I'm sorry," said Sohlman. "It can't be helped."

He sounded as if he meant what he said. Ten years earlier a female night clerk had been murdered at the Wisby Hotel—it was one of only three unsolved homicides in Gotland's history. The murder had attracted national attention, and the case had popped up in the news for years afterward. Now and then it was still discussed on crime shows on TV.

Sohlman was the first to enter the suite, and he motioned for the others to wait. They crowded into the doorway.

Cautiously he took a look around. The rooms seemed stuffy and smelled of smoke. The bed was unmade, and someone had knocked a table lamp onto the floor. In the living room a half-empty glass stood on the table, along with an ashtray containing several cigarette butts.

Sohlman pulled aside the heavy curtains and discovered at once that the window had been forced open. Malmberg's clothes had been neatly folded and placed on a chair near the bed, and his suitcase stood in the small entrance hall.

"How many people have been in the rooms?" Sohlman asked the manager after completing his survey of the suite.

"Just myself and Linda, who's working at the front desk today. She was the one who noticed that he hadn't checked out. A cab had been ordered, and the driver came into the hotel to pick him up and take him to the airport. But as you can see, he's missing."

"Did both of you come into the suite?"

"Er, yes," said the manager uncertainly. "We did. But we were only inside for a minute, at most," he said apologetically, as if he now realized that it might not have been such a good idea.

"Okay, but I don't want anyone else to come in here," said Sohlman to the others. "Someone has forced open the window, and there are clear traces of blood on the floor, as well as signs of a struggle. From now on, we need to consider this a crime scene. What sort of exits are there?"

The manager showed them the fire escape at the end of the corridor. The stairs went down the back of the building and out into the courtyard. From there it was a simple matter to walk out to the street. It was even possible to drive a car to the bottom of the stairs.

Sohlman rang for backup and stayed behind to take charge of the scene-of-crime investigation. Knutas arranged for the hotel employees to be interviewed, and officers be-

gan knocking on doors and asking guests whether they'd
seen or heard anything during the night.

As soon as Knutas was back at police headquarters, he summoned those members of the investigative team who were
in their offices to a meeting. Judging by the focused attention of everyone in the room, Jacobsson's outburst earlier in
the day was forgotten for the time being. For the first time
in days, Knutas felt the old sense of camaraderie come back
to the team. He quickly summarized what he knew about
Hugo Malmberg's disappearance.

"What do we really know about his relationship with
Egon Wallin?" asked Kihlgård.

"They were colleagues and met occasionally whenever
Wallin was in Stockholm, but as I understand it, they mostly discussed business matters," said Knutas.

"So you think that the fact that they both are, or were,
gay has nothing to do with the case?" said Jacobsson, sounding
dubious. "I disagree. There are actually several things con-
necting them now. They were both art dealers, they used
to meet in Stockholm, and they were both homosexuals. It
can't be a coincidence."

"Are we looking for a gay man in the art world of central
Stockholm?" asked Kihlgård. "If so, that would certainly
narrow our search."

"Maybe," said Jacobsson. "Or it could be that we should
just focus on their homosexuality."

"Why's that?" Wittberg objected. "Where does the theft
of the painting come in?"

"You're right. That damned painting, 'The Dying Dandy,'"
said Jacobsson pensively. "Is he trying to tell us something
by choosing that particular painting and no others? Maybe
it has nothing to do with Nils Dardel; maybe it's the motif

and the title of the painting that are important. Isn't a dandy a man with androgynous traits? A well-dressed snob, an elegant fop who frequents exclusive drawing rooms? That applies to both Egon Wallin and Hugo Malmberg.'

"Of course," said Wittberg eagerly. "That's a crystal-clear connection. The murderer is so refined that he stole one of the most famous paintings in the history of Swedish art just to make a point. He's pointing a finger at us—that's what he's doing!"

"Could it really be that simple?" wondered Kihlgård, doubtfully. "Another possibility is that he needs money for some reason."

"Yes, but how is he going to get rid of a painting like that? It'd be nearly impossible to sell it here in Sweden," said Norrby.

"But there could be a collector behind the theft," muttered Knutas.

"I think it sounds like this whole thing has to do with art; that seems to be the key," said Kihlgård. "They're both art dealers, a famous painting has disappeared, and on the day of the murder Egon Wallin held a successful gallery opening. We should be looking within the art world and forget about the homosexual element. We're just bumbling about and can't see the wood for the trees."

"I agree," said Knutas, happy that for once he and Kihlgård shared the same opinion. "They may have had illegal dealings on the side. Both were earning serious money; it's possible that their income wasn't always legally acquired."

"Maybe this is where Mattis Kalvalis and his shady manager come into the picture. He seems anything but a straight arrow," said Jacobsson. "He's a drug user; you can see that from a mile away. What about an art gang with international branches, including the Baltics?" she suggested.

"Our first priority is to find out what has happened to

Hugo Malmberg," Knutas interrupted her. "If we're dealing with the same perp, what has he done with Malmberg? And what's the next step?"

"Unfortunately, it seems unlikely that Hugo Malmberg is still alive," said Jacobsson. "Just before this meeting I checked to see whether Malmberg had received any threats, and it turns out that he did receive an anonymous threat in the mail, as well as some strange phone calls. He filed a police report a couple of weeks ago."

Knutas's face flushed an alarming crimson. "What was done about it?"

"Nothing, apparently. The police officer who took the report thought that Malmberg seemed paranoid, even though it stated in the report that he knew Egon Wallin well and they were supposed to have become business partners."

"Exactly when did these incidents occur?"

Jacobsson glanced through her notes. "The first incident, which took place on Västerbron, was on February the tenth, although at the time Malmberg just thought that someone was following him and it wasn't any sort of threat. But later he received a real threat, on the twenty-fifth."

"What kind of threat?"

"An anonymous note that said 'Soon.'"

"'Soon'?"

"Yes. Evidently that was all."

"And that was two weeks ago?"

"That's right."

Everyone in the room exchanged glances.

"This is crazy," said Knutas tensely. "Egon Wallin is murdered here in Visby. At the same time another art dealer who has had a long-standing business relationship with Wallin receives one threat after another, but nobody bothers to tell us about it. What are those guys in Stockholm doing? This is a serious breach of duty."

Knutas was breathing fast through his nose. He picked up a glass of water from the table in front of him and took several big gulps.

"Well, the only thing we can do now is press on. Sohlman is in charge of the scene-of-crime investigation in the hotel suite, and that's taking place as we speak. The hotel has been partially cordoned off, and we're continuing to knock on doors and collect information. Let's hope we get some leads very soon. In the meantime, what do we think the perp might be planning?"

"Unfortunately, I'm inclined to agree with Karin," said Kihlgård with a sigh. "Malmberg is probably already dead. All that remains is to see what the murderer will do with the body this time."

"Would he be brazen enough to hang it from Dalman Gate? Like he did with Egon Wallin?" Jacobsson suggested.

"Hmm. That seems unlikely," said Knutas. "To do that once, okay, but to dare to repeat such a maneuver? He must realize that we're on his trail and that the hotel staff would discover that Malmberg was missing. Don't you think?"

"That's not necessarily true," objected Kihlgård. "He may not be thinking rationally. He might be giddy from his success and starting to have delusions of grandeur. He might think he's invincible. That's happened before."

"Regardless, we need to keep the area around Dalman Gate under surveillance," said Knutas. "Better to be safe than sorry. We really have no idea who we're dealing with."

"What about Muramaris?"

"We'll put it under surveillance, too. It's always possible that he'll decide to go back there."

S verker Skoglund had been classmates with Egon Wallin from primary school all the way through secondary school. After that their ways had parted. Sverker had gone to sea and lived abroad for many years. When he returned to Gotland, he and Egon no longer had much in common. But their shared past prompted them to keep in touch with each other. The few times that they met in private, it felt as if they'd seen each other just the day before.

Sverker was shocked by Egon's violent death. Like many other people, he was horrified that his childhood friend should end his days in such a cruel way. He had missed the funeral service because he was working on an oil platform off northern Norway at the time. He could only get bereavement leave if the deceased was a close family member.

But now he had returned home, and the first thing he wanted to do was visit Egon's grave. Norra Cemetery was deserted when he arrived. His vehicle was the only one in the parking lot.

The snow had been shoveled off the pathways leading through the cemetery, and it was obvious that many people had walked out to the grave to show their respects to Egon. Apart from that, there were few visitors here in the wintertime.

Egon Wallin had been buried in the family plot, which was visible from a distance. His family was well-to-do, and that was apparent from the size of the monument. At the very top was a cross. Wreaths and flowers were piled up at the base, bearing witness to the recent burial. After the night's snowfall, nearly everything was covered with a frosty white blanket, but here and there a few flowers showed through, and Sverker could make out the contours of the wreaths under the snow.

Just as he stepped onto the pathway that led to the iron fence around the grave, the sun peeked out from behind the clouds. He paused for a moment, letting the sunlight warm his face. How quiet it was. How peaceful.

Reluctantly he continued. He wondered whether he had really known anything about Egon. His friend had never let on that he had a lot of money. He never talked about it, although whenever they had dinner together Egon would always insist on paying the bill. But he didn't boast about his wealth. He insisted on living in that terraced house, even though he could afford a much larger and more luxurious home. Of course, those particular terraces were uncommonly elegant and in a superb location. But still.

Sverker wondered what had happened to his old childhood friend. Whether it was some lunatic who had chosen his victim at random. Whether Egon had been killed by chance, or whether there was some reason for his murder.

He reached the enclosed area of the grave. In front was a row of wreaths, and at first that was all Sverker saw. His eyes took in the velvet ribbons, the flowers, and the printed greetings. Suddenly he caught sight of something on the frozen ground that made the hairs on the back of his neck stand on end. Under a heavy wreath with a pink-and-white ribbon from the Visby Art Association, a hand was sticking up through the snow. It was a man's hand, with the fingers curled. Sverker Skoglund slowly moved his eyes, inch by inch, as he held his breath. The man was lying on his stomach next to the monument, with his arms by his sides. He was naked except for a pair of undershorts, and he was partially covered with snow. There were bruises and wounds all over his body. Around his neck was a noose.

Sooner than he'd expected, Sverker Skoglund had received an answer to his question. There was undeniably a reason for his friend's death.

The call came in to Visby police headquarters at 1:15 in the afternoon. Twenty minutes later Knutas and Jacobsson climbed out of the first car to arrive at the site, followed closely by Sohlman and Wittberg. More police vehicles were on the way. Knutas took long strides as he headed toward the grave.

"Damn it," he said. "There's only one person it could be."

Sohlman caught up with them and was the first to approach the body. He leaned down and studied the parts sticking up from the snow.

"He's covered with wounds. Burn marks from cigarettes and other signs of abuse. The poor devil seems to have been tortured before he was killed." He shook his head.

"Is it Hugo Malmberg?" Knutas let his gaze slide over the lacerated body.

"Let's have a look." Sohlman carefully turned over the corpse. "Yes, it's him all right."

Jacobsson gasped.

Everyone bent down to look at the noose. There was no doubt that it was the work of the same person.

Knutas straightened up and surveyed the deserted cemetery.

"The body is still warm," said Sohlman. "He can't have been dead very long."

"We need to search the area with police dogs. Immediately," said Knutas. He began issuing orders. "The killer may not have got far. He must have a vehicle. When the hell does the next ferry leave for the mainland? We have to stop it and search every single car. All the passengers have to be checked. This time he's not going to get away."

Johan and Pia had worked like dogs ever since receiving the press release stating that Hugo Malmberg's tortured body had been found lying on top of Egon Wallin's grave. The murder launched a feeding frenzy in the media, and in Stockholm everybody wanted material for transmission before it had even been recorded.

This second scandalous murder in Visby had also evoked strong reactions among the locals. All of the galleries in Visby had been closed, and the owners were meeting to discuss the situation. Speculation was running rampant, and everyone was wondering whether the killer was only after people involved in the art world. The police had held a chaotic press conference, with questions hurled from all directions by the fifty or so journalists who were present. The news had even spread to the rest of Scandinavia, and reporters from both Denmark and Norway had arrived in Visby during the day.

After editing the final story for the evening news, Johan decided to stay in the office for a while. He was much too stressed to go home yet. He needed to gather his thoughts. Pia left as soon as they sent off the story because she was planning to go to the cinema. *To the cinema? Now?* thought

Johan. *Who could concentrate on watching a film after everything that happened here today?*

He sat down with a pen and paper and began to summarize the events, starting from the very beginning. The murder of Egon Wallin. The stolen paintings found in the storage room of his house. The theft of "The Dying Dandy" at Waldemarsudde. The sculpture stolen from Wallin's gallery, only to show up at Waldemarsudde at the same time as the painting was stolen. The original sculpture was at Muramaris. The perpetrator had stayed in a cottage there, at least when he committed the first murder. Then Hugo Malmberg was also killed, and his body was found on top of Egon Wallin's grave.

Johan wrote down the points of intersection between the two victims.

Both were art dealers.

Both were gay, as he understood it. Hugo was open about his sexual inclinations. Egon was not.

They were planning to become partners in an art business in Stockholm. *Partners*, thought Johan. *Were they also sexual partners?* He considered that highly likely. He added "sexual partners?" as another possible link between the two.

He sat at his desk for a while, staring at what he had written. As he saw it, there were two main questions. He wrote them down.

1.   Why was "The Dying Dandy" stolen?
2.   Was there going to be another victim?

There was nothing to indicate that the murderer would stop his killing spree. There might be more people he wanted out of the way. Johan wrote down the word "dandy." What exactly did it mean?

He looked up the word on the Internet and found this explanation:

"Snob, fop. A dandy is associated with elegance, cold-heartedness, sarcasm, irony, androgyny, or sexual ambivalence."

Did the killer view himself as a dandy? Or were his victims dandies?

Johan thought about the various individuals who figured in the investigation. Pia had made a note of the names of everyone who had been invited to Egon Wallin's gallery opening. She'd obtained the list from Eva Blom at the gallery, but Johan hadn't asked Pia how she'd managed that. He wasn't sure that he really wanted to know.

What if I start with the list? he thought. It didn't take him long to focus on one name. Erik Mattson. He was the Dardel expert who had made several statements on TV about the theft at Waldemarsudde. That was a strange coincidence. Mattson worked for Bukowski's Auction House in Stockholm. Johan decided to ring him. He pulled up Bukowski's website and found Mattson's name and photograph. Talk about a dandy. Erik Mattson was wearing a pinstriped suit, with an ice-blue shirt and tie under an elegant waistcoat. His dark hair was combed back. He had even, regular features and an aristocratic nose, dark eyes and narrow lips. He was smiling at the camera; it was a slightly superior, even ironic smile. *The classic dandy*, thought Johan. He glanced at his watch. It was too late to call now. Bukowski's would be closed. He would have to wait until the morning. He sighed and got up to put some coffee on while thoughts whirled through his mind.

Who was this Erik Mattson? Did he have any connection to Gotland?

He had no clue where the idea came from; suddenly it just popped into his head. He glanced at his watch again.

8:45. It wasn't too late to call. Anita Thorén picked up the phone herself.

"Hi, this is Johan Berg from Regional News. I'm sorry to disturb you so late in the evening, but I have an urgent question that can't wait."

"What's this about?" she asked in a friendly tone of voice.

"Well, I'm doing some research, and I understand that you rent out the cabins to guests in the summertime. How long have you been doing that?"

"Ever since we took over Muramaris in the eighties, actually. For almost twenty years now."

"Do you keep a record of who has rented the cabins?"

"Of course. I've always kept a record."

"Do you happen to have access to it at the moment?"

"Yes, my office is here at home."

"Have you got time to take a look at it?"

"Of course. I have the ledger here somewhere. Wait a minute."

The ledger? thought Johan. *What century is she living in? Hasn't she heard of computers?*

After a minute she was back.

"Okay, here it is. I always enter the name, address, and phone number of everyone who rents a cabin. I also record the amount they paid and how long they stayed."

"You don't have the information computerized?"

"No," she said with a laugh. "It's embarrassing, but this is the way I've always done things. We've been renting out the cabins for twenty years, after all. I suppose it's a form of nostalgia for me to keep things the way they were always done. Do you know what I mean?"

Johan knew exactly what she meant. His mother was just learning to send text messages, even though he'd been trying to teach her for years.

"Could you do me a favor?" he said.

"Er, yes, I suppose so," she said hesitantly.

"Could you check to see whether an Erik Mattson has ever rented a cabin?"

"All right, but it will take a while. I'll have to go through twenty years' worth of records."

"Take all the time you need."

An hour later Anita Thorén rang him back. "That was so strange. Right after we talked, Karin Jacobsson from the police called and wanted to know the same thing."

"Really?"

"Yes. And I actually did find the name of Erik Mattson listed in the records. Several times, in fact."

Johan felt his mouth go dry.

"Yes?"

"The first time he rented from us was in June 1990—so that was fifteen years ago. Rolf de Maré's cottage. For two weeks, from June the thirteenth to the twenty-sixth, together with his wife, Lydia Mattson, and their three children. I have their names too: David, Karl, and Emelie Mattson."

"And after that?"

"The second time was two years later, in August 1992. But that time he didn't bring his wife and children."

"Was he there alone?"

"No, he rented the cottage with another man."

"Do you have the man's name?"

"Of course. Jakob Nordström."

"And the last time?"

"July the tenth to the twenty-fifth of the following year. Again with Jakob Nordström. He rented the same place all three times. Rolf de Maré's cottage."

It was on that Saturday in November that he realized he was capable of killing another human being. It had taken him two seconds to make up his mind. How he wished he hadn't witnessed that scene, which had lasted no more than a moment. The images would stay with him for the rest of his life.

At first he hadn't intended to follow the man who was the focus of his interest; it was an impulse that made him do it. He was just going to walk past the gallery. He hadn't yet decided how to deal with what he'd found out; he had no idea what to do about it. He was planning to put it all aside until he figured out his next move. But that wasn't how things worked out. Maybe what happened was predestined. That was what he thought afterward. And after what he'd been forced to see, there was only one option. The realization had struck him like the blow of a club. Brutally, irrevocably.

He almost missed him. When he turned onto Österlång-gatan, he saw Hugo Malmberg locking up the gallery, even though it was an hour before closing time. Curiosity got the better of him. He decided to follow Malmberg and find out why the man he was tailing had broken his routine.

He followed a few yards behind, over to the bus stop on Skeppsbron. Malmberg was smoking a cigarette and talking to somebody on his cell phone. Then the bus arrived. He dashed across the street to climb aboard, with Malmberg right in front of him. Uncomfortably close. If he simply reached out his hand, he could have touched the man's arm.

He felt sick at the sight of the elegant woollen coat, the scarf nonchalantly flung over his shoulder. That self-confident, pompous man who thought he was invulnerable; so far he was happily unaware that his life was about to be shattered. Malmberg got off the bus near the NK department store on Hamngatan. He turned down Regeringsgatan and headed along the street for a while, then turned left onto a side street. He smoked another cigarette. Cars passed and people strolled by, going home or on their way into the city. Still curious, he continued following the man. He'd never been in this part of town before.

He was careful to keep a good distance between them, and for safety's sake, he stayed on the opposite pavement. As luck would have it, there were still enough people about to prevent him drawing attention to himself. Suddenly the man he was following disappeared. Swiftly he crossed the street to stand in front of the nearest building. The facade had seen better days, and the display window had been painted black making it impossible to see inside. A small sign on the metal door said "Video Delight," lit up in red and gold. This must be where Malmberg had gone. It wasn't hard to guess what type of shop it was. He waited a minute before entering.

Inside he found a stairway illuminated with tiny red lights that led him downstairs. There he found a big DVD shop offering nothing but porn films, all the hard-core kind. Sex toys were also for sale, and there were small booths for private viewings. Behind the counter stood a young girl wearing a black hoodie. She seemed completely unaffected by the place; she might as well have been selling pastries or sewing supplies. She was chatting happily with a guy her own age as he put price tags on DVDs. Everywhere were close-up images from porn films on big-screen TVs. A few male customers were making their selections from the films.

Slowly he walked around, looking for the man he'd been following. The place was bigger than it had seemed at first glance. He peeked into one of the small, cramped booths. All he saw was a black vinyl recliner in front of a huge TV screen, an ashtray, tissues, a wastebasket, and a remote control. Nothing else.

He made a quick survey of all the empty booths; Malmberg seemed to have been swallowed up by the earth. Puzzled, he went over to the red-painted counter and asked the girl if there were any other rooms.

"Yes," she said, pointing to a door that he hadn't noticed before. "In there. But it's only for guys. Homos, you know." A small sign on the door said "Boys Only."

"And there's a fee. Eighty kronor."

"Okay," he said and paid her the money.

She cast a deliberate glance at a basket on the counter. It was full of condoms.

"They're free," she said, lowering her voice. "Well, you can have two for free. If you need more, you have to pay."

He shook his head, opened the door, and went inside.

It was even darker in there, and the stairway was narrower and steeper than the first one.

The only sound was the roar of the air conditioning. There was a fresh, almost herb-like fragrance, almost as if it were a spa. When he reached the bottom of the stairs, he found a long, narrow corridor stretching out in front of him. It was dimly lit, with red neon lights along the ceiling. The walls were painted red, and the floor was black. On either side were booths that seemed to be the same as those upstairs. Several doors were closed, and faint groans were audible through the thin walls.

A guy who looked to be about twenty-five was standing at a booth with the door half open. As he passed, he caught sight of someone sitting inside. The guy was obviously going to go in and keep the customer company.

Everywhere were screens showing porn films. He wondered where Malmberg had gone. Maybe he was sitting in one of these booths, enjoying himself. He found the thought disgusting.

A man came out of one of the rooms, and his face lit up. The man tried to tempt him into the room without saying a word, just using blatant body language to indicate what he wanted. He hurried past.

The place was unbelievable. The corridors were like a labyrinth, and he soon lost track of where he'd entered. All he saw were more booths and pictures.

He started feeling dizzy, and he longed to get out of there. He tried to find his way back, hurrying in the direction that he thought would lead to the stairs. He turned out to be mistaken. Instead he ended up in front of a door at the end of the corridor where he had heard the moaning. Cautiously he opened the door just enough to peer inside. He was looking at a small projection room. On one wall was a screen showing the same type of film that he'd already seen a hundred times over during his brief visit here. All of the furnishings were black—the walls, ceiling, floor, sofa, and armchairs.

At first he saw only three bodies that were fully engaged on the sofa in front of the screen. He immediately recognized Malmberg as one of the men. Then he saw the face of another, who might have been in his fifties. The man looked familiar, but he couldn't place him. The face of the third person wasn't visible. He was younger, and the two older men were leaning over him. They were all naked, and none of them seemed to notice his presence. All of their attention was focused on each other.

He was seized by a sense of unreality—as if the scene unfolding before his eyes couldn't possibly be happening.

Just as he was about to turn round and leave, he saw the face of the third man.

Two seconds. That was all it took to recognize him.

Quickly he shut the door. For a moment he stood outside, leaning against the wall. Sweat was pouring down his face. He wanted to scream.

He stumbled back along the corridor and finally managed to locate the stairs to the exit. He avoided looking at the girl standing behind the counter.

Out on the street he blinked in the light. A woman pushing a stroller walked past. Daily life was proceeding as usual. When he turned the corner, he threw up. Not only because of what he'd just witnessed, but because of what he was going to have to do.

O n Friday morning Jacobsson knocked on Knutas's office door as soon as he turned up at police head-quarters. Her eyes were shining with eagerness.

"Listen to this—I've uncovered some damned interesting stuff. I tried to call you last night, but nobody answered."

"Come on in."

"I checked out Hugo Malmberg's background. You've got to hear this." She sat down on the sofa in Knutas's office.

"He lived alone in a gorgeous apartment on John Erics-sonsgatan in Kungsholmen, and for years he was part own-er of that gallery on Österlånggatan. He was openly gay, and I had the impression that he always had been, but that turned out not to be true. He was once married to a woman named Yvonne Malmberg, but she died a long time ago, back in 1962. So that's over forty years ago. And guess how she died."

Knutas shook his head without saying anything.

"She died in childbirth. To be more precise, in the mater-nity ward at Danderyd Hospital."

"What about the child?"

"It was a boy. He survived and was given up for adoption when he was only a few days old."

Knutas whistled.

"And that's not all."

"No?"

"Do you know who rented Rolf de Maré's cottage out at Muramaris several times?" She went on without waiting for an answer. "That valuer at Bukowski's. Erik Mattson."

Johan had a busy three days ahead of him. On Friday he took the first plane back to Stockholm. He'd made an appointment to meet Erik Mattson at Bukowski's Auction House at ten o'clock. Then he was going to have lunch with his youngest brother. In the afternoon, the head of the news bureau wanted to see him. Sometime in between he really needed to squeeze in a meeting with Max Grenfors to discuss a pay raise. In the evening there was going to be a family dinner at his mother's house out in Rönninge, and on Saturday morning he'd made an appointment to meet the person who was going to sublet his apartment. Johan had received permission to lease the apartment for a year. The prospective tenant was a colleague from Swedish TV in Karlstad who had been hired for a temporary position in the sports division.

Then on Saturday afternoon Johan had to fly back to Visby because he and Emma were planning to meet the pastor at four o'clock. What a schedule, he thought as he sat on the plane, squashed next to a man who must have weighed over three hundred pounds. He didn't have the energy to change seats.

Erik Mattson was just as elegant in person as in the photo

on the web page of the auction house. He was an attractive man with a distinct sexual aura; Johan wondered if he was gay. They sat down in an empty conference room, and Erik served coffee and Italian biscotti. Johan chose to get right to the point.

"I understand that you've stayed at Muramaris many times. Why is that?"

"I was there for the first time when I was nineteen. Some of my friends and I were studying art history at the university, and we were on Gotland for a cycling holiday. Even back then I was fascinated by Dardel's work, and I knew that he'd spent several summers at Muramaris."

He smiled at the memory.

"I remember how we went down to the beach and pictured Dardel walking along the same stretch of shoreline almost a century earlier. We imagined him with Rolf de Maré, Ellen, and Johnny, and all the other artists who came to visit. What a life they lived. Filled with love, art, and creativity. Carefree in so many ways, and removed from reality," he said wistfully.

"And then you returned later on?"

"Yes," he said, sounding distracted. "When my ex-wife, Lydia, and I were still married, we once rented Rolf de Maré's cottage, and we took all the children along. That was years ago. But it wasn't a very successful holiday. It's not a practical place for young children. Steep steps down to the beach and not much of a play area. And the cottage isn't very big."

"But you went back again?"

"Yes, I've been there twice since then."

"Who went with you, if I might ask?"

"A friend of mine. His name is Jakob," replied Mattson tersely. Suddenly he looked uncomfortable. "Why do you want to know all this?"

"There are actually two reasons," Johan lied. "Partly to get some background material for our report on the murder on Gotland. But I also happen to think that Muramaris is an interesting place, and I'd like to do a documentary about it for Swedish TV."

"Really?" Erik Mattson's voice suddenly took on renewed energy. "That's fantastic. There's so much to tell, and the place is spectacular inside. Have you seen the amazing sandstone fireplace that Ellen created?"

Johan shook his head. He studied Mattson intently. "So you've been married. How many children do you have?"

"Three. But what does that have to do with anything?"

"I'm sorry. I was just curious. You said that you took 'all' the children along, so I was picturing a whole flock."

"I see." Erik Mattson laughed. He looked relieved. "I've only got three. But they're not kids anymore. They're all grown up now. Living their own lives."

Johan didn't really know what compelled him to take that route on his way home. But after having a pleasant dinner at his mother's house in Rönninge and seeing all his brothers, he found himself driving past Erik Mattson's building on Karlavägen. He parked the car outside and looked up at the lovely facade. It was an impressive, well-kept building with an ostentatious front entrance and a profusion of flower beds. Without knowing what he expected, Johan got out of the car and went over to try the door. Locked, of course. There were lights on in most of the windows. Earlier in the day he'd checked to see which apartment belonged to Mattson, and now he saw that there, too, the lights were on. There was both an intercom and a keypad that required a code number. On impulse, Johan pressed the number next to Mattson's name. He tried again several times with no response. Then he heard a man's voice, but it wasn't Mattson's. There was loud music playing in the background. The man sounded speedy and slightly drunk.

"Hi, Kalle. You're late. We almost left without you, damn it."

The man cut off the connection. But there was no buzzing sound, so he hadn't unlocked the door. Johan hurried back to his car. After several minutes three men came out of the entrance; one of them was Erik Mattson. They were all in high spirits and stood outside the door for a moment. Johan slouched down so as not to be seen, but he could hear their voices.

"Where the hell did he go?"

"He wasn't mad, was he?"

"Naw, not Kalle. He must have decided to go on ahead."

The two men that Johan didn't recognize seemed to be about the same age as Mattson. Attractive, fashion-conscious professionals from Östermalm wearing expensive suits under their coats, their hair slicked back.

They walked past Johan's car without noticing him and disappeared into Humlegården Park. Johan got out of his car and followed. When they reached Club Riche they went inside. The place was packed, and Johan was lucky that there wasn't a line. The music was pounding, and everyone was walking around with drinks in their hands.

If only he could stay out of sight. Mattson would recognize him at once, since they'd met earlier in the day. On the other hand, it really wouldn't be so strange to see a journalist in Club Riche on a Friday night. This thought was immediately reinforced when he found some of his colleagues at the bar.

He kept an eye on Mattson, who was mingling with the crowd. He seemed to know everybody. Johan noticed that he downed one drink after the other without seeming to be affected.

All of a sudden Mattson was gone. Johan left his friends and walked around looking for him. He started getting worried. Had he lost the guy? Then he saw him talking to an older man. They were standing close together and seemed to be having an intimate conversation.

The older man abruptly headed for the exit and disappeared. A couple of minutes later, Mattson also left the club. Outside, Johan saw both men get into a cab. He jumped into the next taxi and told the driver to follow. Johan didn't really know what he was doing. He had to get up early the next morning and clean the apartment before his tenant arrived. Then he had to pack his suitcase and fly to Gotland. He didn't have time to be playing spy games.

The taxi ride was a short one. The cab stopped outside a battered-looking doorway in a back alley in central Stockholm. Mattson and the older man got out. Johan quickly paid his own taxi driver and got out to follow them. Down a staircase he found himself in a sort of video shop. There he paid the entrance fee so he could proceed even farther down into the depths of the building.

It didn't take long for Johan to understand what Erik Mattson was mixed up in.

Johan and Pia were in charge of the story for the Sunday broadcast; Gotland was where the hottest news events were happening, for a change. Johan told his colleague what he'd discovered in Stockholm when he tailed Erik Mattson.

Pia's eyes opened wide. "Is that true?"

"Absolutely."

"It sounds unbelievable. But do you think he's the murderer?"

"Sure, why not?"

"Have you told the police about this?"

"No, I wanted to confirm all the details first."

"So you don't think we can use this for our report in some way?"

"Not yet. It's premature. I need to do more research first, find out more about Mattson."

That evening as Johan drove home, his head was filled with contradictory thoughts. Erik Mattson worked at Bukowski's Auction House and was one of Sweden's top experts on twentieth-century Swedish art. At the same time, he frequented obscure gay clubs and prostituted himself. Johan couldn't make sense of the whole thing. It couldn't be because Mattson needed the money. He was an enigmatic figure, and Johan was becoming more and more convinced that he'd had something to do with the murders. And the theft of the painting. He was an expert on Nils Dardel, after all.

His ponderings were interrupted by the ringing of his phone. It was Emma, who wanted him to buy some diapers on his way home.

To Johan's disappointment, Elin was already in bed for the night by the time he got home. How quickly we get accustomed to new routines, he thought. Before, he was used to being away from her for weeks on end; now he hated not being able to say goodnight and nuzzle her neck before she went to sleep.

Emma had made salmon pasta, and they had a glass of wine with their dinner. Afterward they curled up together on the sofa, sharing what was left of the wine.

"So what did you think of the pastor? We've hardly had any time to talk about it," said Emma, stroking his hair.

"She was all right, I suppose."

"Do you still think we should get married in a church?"

"That's what I'd like."

They'd had this discussion many times since they agreed to get married. Emma wanted to get the wedding out of the way without a lot of fuss.

"I've already gone through the whole circus once before," she said with a sigh. "That was enough."

"But what about me? Doesn't it matter what I want?"

"Of course it does. But can't we find some sort of compromise? It's okay that you don't want to go to New York and get married at the consulate, even though I think that would be terribly romantic. I can understand that you want all of our family and friends to be present. But not in a church, and not in a white dress, and definitely not with an awful cake that we have to cut together."

"But sweetheart, I want to walk down the aisle with you. I want to wear a tux and see you in a white wedding gown. That's a dream image that I've always had in my mind."

He looked so serious that Emma had to laugh.

"Are you for real? I thought only girls had those kinds of fantasies."

"What sort of sexist remark is that?"

"Johan, I just can't. I really can't go through that whole thing again. It would be like replaying the past. Can't you understand that?"

"No, I really can't. Replaying? How can you call it a replay? I'm the one you're going to marry, Emma. You can't compare me to Olle."

"No, of course not. But all the work, all the preparations . . . not to mention the expense. I don't really think my parents would want to pay for another wedding."

"To hell with the money. I want the whole world to know that we're getting married. And it doesn't have to be that expensive. We can serve wine in a box and chili. What does it matter? We can have the party in the garden in the summertime."

"Are you crazy? You want to have the party here? Not on your life!"

"If you keep on like this, I'm going to think that you really don't want to go through with it after all."

"Of course I want to marry you."

She showered him with kisses until he completely forgot what they'd been arguing about.

On Monday morning when Johan arrived at the editorial offices, he noticed at once that something wasn't as it should be. He held up his arm to prevent Pia, who was right behind him, from going inside. They collided in the doorway. They were both holding coffee cups, and the hot liquid sloshed over the sides as Johan stopped her.

"What's wrong?" she asked in surprise.

"Wait a second," he said, holding up a finger to hush her. "There's something strange here."

The Regional News office was a long, narrow room; at one end a map of Gotland and Fårö usually hung on the wall. Now it was gone. Someone had put up a photograph in its place, yet in the dim light Johan couldn't tell what the picture was. But that wasn't the only thing. Something was fishy with the computers. All three were on, even though he was sure he'd turned them off before leaving the office the previous evening. He whispered this to Pia. Cautiously he stepped forward. There wasn't a sound. He opened the door to the broadcast booth, but it was empty.

"Huh," said Pia. "Maybe somebody from Radio was working here overnight."

"Shh." Johan gave her another nudge.

When he got close enough to the far wall to see what the photograph showed, at first he couldn't believe his eyes.

It was a picture of himself, sitting in his car outside Erik Mattson's house. The picture was dark, but it was still possible to see that he was staring up at a window.

Slowly he sank down onto a chair, without taking his eyes off the photo.

"What's wrong?" he heard Pia saying behind him. Johan couldn't say a word.

The entire team was present at the police meeting on Monday morning. Someone had made coffee and set on the table a basket of fresh cinnamon rolls from the Siesta pastry shop. Kihlgård was whistling merrily. Knutas guessed that he was the one who had brought the provisions. Kihlgård loved to munch, as he put it.

The murder of Hugo Malmberg had pushed the controversy about Karin Jacobsson's promotion onto the back burner. Knutas was grateful for that.

The meeting began with Jacobsson reporting on what she'd discovered about Hugo Malmberg's background.

"So who's the son who was given up for adoption?" asked Wittberg.

"I think it would be worthwhile checking out one potential candidate," said Jacobsson. "Someone who was invited to Egon Wallin's gallery opening, who was in Visby at the time of Wallin's death, who has a special interest in Nils Dardel, and who also happened to rent the cottage at Muramaris. He's in his forties, and he's been popping up in the investigation like a jack-in-the-box right from the start."

"Erik Mattson," exclaimed Kihlgård. "That soft-spoken, ultra-correct man who has made so many public statements with regard to the theft at Waldemarsudde! Could he really be the perp?"

"But that's impossible. He's much too thin," objected Wittberg. "Do you really think he could have hoisted Egon Wallin up in the gate and dragged Hugo Malmberg—his father—to the cemetery? Not on your life."

"He could have had help, of course. I realize that he couldn't have done it alone." Jacobsson glared at Wittberg. Apparently the promotion controversy wasn't completely forgotten, after all.

"And the motive would be . . . what? The fact that his biological father had abandoned him?" Wittberg looked dubious.

Lars Norrby was quick to chime in. "And what about Egon Wallin? Why would Erik Mattson kill him?"

"Obviously I don't have answers to all the questions," said Jacobsson crossly.

"So you haven't checked to see whether Mattson really is the son given up for adoption?" Knutas gave Jacobsson an inquiring look.

Her face fell. "Well, no . . ." she had to admit. "I haven't."

"Maybe that would be a good idea before we start jumping to conclusions." Even though his tone of voice was a bit stern, he sympathized with Jacobsson when he saw the pleased expressions on the faces of Wittberg and Norrby.

Later that afternoon, there was a knock on Knutas's door. Jacobsson came in and sat down with a dejected look.

"I've talked to Erik Mattson's adoptive parents—Greta and Arne Mattson, who live in Djursholm. Hugo Malmberg is his father, but they never told Erik that he was adopted. He has no idea."

"What sort of relationship does Mattson have with his parents?" Knutas asked.

"It's nonexistent. They broke off all contact with him when it became apparent that he was using drugs and was homosexual."

"Homosexual? He's gay too? That seems to be a common thread in this whole investigation."

"I agree."

"But that sounds rather harsh. Did they really break off contact just because of that? It certainly doesn't sound very loving."

"No, it doesn't," Jacobsson agreed. "On the other hand, they seem to have a good relationship with his ex-wife, Lydia, and his children. Or at least two of them."

"How old are they? His children, I mean."

"The boys, David and Karl, are twenty-three and twenty-one. The daughter, Emelie, is nineteen."

"Which child doesn't have a good relationship with the grandparents?"

"Apparently, David. The eldest. I talked to Erik's father, who by the way sounded very nice, and he said that David was the most sensitive and was hit the hardest by the divorce. Erik and his wife split up because of his drug abuse. And he lost custody of the children because he neglected them when they spent weekends with him. But that didn't seem to bother David. Evidently he has always sided with his father."

Knutas fixed his eyes on Jacobsson for a long time without saying anything. Then, with a resolute expression, he picked up the phone as if he'd suddenly had an idea.

It took Anita Thorén, the owner of Muramaris, less than fifteen minutes to get to police headquarters after Knutas rang.

"How good of you to come over so quickly. As I said on the phone, I'd like you to have a look at some pictures."

"Certainly."

Anita Thorén sat down on the sofa in Knutas's office. In front of her he placed five photographs of men in their twenties. He asked her to study the pictures carefully and take her time. Jacobsson and Wittberg were present in the room as witnesses.

"That's him," she said. "That's the man who rented the cottage in February. I'm absolutely positive."

The silence in the room was palpable as she placed a photo on the table. The picture showed a smiling young man. His hair was cut short and he looked well groomed. He appeared to be muscular and very fit.

The young man staring into the camera was none other than David Mattson.

Knutas decided that both Erik Mattson and his son David should be brought in for questioning. He called Kurt Fogestam, who promised to see to it that both men were picked up immediately. Because Anita Thorén had identified David, the prosecutor decided to issue a warrant for his arrest. Traces of Egon Wallin's hair and clothing had been found both in the cottage and in the van, so there was a definite link to the man who had rented the cottage. They now knew that he was the murderer. The only question remaining was whether he had acted alone or together with his father. Knutas still couldn't explain what Egon Wallin had to do with the case, or why "The Dying Dandy" had been stolen. But he hoped that everything would become clear during the interrogation.

Knutas cursed himself for not thinking to check up earlier on the people who had rented cabins at Muramaris. They'd been so preoccupied with trying to locate the person who'd rented the cottage when Egon Wallin was murdered that they hadn't thought about going back in time. That infuriated him. His oversight might be partially due to all the turbulence created by Jacobsson's promotion to assistant superintendent; it had made him shift his focus away from the investigation.

While they waited to hear from the Stockholm police, a mood of tense anticipation prevailed at police headquarters.

Knutas stood at the window in his office and lit his pipe. He inhaled deeply and then blew the smoke out through the window.

He was on tenterhooks. They were finally on the verge of untangling the Gordian knot that had grown more complicated and mysterious as time passed. He rang Lina and told her what was going on, explaining that he wouldn't be home for dinner or perhaps at all that night. She was happy, for his sake, as well as for herself and the children. Now they'd finally be able to see him in the evenings again.

It took exactly an hour for Kurt Fogestam to call. He sounded shaken. "You'd better sit down," he said.

"What's wrong?"

"Just sit down, Anders, before I tell you." Knutas sank down onto a chair without taking the pipe out of his mouth.

"What's happened?"

"The officers who were supposed to pick up Erik Mattson went to Bukowski's first, but he hadn't turned up for work today. His boss didn't seem surprised. He said that Mattson occasionally doesn't come in. Clearly he has an alcohol problem. Or rather, had."

"What do you mean by 'had'?"

"They just phoned from Karlavägen, where Mattson lives. No one opened the door when they rang the bell, so they decided to force their way in. They found Erik Mattson lying in bed. He was dead."

Knutas couldn't believe his ears. "Murdered?"

"We don't know yet. The ME is on his way over there right now. But that's not all. Do you know what was hanging above the bed?"

"No."

"That painting that was stolen from Waldemarsudde. 'The Dying Dandy.'"

The house stood at the intersection of two residential streets in an idyllic neighborhood, close to the school in central Roma.

It was nine thirty in the morning. He had purposely waited until the worst of the morning rush hour was over, with people going off to work, children heading to daycare centers or to school, owners walking their dogs and coming out to pick up the morning newspapers. By now an air of calm had settled over the neighborhood, and the street was quiet.

From where he was standing he could see the woman moving from room to room on the ground floor of the house. That must be Emma Winarve. Discreetly he took out his binoculars. He was hiding behind some shrubbery so that he wouldn't be seen from any of the well-tended houses lining the street.

She was beautiful, dressed in a long, pink bathrobe made of some soft fabric. Her hair was sandy colored, her eyes dark under distinctive eyebrows. She had high cheekbones and regular, classical features. No longer really young, of course, but still attractive. Tall and stately. He wondered how strong she was.

He saw her bend down and pick up the child. The next minute she appeared upstairs. He could just make out her shape as she moved from room to room. Through the cold lenses of his binoculars, he could follow her movements. Now she was leaning down, presumably to put the baby to bed. She stood there for a moment, doing something.

Then her bathrobe fell away, and he caught a quick glimpse of her bare back before she disappeared from view. She must have gone into the bathroom to take a shower. That was perfect. Swiftly he crossed the street, opened the gate, and resolutely entered the property as if it were the most natural thing in the world. From a distance he could tell that the front door wasn't locked. *Great*, he thought. That would only normally happen way out in the country.

He looked around before he opened the door. Not a soul as far as the eye could see. Quickly and quietly he slipped inside, finding himself in a messy hall filled with clothes, shoes, and gloves all jumbled together. He could smell coffee and toast. Deep inside of him a feeling surged up that confused him for a few seconds. He made a concentrated effort to regain control of himself. Stay focused, he thought. Right now everything depended on staying focused. He peeked inside the kitchen. A radio was on, playing music at a low volume; there were dirty dishes in the sink and crumbs on the table. He made his way into the living room, where two large sofas faced each other. He saw a fireplace, a TV, rugs, books and newspapers, a bowl of fruit, and a pair of ceramic candlesticks with candles that had burned down. Again that feeling welled up inside him; he pushed it back.

As he climbed the stairs, he heard the shower running. She was singing. He crept over to the door, which had been left half open. It was a big bathroom with two sinks, side by side, a toilet on the opposite wall of the room, a bathtub with a Jacuzzi, and a shower booth with frosted glass. He could see the woman's body in silhouette through the glass. Her loud, clear voice bounced off the walls.

The feeling came over him again. His eyes burned. Suddenly he was furious at her. There she stood, naked and beautiful, singing without a care in the world. She had no idea what was going on around her. What was happening inside of him. Fucking idiot. Rage shot up into his forehead, clouding his vision. He would show her. He gripped the piano wire between his fingers. Closed his eyes for a second to concentrate before he attacked.

Suddenly he was interrupted by a sound behind him. A few cries that threatened to become sobs. The woman didn't seem to notice. She kept on singing while the shower water poured out.

Abruptly he turned around, slipped out of the bathroom and into the room where the sound was coming from. The blinds were pulled down, and in the darkness stood a crib. In it lay the baby, now crying louder.

In a flash he picked up the little girl, wrapped in her blanket, and dashed down the stairs to the ground floor and out into the hall.

He could still hear the woman singing as he closed the front door behind him.

U nsuspecting, Johan picked up the phone. All he could hear at first was a hysterical person crying and screaming as she rattled off a string of words that didn't make any sense. It took several seconds before he realized it was Emma and that she was shouting something about Elin. When Johan heard the name Elin coupled several times with the word "gone," his blood turned ice cold.

"Calm down. Tell me what happened?"

"I . . . I was in the shower," she sobbed. "I had put Elin in her crib, and when I came out, she was gone, Johan. Gone."

"But have you looked everywhere? Maybe she somehow managed to crawl out."

"No!" she shrieked. "No-o-o! She can't crawl out on her own! Didn't you hear what I said? She's gone! Someone must have come in and taken her!"

She burst into such heart-rending sobs that Johan felt his nerves shatter. He could feel himself starting to cry. It couldn't be true. It just couldn't be.

Pia was sitting next to him and had heard every word that Emma said. She cast a glance at the photo on the wall.

The picture of Johan sitting in his car outside Erik Mattson's apartment was still hanging there.

Suddenly the threat felt very real.

When the police arrived at Emma's house in Roma, she was collapsed in the nursery upstairs. She was totally unresponsive, and the officers had to call an ambulance to take her to Wisby Hospital.

The police cordoned off the house and street. Roadblocks were put up at all the routes to and from Roma, and also at the entrances to Visby and down by the harbor. The next ferry to Nynäshamn was due to depart at four o'clock, and all the vehicles waiting at the dock were searched. At the airport every passenger was checked. It would be impossible for the kidnapper to leave Gotland with the child, at least by the usual means of transport.

At first Knutas couldn't believe it when he heard that Johan Berg's daughter had been kidnapped. But he realized immediately that the reporter must have been conducting his own investigation and provoked the perpetrator in some way. He evidently hadn't learned from previous experience to stay out of police business. Last time it had nearly cost Johan his life; now it was his little daughter's life that hung in the balance. Knutas truly felt for Johan, and he called him as soon as he found out what had happened. No answer, of course. Knutas then discovered that

Johan was at the hospital with Emma, and he contacted him there. The reporter's voice was barely audible when he at last picked up the phone.

"I feel terrible about this," said Knutas. "I want you to know that we're doing everything we can."

"Thank you."

"I need to know what sort of contact you've had with the killer," said Knutas. "Have you talked to him?"

"No. But something else happened."

"What?"

Johan told the superintendent about the photo that was left on the wall of the Regional News office.

"Do you know who the murderer is?"

"I think it's Erik Mattson. The man who's an art valuer at Bukowski's."

"No, it's not," said Knutas. He didn't want to mention that Mattson was dead, because he thought that would alarm Johan further. The situation was bad enough as it was. "He's not the one. It's his son. David Mattson. It's possible that he might try to contact you. We don't know what he wants, but if you hear from him, you need to call me immediately. Do you understand, Johan? It's tremendously important that you call my direct line at once. Then you and I will discuss how to handle the situation. Okay?'

"Okay," said Johan tonelessly. "Now I'd better get back to Emma."

T he night passed without a word from David Mattson. The police maintained their tight control on all exits from Gotland. For safety's sake, Muramaris was kept under surveillance, but nobody really thought he would be stupid enough to go back there. They were dealing with a dangerous man who had already killed at least twice. It was still not clear whether David Mattson had also murdered his father. A post-mortem needed to be performed before the ME could answer that question.

Knutas sat in his office at police headquarters in a state of anguish. A kidnapped child was the worst scenario he could imagine. The most frustrating part was that he felt so helpless. As long as the kidnapper refused to make contact and remained holed up somewhere, brooding, it was virtually impossible to track him down. A team of police officers was at the house in Roma, and the phone was being tapped. Emma Winarve was still in hospital. They had tried to interview her, but it was proving nearly impossible to get anything out of her. She was suffering from a complete nervous breakdown.

Where was the kidnapper? In the summertime he might pitch a tent or slept in a camper, or even in his car if need be. But at this time of year? It was most likely that he'd broken into a summerhouse somewhere—there were plenty on Gotland. But where should the police start looking? Summerhouses in remote locations were everywhere on the island, and on Fårö. But if he decided to let the child live, he would need food and diapers. What was his intention when he kidnapped Elin?

Sooner or later David Mattson would make contact.

Nothing was so desolate in winter as a campsite. Johan parked his car close to the shoreline. He got out and trudged toward the public lavatories. The whole place was quiet, deserted, and closed down. The snowdrifts were higher here. It probably hadn't been plowed all winter. And the steep slope he was descending hadn't been sanded either. The question was whether he'd be able to make it back up, but he wasn't worried about that at the moment. All he wanted was to have Elin in his arms.

David had said that he wanted to make an exchange, but he refused to reveal on the phone what his demands were in order to give Elin back. He said that he would tell Johan in person. Johan didn't think he had any choice but to go along with this condition. He'd been sternly warned not to contact the police. If David got the slightest indication that Johan wasn't alone, that would be the end of Elin.

Utter silence had settled over the beach. The open water was gray and inhospitable. The cold was raw and damp, seeping in under his clothes. As Johan approached the building with the showers and toilets, he saw a car parked some distance away, a blue Citroën. There was no one in sight. His nerves were stretched taut. He didn't know what David looked like, only how old he was. Johan walked around the wooden building. The windows were boarded up and the doors locked. It was easy to see why David had wanted to meet him here. Close to the city, but as deserted as could be.

Suddenly he caught sight of a tall, dark-clad figure approaching from the sea. He was powerfully built, wearing a down jacket with a knitted cap on his head. Johan felt the ground swaying under his feet. The man who was walking toward him had killed two people in cold blood and taken an eight-month-old child hostage. Johan was about to stand face to face with a psychopath.

At that moment he realized what an idiot he was for not contacting the police. He was unarmed and completely at the mercy of a madman. What was he thinking? That David would simply hand over Elin?

He stood motionless, waiting, as his brain shifted up a gear. Of course David didn't have Elin with him. Johan felt so helpless. He wondered wildly what he should say or do in order to have the greatest chance of seeing Elin again.

David stopped a few feet away.

"You need to stop following my father," he said. "Leave him alone from now on and you'll get your daughter back. You have to promise, on your honor. Leave Pappa alone."

So that's what it's all about, thought Johan. His visit to Erik Mattson, the fact that he'd been tailing the man. David wanted to protect his father. That was why he'd kidnapped Elin. It was that simple.

"Yes, of course. I promise to stop at once. My daughter is much more important to me. I'll quit right now. Just give Elin back."

"Elin? Is that her name? I didn't know what I should call her."

He smiled. Johan saw the insanity in his eyes. The man looked drugged. It was impossible to make eye contact. David kept evading his glance. Maybe he was taking anabolic steroids, considering his size.

"Where is she?" Johan controlled his voice, not wanting his desperation to show. He needed to stay calm.

David opened his mouth to reply, but was interrupted by a bellow coming from the roof of the lavatory building.

"Police! Put your hands up. Don't move."

David looked around in bewilderment. Johan stood as if paralyzed, incapable of thinking sensibly. This couldn't be happening.

The arrest of David Mattson proceeded without incident. Four police officers overpowered him before he even knew what was happening. He was handcuffed and led away to a police vehicle. Johan stayed where he was, watching mutely.

Out of the corner of his eye he saw Knutas coming toward him. He turned to face him.

"How did you know?"

"Emma called me."

"Where's Elin?"

"We're searching the campsite now. There are a lot of buildings here, and she's probably in one of them. Don't worry, she's here somewhere."

The interrogation of David Mattson was conducted immediately. The impressive bulk of the suspect seemed even greater inside the cramped interview room. He sat down opposite Knutas, who was in charge of the interview. Jacobsson was also there as a witness, and she stayed in the background.

So here I am, thought Knutas, *sitting in front of the killer we've been hunting for more than a month.* It was an unreal feeling. This was what the man looked like. The murderer who had attacked his victims from behind with piano wire, who had hoisted one man up on Dalman Gate and later dragged another body to the first victim's grave. The person who had carried out the improbable theft of a painting from Waldemarsudde. The one question that overshadowed everything else was: why? Why had he committed those terrible murders? What was behind it all? And had he also killed his own father? Knutas was longing for an explanation, but first and foremost they needed to solve a more urgent mystery. Where is Elin?

While Knutas switched on the audio recorder and arranged his papers, he studied David Mattson. He was wearing jeans and a shirt, sitting on the chair with his legs set apart and his hands clasped. So this was the face of the murderer, a twenty-three-year-old man who lived with his girlfriend in one of Stockholm's northern suburbs and was enrolled at the university. He had no police record.

Knutas and Jacobsson did their utmost to get him to say where Elin was, but it seemed completely futile. David could not be budged. He thought that Johan had broken his promise by notifying the police about their meeting. That was why he refused to say what he'd done with Johan's daughter. It made no difference that the police tried to convince him that Johan was innocent and that it was Emma who had told them where the meeting was taking place.

The police quickly realized that David was unaware of his father's death. In the middle of the interrogation, the ME's preliminary report arrived, stating that all indications were that Erik Mattson had died from an overdose of cocaine.

Wittberg summoned Jacobsson and Knutas, who briefly interrupted the interrogation to listen to him report the new information.

"There's something that we have to tell you," said Jacobsson when they returned to the interview room.

David Mattson didn't even look up. He was stubbornly staring at his clasped hands on his lap. He'd answered their questions in monosyllables, and kept asking for more cold water. Karin had already refilled the carafe on the table numerous times.

"Your father is dead."

Slowly David lifted his head. "You're lying."

"I'm afraid not. He was found this morning, at home in his apartment. He was lying in bed, and according to the medical examiner, he died from an overdose of cocaine. We also found 'The Dying Dandy' hanging above the bed. Your fingerprints were on the canvas."

David Mattson stared at her for a long time, a look of

incomprehension on his face. The silence in the room was palpable. Knutas wondered whether it had been wise to tell him about his father's death before they managed to find out what he'd done with Elin.

"When did you last see Erik?" asked Jacobsson.

"Saturday night," he replied without emotion. "I went over there to have dinner. I gave him a present. We talked and talked. Then Pappa got mad, and I left . . ."

His voice faded away. His face changed completely. The hard, arrogant mask cracked for a moment, and without uttering a sound, the big man collapsed onto the table.

Johan was taken straight to Visby Hospital, where he was given a sedative until he could speak to a psychologist. The nurse had left his room, assuring him that she'd be back soon. In the meantime, Johan should lie down and take it easy. He felt empty and numb, as if he wasn't really there. When the door opened again, it wasn't the nurse who came in. Instead, he saw Emma's face in the doorway.

"Hi," he said, attempting to smile. Her expression was stony, her face swollen, and it looked as if all her features were in the wrong place: her eyes on her chin, her nose on her left temple. She had no mouth at all. Just a dry hole.

Emma didn't respond to his greeting. She stood some distance away from the bed, staring at him with disgust.

"You didn't tell me about that photograph of you in the news office," she snarled. "You were tailing a man you assumed was a murderer, just because you thought it would be fun, without giving the least thought to us—me and Elin— or our safety. And now she's gone. My Elin, my beloved Elin is gone, and it's your fault. Your fucking fault. If you hadn't been doing what you did, this wouldn't have happened."

Johan was shocked by this unexpected attack, and he tried to protest.

"But Emma . . ." he said weakly.

"Shut up." She crept closer. Stood leaning over him, staring angrily into his eyes. "He came into my house, my house. When I was taking a shower, he was creeping around. He took my daughter and disappeared. Now all we can do is hope that the police get him to say what he's done with her, and that my Elin isn't dead. That she's still alive."

"Yes, but—"

"She's eight months old, Johan. Eight months old!" She tore off her engagement ring and threw it at him. "I will never forgive you for this!" she screamed.

She left the room, slamming the door behind her with all her might. Johan sat there in the hospital bed, anaesthetized, annihilated, incapable of taking in even a fraction of what had just happened.

It was horrible, just too horrible.

The search for Elin continued nonstop out at the Snäck campsite. Police dogs combed every nook and cranny: the cafeteria, the grocery shop, the reception building, the lavatories, and shower booths. They didn't find the child anywhere, and everyone feared that she had been killed and her body dumped somewhere. David Mattson's car was found, but it provided no clues.

Reluctantly Kihlgård, who had come to the area with Wittberg, began to despair. If Elin had been hidden somewhere here, they should have found her by now.

As he stood looking at the Snäck block of apartments, an idea came to him. If David Mattson had been certain that the exchange would take place, he could have left the baby some distance away, pointed Johan in the right direction and then driven off in his car, which he'd parked next to the lavatory building.

"Come with me," he shouted to Wittberg.

His colleague ran to catch up with him. "Where are we going?"

"I just have a gut feeling," said Kihlgård. "Aren't those time-share condos over there?"

"Yes," said Wittberg, gasping for breath.

"Does anybody live there in the wintertime?"

"I assume so. They must pay for the weeks they want to be here, and I'd think that some people would want to live here year round."

They headed up the slope to the block of apartments, located in a lovely spot near the sea.

"Do you think he hid her somewhere inside?" asked Wittberg.

"Why not? If he can get into Waldemarsudde, surely he could get into this building too."

They found nothing suspicious in the area, but were soon joined by more police officers who took over the search.

Wittberg turned to Kihlgård. "Come on, let's check over there."

"Where?"

"There are some summerhouses up on the ridge. Maybe he broke into one of them."

"How far is it?" asked Kihlgård doubtfully. "Shouldn't we go and get the car?"

"It'll take longer to walk back and get the car than to continue up to the summerhouses. Come on." Wittberg began jogging up the slope.

"Take it easy," Kihlgård panted. He had a hard time keeping up with the pace set by his younger colleague.

When they reached the top of the ridge, they found a small side road leading to a wooded area. The cabins were scattered among the trees, simple wooden structures on small plots of land. The area was deserted. They went in separate directions and started looking for signs that someone might have been there earlier in the day. It didn't take long before Wittberg gave a shout.

"Here, Martin. Come over here. I think I've found something!"

A yellow-painted cabin stood at the edge of the area,

near the side road. Fresh tire tracks were visible in the snow. They rushed toward the cabin. Suddenly Kihlgård started yelling.

"Look, someone broke open the door!"

"Yes, I see that, damn it," gasped Wittberg excitedly. "But what's that?"

For one icy moment they both thought that the red patch in the snow was blood, but when they got closer, they saw that it was a tiny baby's sock.

They were in the right place. Wittberg went first, tearing open the door. The hallway inside was dark and cramped, and there wasn't a sound. When Wittberg later recounted the story to his colleagues, he described the feeling he had as "nightmarish." He and Kihlgård hardly dared breathe, fearing what they might find. Their eyes scanned the rag rugs on the floor, the simple furniture, the clumsily painted pictures, the wall clock that had stopped at 4:45, and the pots of plastic flowers in the windows. The raw cold, the faint smell of mold and rat poison.

Wittberg was the first to enter the small bedroom with two narrow beds on one side. In a corner on top of one of the beds stood a dark blue crib, shoved close to the wall.

Wittberg slowly turned around to look at his older colleague. Kihlgård calmly met his glance and nodded for him to proceed.

At that moment, Thomas Wittberg felt smaller and more insignificant than he'd ever felt before. For a second he shut his eyes, unable to remember ever experiencing such silence. He would never forget the moment when he leaned over the crib. The sight that met his eyes would change his life forever.

There she lay. Under a blanket with a pink knitted cap on her head. Her eyes were closed and her face peaceful.

Her little hands lay on top of the blanket. Then Wittberg bent even closer and listened to the most beautiful sound he could imagine.

The regular in and out of Elin's breathing.

Epilogue

The springtime sun had finally begun to loosen winter's harsh grip on the island, and the icicles were falling from the eaves. During his morning walk to police headquarters, Knutas could feel the sunlight warming his back. The birds were chirping, infusing new hope into life.

And there was certainly a need for that.

As usual, he climbed the stairs to the criminal division, the first to arrive, and sat down at his desk with a cup of coffee. In front of him lay a thick folder with material from the investigation. On top was a stack of photocopies of the diary entries that the killer had made, describing his plans for the murders.

David Mattson lived with his girlfriend and a little kitten in an apartment in one of Stockholm's northern suburbs. He was studying economics at the university, but his studies were not going well. During the past six months he had skipped more classes than he had attended.

His girlfriend had been deeply shocked to hear that he was the one who had killed both of the art dealers. According to her, he was the nicest, most gentle person you could possibly meet.

The whole thing started one day in the autumn when David happened to overhear a conversation between his paternal grandparents. They were talking about the fact that Erik was adopted. This had come as a complete surprise to David. His whole life, he had assumed that these two people were his grandparents, yet they weren't related to him at all. Not really. His real grandparents were somewhere else, but had never made themselves known. When he found out the truth, it was easy to work out the rest.

The fact that Hugo Malmberg had given Erik up for adoption on the very day he was born had seemed to David an enormous act of betrayal. That he was wealthy and able to throw money around while Erik struggled to pay his bills had filled David with contempt. He started tailing Malmberg, following him to the gallery, as he went about town, and at the gym. He soon discovered that his real grandfather was gay.

In the diary entries, David described the terrible incident that became the springboard for everything else. One afternoon in November, David had followed his biological grandfather to an underground club for gay men. There he had witnessed Hugo Malmberg, along with Egon Wallin, using his own son for his sexual pleasures, although without being aware of their kinship.

David was the only one who knew the truth of the matter. It took only a couple of seconds for him to understand what he was seeing. Those seconds turned him into a murderer.

During the investigation, it turned out that Egon Wallin and Hugo Malmberg had not only had a relationship, but on several occasions they had also paid to have sex with male prostitutes. Knutas thought this must have been the reason for Malmberg's reluctance to admit to the police that his relationship with Egon Wallin was more than a business partnership. And that was also why he didn't want to admit that his colleague on Gotland was homosexual when the police asked him about that.

The basis for the murders seemed to be David Mattson's complicated and deluded relationship with his father, Erik. As far as Knutas understood from the detailed descriptions in the diary, David had always loved Erik and looked up to him. At the same time, he seemed to have longed for a father who didn't really exist—the kind that others seemed to have, someone who could give him encouragement, solace, confirmation, love, and a sense of security. This hope remained so strong that David hadn't been able to free himself from Erik. The diary entries were permeated with a striving to make his father happy, to straighten out his life, to please him. Maybe David was hoping that his father would then be able to give him what he needed in return.

The theft of "The Dying Dandy" was, of course, pure insanity. But in David's eyes, it was a way to redress the wrongs done to his father.

Knutas interpreted the fact that he'd wanted to show a connection with the sculpture as proof that deep in his heart David Mattson wanted to be caught, that he wanted the world to see and understand the suffering he had been forced to endure. That was undoubtedly also why he'd arranged his victims the way he had done. Everything had to do with revenge and redress and going back to the past.

As for the stolen paintings, Wittberg's persistent efforts had finally paid off. It turned out that Egon Wallin had been collaborating with Mattis Kalvalis's manager, Vigor Haukas. The paintings were stolen by professional criminals from the Baltics and later sold from there on the international market. Haukas had run the whole operation, with Wallin acting as a middleman while the paintings made their way out of Sweden. It had been a lucrative business for several years.

Knutas sighed as he continued reading. It was a deeply tragic story. And there was one theme that had run through the whole investigation: secrets. First there was the murder of Egon Wallin and everything that he'd kept hidden from his family, then Erik Mattson's double life, and, finally, all the secrets that were part of Hugo Malmberg's past.

Knutas took out his pipe from the top drawer of his desk, got up, and went over to the window. There wasn't a cloud in the sky, the sun was shining, and in the distance the sea was gleaming bright blue, the way it did only in the springtime. He glanced over at Dalman Gate. That was where it had all begun, two months earlier.

It seemed like a very, very long time ago.

Acknowledgements

This story is entirely fictional. Any similarities between the characters in the novel and actual individuals are co-incidental. Occasionally I have taken artistic liberties to change things for the benefit of the book. This includes Swedish TV's coverage of Gotland, which in the book has been moved to Stockholm. I have the utmost respect for SVT's regional news program Östnytt, which covers Gotland with a permanent team stationed in Visby.

The settings used in the book are usually described as they actually exist in reality, although there are a few exceptions.

Any errors that may have slipped into the story are mine alone.

First and foremost, I would like to thank my husband, journalist Cenneth Niklasson, who is always ready to be my sounding board and offer me the greatest support.

Special thanks to:

Gösta Svensson, former detective superintendent with the Visby police; Magnus Frank, detective superintendent with the Visby police; Hans Henrik Brummer, chief curator at Waldemarsudde; Martin Csatlos, the Forensic Medicine Laboratory in Solna; Ylva Hilleström, Museum of Modern Art, Stockholm; Johan Jinnerot, curator at Bukowski's Auction House; Johan Gardelius, crime technician, Visby police; Ulf Åsgård, psychiatrist; Birgitta Amér, owner of Muramaris. Thanks also to Nicklas, for his valuable help, and a big thanks to Ingrid Ljunggren. And I would like to thank my dear author colleagues—thanks for being there!

Thanks also to my readers for their valuable opinions: Lena Allerstam, journalist, Swedish TV; Kerstin Jungstedt, consultant, Provins fem; Lilian Andersson, editor at Bonnier Educational Books; Anna-Maja Persson, Moscow correspondent, Swedish TV.

My thanks to Albert Bonniers Förlag, and especially to my publisher, Jonas Axelsson, and editor, Ulrika Åkerlund. Thanks to my designer, John Eyre, for the cover of the Swedish edition, and to both Niclas Salomonsson and Emma Tibblin at Salomonsson Agency.

Last, but not least, I want to thank my wonderful children, Rebecka and Sebastian.

Mari Jungstedt
www.marijungstedt.se/en

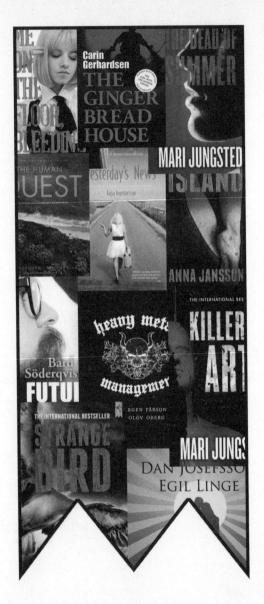

www.stockholmtext.com